NEW DARK VOICES II
Edited by Brian Keene

Featuring:
Ronald Damien Malfi
Nick Mamatas
Brett McBean

First Edition Paperback
January 2009

Published by:
Delirium Books
P.O. Box 338
North Webster, IN 46555
sales@deliriumbooks.com
www.deliriumbooks.com

New Dark Voices II © 2008 by Delirium Books
"Sins of the Father" © 2008 by Brett McBean
"Eliminate the Improbable" © 2008 by Nick Mamatas
"Borealis" © 2008 by Ronald Damien Malfi
Cover Artwork © 2008 by Mike Bohatch
All Rights Reserved.

Copy Editors: David Marty & Mark Sylva

ISBN 978-1-934546-06-2

This book is a work of fiction. Names, characters, places and incidents are either a product of the author's imagination or are used fictitiously. Any resemblance to actual events, locales or persons, living or dead, is entirely coincidental.

TABLE OF CONTENTS

Introduction — Brian Keene
5

Sins of the Father — Brett McBean
11

Eliminate the Improbable — Nick Mamatas
87

Borealis — Ronald Damien Malfi
141

Biographies
217

INTRODUCTION

I'm not getting paid for this.

Not a dollar. Not a cent. Not even in copies. It's true. Not only am I writing this introduction for free—I'm not even getting paid for editing the anthology.

Now, I know what you're thinking. "How crass. How rude. What a terrible, self-centered way to open a book." And perhaps you'd be justified in saying those things. But what do you do for a living? And regardless of whether or not you love your job, would you spend four months working there for free? Probably not. But I just did. Writing and editing are how I earn my living. This is how I feed my family and pay the mortgage. So perhaps you'll pardon me if I state one more time that I'm not earning a cent with this book.

And I'm happy about that.

And it's all Nick Mamatas's fault.

Last year, Nick Mamatas released a novel called *Under My Roof*. It was about a father and son who build a small nuclear bomb and hide the device inside a garden gnome. Then they secede from the United States of America, and declare their home sovereign territory. Others are inspired by their actions, and soon, America is a crazy-quilt landscape of nation-state 7-11s, Blockbuster Video stores, and apartment buildings. *Under My Roof* was a brilliant, fun, clever novel. I enjoyed it very much and thought that others might, too. I shared my enthusiasm for the book on my Blog. A few weeks later, I got an email from a 16-year old kid. Apparently, this young man reads nothing but Brian Keene novels, but he took a chance on *Under My Roof* and loved it as much as I had. He ended his email with: "Can you recommend any other new authors?"

In fact, I could recommend quite a few. I can list a dozen without even taking a breath: Darren Speegle, Greg Gifune, Sarah Langan, Mary SanGiovanni, Lee Thomas, Brian Knight, Wrath James White, Nate Southard, David Jack Bell, Nick Kaufmann, Maurice Broaddus, Kealan Patrick Burke. I could keep going, but I won't, because of space limitations. My point is this: the current popularity of the genre and the subsequent growth of the small press over the last decade has led to the emergence of many talented new authors—writers who have an exciting amount of skill, energy, voice, and imagination. Sadly, because of the sheer number of competing voices, these new authors are often not as widely-read as they deserve. There are a number of writers who could easily win readers over—if only the readers were exposed to their work. All these authors need is a chance to have their voices heard.

A few years ago, Delirium Books released an anthology called *New Dark Voices*. It evoked memories of the classic *Night Visions* anthology series. *Night Visions* and other annual anthology series (*Whispers, Shadows, Year's Best Horror*, etc.) were a big part of my formative years, but it occurs to me that many younger readers might not be familiar with them. *Night Visions* was conceived as a showcase for the best established authors in the genre, and featured work from writers like John Farris, Joe Lansdale, Richard Laymon, F. Paul Wilson, Chet Williamson and many more.

New Dark Voices had a similar intent, but rather than focusing on the already-established masters, it showcased the talents of newer writers who hadn't yet garnered a huge audience but certainly deserved one. The first volume featured novellas from Michael Oliveri, Gene O'Neill, and John Urbancik (all of whom have indeed gained a following in the years since its publication). It also had an introduction by myself.

So, lets get back to *Under My Roof* and the email from the reader. I called Shane Ryan Staley, the head of Delirium Books, and I told him about what this kid had asked me. I mentioned that there were a whole bunch of new authors that I wanted to endorse and recommend because I thought readers would enjoy their work. I suggested to Shane that he edit a second volume of *New Dark Voices* and showcase some of them. Shane said he couldn't do it. According to him, anthology sales were down. Nobody read them anymore—especially if they were anthologies featuring unknown or lesser-known writers, rather than "name brands." But I was insistent, and before I realized what I was doing, I'd volunteered to lend my name to the project. Not only that, but I'd select the authors, work with them, and edit the book for free.

"Damn," Shane said, "this must be really important to you."

"It is," I replied. "I want to help readers find new authors and help new authors find readers."

So here we are. *New Dark Voices* is now an annual anthology series spotlighting the best new authors in the genre—authors who you might not have read yet, but who I'm sure you'll enjoy. It is my sincere hope that you will seek out more from them after you've sampled their work herein.

Selecting three authors for this volume was no easy task, but ultimately I settled on Brett McBean, Nick Mamatas, and Ronald Damien Malfi. Each of them has a loyal readership, and yet, each one deserves a much wider audience. If you've never had the pleasure of reading their work, please allow me a moment to give you a bit of background on each of these uniquely talented new authors.

Brett McBean has had some mass-market success in his home-country of Australia, but, outside of the small press, he's still relatively unknown in the United States. I think this will soon change, and I'm positive that you'll agree with me once you've read the novella in this book. Brett McBean has the potential to become a major voice in horror fiction. Reviewers often compare his prose to that of the late Richard Laymon, and justifiably so, since Laymon was a major influence on him. But while Laymon's impact might echo through his fiction, Brett's strong and self-assured voice often transcends it—delving into characterization, motive, and the emotional aftermath of events in ways that Laymon never did. I do not say that to disparage Richard Laymon (the man was a good friend and I consider myself a big fan of his work), but to point out the uniqueness of Brett's work. Even the absolute best Laymon novels can usually be summarized like this: the beautiful blonde flashes her boobs and the crazed killer stabs her. The end. Now, that's fun and entertaining, but we don't really know much about our victim other than her cup size. Not so, with Brett McBean. Yes, he's writing commercial horror fiction, but he's also reaching beyond it. His characters live and breathe, and we feel it in our gut when the beautiful blonde gets stabbed because she could have been our girlfriend or our sister or our mother. His characters have heart, and those hearts pump real blood. We know these people, for they are us. Their hopes and fears, victories and defeats—all of these are things we've experienced in our own lives. Brett's previous books include *The Last Motel*, *The Mother*, *The Familiar Stranger*, and *Tales of Sin and Madness*.

Nick Mamatas does not suffer fools gladly. He comes armed with a sharp, acerbic wit and an unerring willingness to speak the truth, no matter how unpalatable or unsavory that truth might be to some. His daily online musings (which can be found at nihilistic-kid.livejournal.com) are an eclectic and entertaining mix of observations on writing, the genre, the publishing business, pop culture, society and politics. It's the second website I visit each day (after reading the morning's news). Nick Mamatas is like the demented offspring of a Nazi experiment combining the DNA of Bill Hicks, Hunter S. Thompson, Jack Kerouac, Abbie Hoffman, Che Guevara, and the Hernandez brothers.

Nick is an enigma, wrapped in a riddle. His prose crosses genres—as well as socio-economic classes and political spectrums. His fiction is peppered with influences, from his Greek-American, blue-collar roots to his days spent as a student at New York's State University at Stony Brook. He is equally as comfortable at a political rally in Berkeley, holding a Molotov cocktail in each hand, as he is at some waterfront bar in Long Island, discussing pro-wrestling with longshoremen—and he'd come off as genuine and knowledgeable in both camps. This is dangerous writing, folks—charming, perhaps even disarming—until it cuts your throat and leaves you bleeding in an alley. Nick's previous books include *Move Under Ground*, *Northern Gothic*, *3000 MPH In Every Direction At Once*, *You Might Sleep...*, and the aforementioned *Under My Roof*. He is also the editor of *Clarkesworld Magazine* and he co-edited *Haunted Legends* with Ellen Datlow.

Ronald Damien Malfi rounds out this volume. Like McBean and Mamatas, he's a unique voice. His stories are rich in mood, atmosphere, and setting. They drip with imaginative imagery. The first novel I read by him, *The Fall of Never*, had a wonderfully bizarre, Alice in Wonderland-like quality to it. It was a darkly surreal trip down the rabbit hole and out the other side of the looking glass—the portion that gazes into Hell. I anticipated a similar gothic dark fantasy with the next book I read by him, *The Nature of Monsters*, and was surprised to discover that it was nothing like the former. That is the mark of an author who is writing to please himself, rather than the whims of the marketplace. Indeed, Ronald Damien Malfi is a remarkably versatile writer. He is comfortable with different genres and he deftly wields various styles with equal fervor. His work has the potential to appeal to both the literati and the readers of commercial fiction (something that is very hard to do, as the two groups are usually quite disparate). In addition to the aforementioned *The Fall of Never* and *The Nature of Monsters*, his books include *Via Dolorosa*, *Passenger*, and *Shamrock Alley*.

Three different authors with three very different styles. Three unique visions of horror. Enjoy these discoveries, as I have, and add these authors to your "must-read" list when you're done.

Brian Keene
March 2008

SINS OF THE FATHER
Brett McBean

The boy gazed out the bedroom window and wondered yet again when daddy was coming back.

And Bluey; don't forget Bluey.

The day had just begun, the sun was poking its head over the horizon, burning off the morning mist; it looked like it was going to be another bright autumn day.

Day number 29 since the big storm.

Twenty-nine days since the light and the smell and the screaming had stopped, and yet the boy could still smell the horrible odor, could still hear the people's screams. They hung in the air and in his head like moths buzzing around a light.

At least the sheep had stopped crying. He didn't know how much longer he could've stood their pained bleating.

The boy sighed.

Just another day, alone, waiting for dad's return, waiting to see his lean, muscular body come striding through the front door, Bluey, their spritely kelpie, trailing behind, wagging his tail.

But standing in the shadowy, frigid room, hunger pains stabbing at his gut, the boy felt a shift in the air. It was subtle, barely perceptible, but he had felt it all the same.

There was a change coming.

Someone was coming.
Daddy?
He hoped so.
But the boy knew better — deep in his heart, where dark secrets were kept, he knew better.
Still, he remained by the window and waited.

* * *

When Tony Christopher laid eyes on the railway crossing, his heart filled with happiness. He had made it.

He was home.

He had only been gone a day over two months, but Christ, it felt like a thousand sunsets since his Ford Ute had rattled over the train tracks, the tiny northwest Victorian hamlet of Gainesville shrinking in the rear-view mirror.

He had been a different person then: the eyes staring back blood-shot and weighed down with dark rings; hair down to his shoulders, greasy and stringy; face the color of pale urine, the skin pulled tight like a drum over jagged cheek bones; and body equally starved and racked with withdrawal spasms, which, at the time, he thought couldn't get any worse.

How wrong he had been.

If he knew then, as he had driven away from family and friends, just how worse the pains, the cramping, the sickness, the madness would get, he doubted he would've made it far past the train tracks, let alone all the way to the farmhouse in the mountains. He most likely would've turned his truck around, driven straight back into town and parked his butt on his favorite stool at the Cresland Hotel and ordered two beers and a shot of whisky.

But he hadn't known and now he was clean; sober for two months (and one day), thank you very much, and he hadn't needed any doctors or twelve steps to get there. All he needed was to get away from civilization, to breathe crystal clear air, and do nothing all day except chop wood, cook meals over the stove (or campfire, depending on how he was feeling that day), and read.

No television, no computer, no radio, no Xbox, no mobile phone — and certainly no visitors. Just Tony, nature, and a shit-load of canned food and bottled water.

Two months staying in his long-dead Uncle Wilbur's empty farmhouse, nestled deep within the Pyrenees Ranges; that's what it took to get Tony off drugs and booze.

Two of the hardest fucking months of his life.

But he proved that he could survive without those addictions; he had broken free from the drug and alcohol chains that bound him, destroying his life and those around him.

As he rolled his Ford over the tracks, Tony glanced up at the rear-view mirror. "You handsome bastard," he said with a chuckle.

Nobody'll recognize me, he thought as he pulled his eyes back to the road.

Hair cut short (a homemade job, but he thought it looked all right), eyes alert, face healthy and body toned, tanned. His wife would say he looked like a movie star; his ten-year-old daughter like one of the Backstreet Boys, or whatever pop band she was into at the moment; his dad would pat him on the back and say, "Well done, Anthony," and his friends would all hang shit on him, but in a well-meaning way. The whole town would be pleased — but amazed — to see him: all two thousand, three hundred of them. Most probably expected him to either run back after a day of self-imposed exile, or not make it back at all.

Tony had to admit; there were times when he thought he would never see his family and friends again.

But all that was behind him.

Standing on the front porch of the farmhouse just after sunup this morning, drawing sweet mountain air into his lungs, he had promised himself he wasn't going to dwell on those dark times; he vowed to leave all that shit in the past, think only of the future.

So that's what he aimed to do.

Tony cruised along Wickes Road, a crisp autumn wind

blowing in through the open driver's side window, slapping his face like a wet blanket.

He glanced down at the car's clock radio. It was just after seven o'clock.

His wife and daughter would probably be up by now — Amy sitting at the kitchen table sipping the first of three cups of coffee and reading the newspaper; Heather transfixed in front of the television, munching away at her cereal.

His dear old dad would be groaning out of bed in an hour's time, asking Mildred for his morning coffee, and then realizing with a horrible gut-wrenching sting that Mildred had been dead ten years come November. Tony knew this because, even though he hadn't lived at home for over fifteen years, he frequently shacked up with his old man whenever he was kicked out of home by Amy for coming in stinking of booze or flying higher than a 747. All his friends were married, most with kids, and he didn't fancy park benches and the kennel was too smelly, not to mention crowded. So that left his old childhood home, located across town, where his dad still lived, still pining for his wife who died ten years ago of a stroke. It was during those stays that, in the morning, his head still foggy with hangover, Tony would hear his dad call out for Mildred to get him his coffee, and then, after a short pause, he would hear a heavy sigh, followed by, "Oh, Mildred."

Such was the pace, regularity and familiarity of Gainesville.

Off to the right, Cemetery Road, which lead to Gainesville's one and only cemetery; farther down the road was Hammond's farm, with its green pastures and fat cows (which, curiously, were nowhere to be seen — old Burt must've placed them in another paddock). Coming up on the left was Gary's Auto, which Tony's Ford was well-acquainted with.

He knew this area like a camel knows the desert, and yet, as he continued along Wickes Road, things seemed different, quieter than usual, even for a Sunday morning, like the world was on pause.

It's just you, knucklehead. You've changed. Haven't seen this place through sober eyes in a long while.

But there was also a strange smell in the air, a metallic tinge, like the coppery smell of blood, or like when he was a boy and used to stick the end of his tongue on batteries, and would get a small buzz and a sharp acidic taste.

Tony leaned out the window, drew in a breath, and coughed.

No longer the sweetness of dew and mist. Instead, a caustic bitterness caught in his throat.

Strange...

He leaned back in. What had been Boston's "More Than a Feeling" softly playing on the oldie's station a few moments ago was now static. He switched off the radio.

He turned onto Camp Street and soon Gainesville proper rolled into view.

The small farming town was nestled in a valley. It was like the town once rested on an even plane with the surrounding farmland, and slowly, as more houses were built, sunk down until it couldn't go any farther. A piddling amount of gold had been found in 1853 and hungry prospectors converged in the hopes of striking it rich. But the precious resource proved to be scarce, and unlike other towns in the area, such as Clunes, Dover and Ballarat, it didn't go on to become a popular tourist destination. Nobody went out of their way to visit Gainesville.

Tony headed down into the town center. On the right was St. John's Anglican Church, the post office and then a string of shops which included the news agency where he had stolen many packets of gum and football cards over the years (and which had ads for a 30 million dollar Tattslotto draw plastered over its windows, which, according to the date on the posters, was supposed to have been drawn about a month ago—strange then that old Bruce Jensen still had the posters up); the hardware store where he worked, and the bakery which made killer lamingtons and vanilla slices. On the left, taking up a great deal of real estate was the Cresland Hotel, then the butcher, the I.G.A. supermarket, and his wife's favorite op-shop, where she got a lot of her wardrobe from.

All of it so familiar, most of the shops had been around since Tony was a kid and probably long before that, but as Tony cruised down Main Street, he was struck again with how lifeless the town seemed. And stranger still was that while no shops were open, there were cars parked in front of the local pizza restaurant, the hotel, the bakery — yet there wasn't a soul around.

Only lots of paper swirling about, like tiny white tumbleweeds.

And that metallic smell was stronger in the heart of town.

Tony's unease grew.

He pressed his foot on the accelerator. He had been eager to get home to see his wife and daughter, to hold them in his arms and smell their beautiful, familiar smell, but now he just wanted to get home because he was worried.

About what? So the town's quieter than usual. It is a Sunday morning.

He left the main strip of shops behind. The western residential area of Gainesville where Tony lived was just as desolate as the center. He couldn't even hear any animal noises, now that he listened. No roosters calling, no birds cheeping, no dogs barking.

He rolled the window back up, partly because of the bitter smell that was in the air, tickling his nose and burning his tongue, but mainly because he was shivering — and Tony didn't usually feel the cold.

It's being back in town again, that's all. It's messing with your head. You're just being paranoid. Worried because you haven't faced your family sober in a long time.

Tony shifted in the seat.

He thought back to the first two weeks alone at the farm. The time when his world was at its darkest and it felt like a thunderstorm was booming and crashing inside his head.

As he lay dying in that farmhouse, sweating, shivering, floor coated with his puke and tears, he would think of Amy and Heather and cry even more. He missed them so much it was a physical pain, and he knew that if he survived those initial few weeks, he would hold them in his arms and assault them with hugs and kisses, tell them how much he loved them and never let them go.

But then the guilt would surface, how much he had hurt them; not physically, no, he had never hurt them like that, but how he had abused them emotionally, was a mostly absent father and husband, and even now, as he turned down his street, he felt his eyes well up and a heavy sickness lay in his gut at the thought of all the times his daughter had seen him off his face, either drunk, or high—often both.

She didn't deserve that, neither of them deserved that, and all of these thoughts and emotions pumped through his body as he pulled into the driveway.

He wanted to see the two most important people in his life more than anything in the world, they were what ultimately got him through the last two months, yet he couldn't help but also feel a little hesitant. He had caused them so much pain and grief, would they ever truly forgive him?

And on top of all these worries was the added concern that something was wrong in Dodge. He was sure he would be laughing about it in a few hours, could hear Amy now: *You silly man, it's always like a ghost town Sunday mornings. You just never realized it before, you were always too hung-over to notice. What did you think could have possibly happened?*

Tony parked the Ute behind Amy's Land Cruiser, killed the engine and jumped out. He didn't bother getting his bags, they could wait.

The strange warped metallic smell was still present in the air and as he crunched over the gravel pathway up to the front door, he heard the noise of the television. He saw lights on inside.

Tony smiled.

All tension lifted from his face and shoulders.

"You silly man," he said to the wind, and with keys in hand, he unlocked the door.

He pictured Heather sitting crossed-legged or on her belly gazing wide-eyed at the colorful cartoons on TV. He pictured himself creeping into the lounge, and then stepping into the room and saying, "Hey there kiddo," and Heather's eyes widening even more, a smile breaking across her angelic face, and then her jumping up and running into his arms.

But as he closed the front door, he frowned at the sound of static coming from the lounge. Static interspersed with snatches of dialogue, like the TV wasn't tuned in properly and was only receiving an extremely fuzzy signal.

That was the first sign that something wasn't right.

The second was the smell — a heady mixture of spoiled meat, off milk and that musty odor of a place that hadn't been aired in a while.

He walked into the lounge and found it empty. No Heather, no empty bowl of Corn Flakes and half-finished glass of orange juice resting on the carpet.

There was a half-full bowl of popcorn, an almost full glass of what looked like Coke on the carpet. And on the small table beside the couch, was an almost drained bottle of white wine.

And behind the couch, the window was smashed. Only jagged bits of glass remained along three of the edges — the rest of the glass was scattered over the couch and the carpet in front of the TV.

Tony panicked. He darted through the house, popping his head into each room. They were all empty. In the bedroom, Tony checked the wardrobe — all of Amy's clothes were still hanging in there and no suitcases were missing. He raced through the kitchen and flung open the back door and standing on the back porch, staring out at the expansive green lawn, he cried, "Amy! Heather!"

He got back nothing. No response, no Copper — their two-year-old Golden Retriever — running over to greet him.

Not even the next-door neighbor's dog, Pepper, yapped, and he yapped at the drop of a leaf.

"What the hell…?" Tony started, but he didn't finish the question. He knew he would get no answer.

He shut the back door, stood before the kitchen—which was messy with plates that still had bits of last night's dinner on them (though it smelled more like last month's); pots and pans that had yet to be cleaned; and things left on the counter that Amy always made sure to put back, like the tub of margarine and carton of milk—and felt tears wash down his cheeks.

"Amy!" he shouted, and the stillness that followed was like the aftermath of a bomb exploding.

Something was most definitely wrong.

And outside storm clouds gathered.

* * *

Tony sat shivering on his father's couch, clutching the bottle of gin.

His mouth was dry, the gin untouched, but he ached to take a good long drink. So far he had yet to succumb, but he was slipping—after all, he could've poured the gin down the sink instead of taking the bottle and holding it like it held the breath of life.

Amy…Heather…dad…where are you…?…what's going on…?

He couldn't stop shivering and even though it was only ten o'clock in the morning, outside was thick with shadows. It was more like five o'clock on a winter's evening.

Three hours.

That's how long it had taken for Tony's life to go to total shit.

Three hours since arriving back in town, only to find his wife and daughter gone. Three hours since finding out that the whole town had seemingly vanished.

Tony almost giggled at the idiocy of it all. *Things really do come full circle, don't they?*

He had gone from lonely drunk, on the verge of killing himself, to rehabilitated and looking forward to the future, back to feeling like a sniveling mess, all in the space of a few months.

After discovering Amy and Heather were gone, he had stormed over to the phone and dialed his dad's number. The line crackled at him, like someone was crumpling cellophane on the other end. He had hung up and desperately tried again; same deal. He got static when he tried Paul Dobson, one of his best mates, as he did when he rang Gay Heathmont, Julian Barnes and a bunch of other Gainesville residents, including the local police station.

He had then stormed into his bedroom, where his mobile phone lay on his bedside table, untouched for over two months. He picked it up, turned on the power. The battery still had some juice in it. He pressed zero three times, held the phone up to his ear and listened as the phone beeped at him.

He glanced at the screen.

No coverage.

"Fuck," he growled and threw the mobile phone to the ground. "Useless piece of shit."

He had left his house — turning off the TV that was still airing nothing but snow with jabs of dialogue and occasionally music, faint and sporadic. Next door was also in a kind of limbo, almost a mirror image of his own house — the TV on, also broadcasting static, dirty plates stacked in the sink, shoes and clothes flung on the floor. The back door was swinging wide open, which was probably why the stink had been less there than in his own house, and a front lounge window had been smashed. But it had been empty.

So was the next house, and the house after that. It was the same situation in each house on the street — TV (or radio, sometimes both) left on, food left half-eaten, one window obliterated, everyone gone. In one house — the Brady's — even their budgies were gone, even though the cage was still securely locked.

After yelling his throat raw for someone, anyone, to

answer him (nobody did) Tony had stumbled back into his truck and driven over to his dad's, fear, like a woodpecker pecking away at his gut as he drove over to the other side of town, intermittently honking his horn, hearing only an echo.

It seemed like a dream, or a nightmare. There had to be a simple, logical explanation. Tony was a rational man, he believed in science, things he could actually see, touch or experience.

But he had no explanation for this.

He had driven through the empty streets of Gainesville, face pale, eyes glazed, confusion filling his head like the muddy clouds that were gathering over the town.

Finally he came to the old weatherboard. The place of his childhood. Hardly changed in all his life, just a new paintjob here, a new roof tile there.

Surely he would find some answers inside. Some things never changed, and he was sure the moment he stepped into the lounge room his dad would look up from the newspaper, that well-worn crease lining his brow and looking over the top of his reading glasses he would grumble, "Anthony, what the hell are you doing here?" and then Tony would break down and cry when he learnt that a bunch of people from the town had gone on an overnight trip to Hepburn Springs or Ballarat, Amy and Heather included.

But when Tony entered the house, he found it to be like all the others—empty as a gambler's wallet, stinking to high heaven of moldy food, the TV crackling the only sign of life.

Tony had lost it. He had staggered over to his old man's liquor cabinet, grabbed a bottle of dry gin, and then staggered over to the couch, where he flopped down, opened the bottle cap, and froze, the bottle clasped in his clammy hand, his body aching to taste the alcohol, his mind shouting at him to put the damn bottle down.

And he had remained in that state ever since, unsure of what to do, what to think.

He had run over in his mind what might've happened to the town until his brain felt like it had melted. He thought of all kinds of possibilities—none of them seemed the least bit plausible. The best, and most rational, explanation he had come up with was that the town had been evacuated due to some toxic chemical leak. That would explain the absence of people, the fact that homes looked like they had been left as is, no time to clean up or pack. That would even explain the strange smell in the air.

But unfortunately it didn't explain everything; there were too many loose ends that didn't fit.

Like where was the army? Surely an entire town could only be evacuated by the army, only they would be able to carry out such a task. But if that were the case, then where were the barricades? The tanks? The men in those white jump-suits and gas masks?

And if the entire town had been evacuated, including his family, then why wasn't he notified? His family and friends knew where he was staying; it wouldn't have taken much to send word to the farm to let him know what was going on. At the very least, Amy would've thought to leave a note, telling him where she and Heather had gone. All he had found was an abandoned Tattslotto ticket sitting on the couch, just like he had found in most of the homes he had checked, including his dad's.

I know, Tony thought, *the army came in too sudden for Amy to leave me a note. She wanted to, but they ordered her to get out, now!*

That made sense.

But it didn't explain the lack of army presence.

The evacuation took place a few weeks ago. The army has already taken down the barricades and have moved on.

Then why haven't they let everyone come back?

Tony had to face up to reality—as much as he wanted the evacuation theory to be true, it just didn't add up. Aside from a lot of empty houses, there just wasn't any sign that a military evacuation had taken place.

Then what…the fuck…is going…on!

Tony gazed down at the bottle of gin. His chin trembled, his hands shook. He had worked so damn hard to kick the habit, to get clean. Would he slip so easily into old habits?

Well Jesus Christ, the whole town has disappeared, what else am I supposed to do? One little drink won't hurt.

Maybe not the whole town, he told himself. He hadn't checked every house, every shop. But nobody had answered his cries. And if there were people here, surely someone would've heard his car horn blaring.

He sighed, his gaze boring a hole through the gin bottle, heavy in his hand.

Just a small nip, and then I'll get moving.

He didn't know what he planned on doing after the small nip — drive around, checking every single building in and around town? That would take hours, not to mention a lot of breaking and entering, only to find out what he already knew was true. Maybe he should drive to Dover, let the authorities there know what's happened. Maybe he would find Amy and Heather and everyone else there, smiling, wondering when he'd turn up.

Tony closed his eyes, lifted the bottle to his mouth.

Saw a smiling Amy and a laughing Heather. Then he saw the smiling visage of a skeleton behind, looming large over them.

And that's when it hit Tony, that proverbial ton of bricks crashing down on him.

They weren't dead. He could feel their presence; weak, but still with a pulse. They were close by, he just knew it.

He remembered when his mum died. He already knew she was dead before his dad called him from the hospital; somehow, he had just known, her presence that he didn't even know existed in him until that moment was snuffed out, like a candle flame licked by a puff of wind.

Well he didn't have that feeling now, not about Amy, Heather, nor his dad.

Maybe it was just wishful thinking. But he was sure his family was still alive, somewhere, and he knew he had to find them.

He opened his eyes. Threw the bottle of gin. It shattered against the wall, showering the TV with glass and alcohol.

Gin, strong and bitter, filled the lounge room, but instead of jumping up and lapping it off the carpet like a ravenous canine, the alcohol turned his stomach, and he allowed a brief flicker of a smile to caress his face.

Tony, one; alcohol, zip.

But the smile dropped when he thought of the problem which lay before him.

A town with no residents. A town seemingly left behind. A town littered with spoiled food, faulty phones and TVs, a strange electric tinge in the air, and a bucket-load of lottery tickets.

Lottery tickets, Tony thought. *Most of the houses I went into there were lottery tickets lying about on floors, couches or on tables. And the news agency, it still had the posters for the $30 million draw that was supposed to be...*

Tony hopped off the couch. He turned to his dad's much-loved chair, its fabric frayed and as thin as a wafer where it wasn't torn, exposing the cushion underneath. He spotted the small lottery ticket resting on one arm of the chair. He picked it up.

Glanced at the date of the draw. Sat. 21st April.

That was a month ago, yesterday.

None of the numbers had been crossed off. So his dad hadn't watched the lottery broadcast.

Could whatever happened, have happened on this night?

Tony pocketed the ticket and headed outside.

It was even darker than it was an hour ago. Thick black clouds like inky balls of cotton blanketed the sky, swirling about with the promise of rain, maybe even thunder and lightning.

A startling contrast to the crisp, sunny morning only three hours ago.

Tony flicked his eyes about; soon spotted one of the white bits of paper that were kicking around the desolate streets. He grabbed it. The lottery ticket was unsullied, no numbers had been marked off, and the date was Saturday a month ago, just like his dad's.

He drove home, stormed into the house — half-expecting (or was that hoping?) to find Amy or Heather, but finding only silence — and snatched up Amy's lotto ticket. Same date, unmarked.

So whatever happened, happened on that night.

Tony stood in the hollow lounge room.

One month ago. What happened one month ago?

He was up in the Pyrenees, fighting his demons, feeling close to death.

Meanwhile something was happening back here in town. Something happened on the 21st of April, while the people of Gainesville were getting ready to watch the $30 million Tattslotto draw, hoping to strike it rich, something their ancestors had failed to do.

But really, what did that tell him? So he knew the date of whatever it was that happened. Knowing that fact didn't tell him where everyone had gone, where his wife and daughter had vanished to.

He crumpled the ticket into a tight ball and tossed it to the floor.

It was hopeless. He had no idea what was going on, and by himself, he would never find any answers. He needed to get to another town. From there he could contact the proper authorities. Hopefully someone would be able to find out just what had happened here on Saturday the 21st of April.

But he wasn't thrilled with the idea of leaving his town, leaving Amy and Heather — wherever they were. This was his town, damn it, and he wanted to find his wife and daughter as quickly as possible. Driving to Dover would take around half an hour, twenty minutes if he sped, time that could be spent looking for his loved ones.

Maybe they needed his help, and the more time he wasted, the less time...

Wake up. Even if they are around here someplace, you've already wasted three hours grieving, trying to decide whether or not to drink yourself into a drunken stupor. And if they do truly need your help, best go and get help rather than tackling it on your own.

Then again, what if the police in Dover thought he was a nut-case and locked him up? Or simply thought he was a joker and told to get back to whichever hole he crawled out of? Because really, how could he expect anyone to believe that a whole town had just evaporated into thin air? It was a ludicrous notion, unless you actually witnessed the desolate streets and empty homes for yourself.

Tony felt anger building. A concoction of confusion, fear and a sense of helplessness. When it got too much he lashed out, kicking the wall, putting his foot through the plaster, and screaming to the heavens with an anguished cry.

Thunder cracked in the sky, cutting Tony's scream short.

He pulled his foot from the hole in the wall. He shook his head. What a fool he was. He wasn't even drunk and yet he still destroyed things.

Why couldn't it have been you? You should be the one to vanish, not Amy, not Heather, and not dad. You deserve to disappear, all the pain you've caused. What the hell has Heather ever done?

Part of him wanted to curl up in a ball and sleep forever, to let all the pain and confusion drain away. But the need to find his wife and daughter was stronger.

He formed a quick plan in his head. He would stay and search every house and shop. Maybe he would find a lonely soul who was still here in town, someone who could tell him just what the hell had happened, or a stray family, hiding in their home, for whatever reason too scared to come out.

Maybe Amy and Heather will be with them, maybe that's why I feel them close by.

And if I don't find anyone here, then I'll go to Dover.

With a faint glimmer of hope pushing its way through the dense layer of fear and confusion, Tony headed for the front door.

Outside, the winds whipped at his hair and tussled with the trees. With darkness pressing in on him like the walls of a prison, he strode over to his car, wondering where to start searching. He had already checked the houses down his street, but there were so many more houses, so many shops.

And then there were the farms on the outskirts.

The farms!

Maybe that's where some of them were hiding. Maybe that's where Amy and Heather and his dear old dad were. Not vanished off the face of the earth, but hiding for whatever reason in one of the farmhouses, or in a shed.

He knew it was a long shot, but he had to hope.

He had to believe that Amy and Heather were safe, and that his dad was with them, grumbling about being cold, or being hungry, or maybe even wondering where Mildred was.

He hopped into his Ute.

In the late morning sky, dark clouds were hovering, a threatening force that refused to go away, and as he sparked the engine, sparks of light danced in the sky.

* * *

He stopped by the Gainesville Police Department on his way to the outskirts of town—just to satisfy his curiosity.

He doubted he would find anyone there, but he had to hold out hope that something, anything, would turn up to point him in the direction of what had gone down in his sleepy town a month ago.

He had to put on the Ute's headlights as he drove through town, and when he arrived at the small, modern red-brick building, he found it locked. He peered in through the glass door, saw the station was in darkness, the desk unmanned. He rapped on the door. Waited. Nobody came out to greet him.

There didn't appear to be any broken windows. He considered smashing one and checking the place out for himself, but despite his many bad habits, breaking and entering wasn't one of them. He would only break into places if necessary.

With a heavy sigh, Tony left the police station and drove back to Main Street and continued towards the outskirts.

The storm was building in the sky above. Light sparkled in the clouds, thunder grumbled like an old man's stomach at dinnertime.

Tony had rarely seen such a display of light and noise. It was as scary as it was breathtaking, and at times Tony thought he even saw splashes of red and pink when the lightning broke across the dreary morning sky.

That sizzling metallic smell was still all around him, even in the Ute with all the windows up. It was in his clothes, in his hair. His skin was even tingling, like his whole body had pins and needles.

He continued up one of the steep roads leading out of town. The road soon leveled out and at the T-intersection, he turned left onto Wickes Road, and headed for the Hammond farm.

As he neared he saw that lights were on inside the main house, and there was an initial rush of hope that someone was home.

But he reminded himself that most of the houses still had their lights on, it didn't necessarily mean anything.

He slowed the car, turned, and wound his way up the long driveway, stopping behind old Burt Hammond's Ford Fairlane. Tony hopped out and started towards the house.

Please let there be someone home, please let Amy and Heather be inside.

He trudged up the porch steps and at the front door, tried the knob.

The door was locked.

So he knocked. Then rang the doorbell when his knocking yielded no answer.

When the doorbell failed to bring anybody to the door, he worked his way around the house, seeing if Burt had left any windows open. But luck wasn't on Tony's side today. He did find a window smashed on one side, but it was too small to crawl through.

The back door was also locked, and when he searched

the few sheds out back, he found them empty. Just a lot of old broken cobwebs and farming equipment, not even a spider, a rat or an old mangy dog to greet him.

Standing out in the back of Burt Hammond's house, the 90 acres of farmland stretching out before him, hazy in the gloomy light, Tony was again struck by how quiet the world was.

Even with the storm brewing above, he still expected to hear the usual farm noises; all he heard was the howling wind, the occasional slap of thunder.

Was it really possible that all the animals in Gainesville had vanished, too?

Tony turned from the paddock, and strode over to the back door of the farmhouse. Now was the time to start breaking doors — he would pay for the damage later, if — no, *when* — things turned out okay. Paying for property damage was the least of his concerns; he would gladly pay his entire life savings if only he could have some normalcy back in his life. He had worked hard to get clean and live a normal life with his family, and he wasn't about to let that go without a fight.

He picked up an axe he found imbedded in a nearby stump and hacked away at the door until it broke open.

The now-familiar stench of rotting food slapped him in the face.

Not a good sign.

Still he entered, keeping a hold of the axe, though he didn't know why he kept it. What was he expecting to encounter inside? Zombies? Vampires? Jason-fucking-Voorhees?

The kitchen was neater than most others he had seen this morning. There were no dirty plates piled in the sink. There was a carton of milk, but that didn't account for the rank stench.

Must be the garbage bin, Tony figured, and he left the kitchen and headed down the hallway.

In the lounge, the TV was hissing, static interspersed with snatches of talking. He was beginning to really hate that sound.

He strode over, thought about taking the axe to the small square box, but decided that was a little too much vandalism and besides, wouldn't he get electrocuted?

Instead he reached down, was about to switch it off, when he heard a muffled, tinny voice crackle, "Unknown… spreadi…va..sh…eop…pol…e…"

Tony frowned. "Huh?" he said to the TV. He turned up the volume. Static continued to hiss and crackle. The voice had grown even more faint and harder to hear. "Come on," Tony muttered and banged the sides of the set. The reception didn't get any better.

After ten minutes of flipping through channels, banging the TV set some more, he decided whatever it was he had heard, it was either nothing, just his imagination, or something, but he was destined never to know, unless he got his arse moving.

So he switched off the TV and moved through the house.

The bedrooms were cold and empty, just rooms that used to house a kind, elderly farmer, now just space waiting to be filled again.

Tony left the Hammond farm with heavier shoulders and heart than when he'd entered.

Still more farms to go. And then the whole town to explore.

It was a daunting prospect, and time would tell how far he got before he gave up and decided instead to drive to Dover.

He stopped at the McKenzie farm, the Hood farm, the Kroenert farm, and the Livings farm. All were empty, except for radios and TVs speaking to no one and lottery tickets left to fade.

Jesus, did every single person in town buy a ticket? Tony wondered as he left the Livings farm and hopped back into his Ute.

With headlights spearing the darkness, Tony continued along Wickes Road, heading west.

There was one last farm he had to check. It was the farthest from town, scarcely within the town limits.

Hank Reynolds, the area's prime lamb breeder, lived up there in a crumbling old farmhouse with his eight (or was it nine?) year-old son, Shaun. Hank's wife and Shaun's mum, Doris, died when Shaun was five: an accident according to Hank, a simple case of gun malfunction; suicide according to everyone else.

Hank hardly ever ventured into town. He was a ghost, his presence felt throughout Gainesville, but rarely seen. Most people in town, Tony included, thought of Hank as a right arsehole. The rare times Tony saw Hank around town, he always had a scowl on his hard, slim face. He always looked to be in a hurry, too, which he probably was. In a hurry to get out of town, away from people, and back to his crummy shack way up in the rolling hills.

Shaun was another matter entirely. A tiny boy, he had a sad quality about him, though he always had a shy smile for Tony on those rare occasions he came into the hardware store with his dad.

Tony felt sorry for the boy, living with such a hard-arse like Hank Reynolds. Tony wouldn't have been surprised if Hank had Shaun working on the farm from sunup till sundown on weekends, on top of him going to Gainesville Primary during the week, and Tony always imagined Hank as a bible-belting disciplinarian, though that was purely conjecture on his part.

When Tony arrived at the Reynolds farm, he turned onto the long dirt road that served as a driveway. As he neared the house, he noticed that the windows were dark—every other house in town seemed to have at least one room lit.

Something stirred in Tony's gut, but he told himself not to get too excited. Probably meant nothing. Most likely the lights had burned out, or they weren't on in the first place when the house was vacated.

Tony pulled to a stop at the top of the driveway, behind Hank's old dirt-splattered Ute. He turned off the headlights, the engine, then he stepped out of the car.

He paused. Sniffed the air.

Now that certainly was strange, he thought. The air smelled cleaner here, free from that bitter metallic smell.

Though he did detect another smell, faint, and only when the wind blew in his direction. It was different from any smell he had come across this morning, not of rotten food and spoiled meat, but of dead things — a smell he knew all too well living in a small farming community.

He started forward and when he reached the front door, tried the doorknob. It was locked, so he knocked on the door (the Reynolds didn't own a doorbell — didn't own a lot of modern conveniences, according to some people). He waited, gut clenched in nervous anticipation.

All that answered was a short, sharp clap of thunder. So he knocked again. "Hank, you home!" he called. "It's Tony Christopher. Hank! Shaun! Please, open..."

Tony froze at the sound of banging inside.

The noise had been faint, but it had sounded like a door shutting, or a wooden table shifting on a hardwood floor.

Tony's heart hammered in his chest, the sound booming in his ears.

Don't get carried away. Could've been the echo of the thunder, or your imagination.

Mouth dry, he knocked on the door again. "Hello," he said, voice almost breaking. "Hello, is anyone in there?"

He pushed one ear against the cold wood and listened. And thought he heard a noise a lot like footsteps.

He pounded on the door. "Hey, open up! It's Tony, please, open up!"

He waited, but the door remained shut.

Fuck it. I'm going in. No matter who — or what — I find, I have to get in there.

"I'm coming in. I'm unarmed, so please, don't shoot."

Tony stood back, heaved a deep sigh, and then shot out his right foot. He hit the wood with a jolt. Pain coursed through his leg and up his body.

Damn!

He tried again, and this time the door gave way a little.

His leg sore, he opted for his shoulder, and so, with a running start, he charged towards the slightly bowed door and broke it all the way open.

His shoulder cried out in pain, but at least he was in.

The house was dim, with only gray, muted light spilling through the windows. There was a musty smell, but no stench of spoiled food.

And the house was quiet; Tony couldn't hear any television static.

"Hello, is there anybody here?"

His voice sounded scared, but loud, in the stillness.

He started forward, treading slowly, letting his eyes become accustomed to the darkness. He darted his gaze around the small shack, not wanting to be surprised by the barrel of a shotgun suddenly pointing at his face.

To his right was a room containing an old couch, a few worn chairs, and a fireplace that held blackened logs. Some rifles were perched on one wall. Behind the lounge room was a small kitchen, which housed an old fashioned refrigerator, a stove, and a table that looked handmade. Sitting atop the table was a bowl of half-eaten cereal and a carton of long-life milk. It had to be fresh, or else there would've been a noticeable smell of sour milk.

Taking his chances, Tony crept into the lounge, eyes continually scouting for any movement, and headed towards Hank's firearms. There were two rifles resting on hooks against the wall, the bottom one was sitting slightly crooked. He took the bottom rifle carefully down from its cradle. He never was much into guns, but living in a farming community, he couldn't help but be a little familiar with firearms. The rifle in his hands was a Mauser 98 bolt action. Sliding back the bolt, Tony saw the chamber was empty.

Ah well, didn't hurt to check.

He placed back the rifle, didn't bother checking the other one, and headed back out of the lounge.

As Tony worked his way down the hall, he spotted two doors. He took some much-needed breaths (he hadn't realized he was holding his breath until his lungs started burning) and stopped at the first door.

He gripped the handle and pushed.

He gazed in at the modest bathroom, saw it was empty, closed the door and moved down to the second, a board creaking as he stepped. Tony winced, but then realized how silly it was to be worried about a little creak. If somebody was here, they already knew he was inside—breaking down the door sort of gave that away.

Still, he was scared. Not only of what might be waiting for him behind door number two, but scared of what *wasn't* waiting for him.

Admit it, if either Amy or Heather were in here, they would've come bolting out the moment I identified who I was.

Unless they weren't able to...

A whole slew of unwanted and horrible images popped into Tony's head, of Hank and ropes and blood and sex and...

Stop it!

He considered going back, trying to find cartridges for the Mauser, but then he heard what sounded like a child whimpering from behind the second door.

Shaun?

Tony gripped the doorknob and eased the door open.

He saw the tiny figure curled up at the head of the bed, eyes wide and looking fearful. Tony exhaled and said with a quivering voice, "Hey there Shaun. It's Tony. Tony Christopher."

The boy blinked in the dim light.

"It's okay, I'm not going to hurt you."

Tony wanted to rush over and both hug the boy until all breath was squeezed from his skinny body, and shake him, demanding he tell him what the hell was going on and why he was seemingly the only person left in town.

But Tony knew, even amid all his fear and confusion that he had to proceed delicately. He didn't want to frighten the boy. Who knew what horrors he had witnessed? If Tony, a grown man used to dealing with pain, was terrified after only a few hours of this nightmare, he could only imagine how a young boy left alone for a month must be feeling.

"Are you hurt Shaun?" Tony asked.

The boy hesitated, then shook his head.

"Can I come in?"

Tony itched to find out what the boy knew; he sweated fire waiting for the boy to answer. Finally Shaun nodded.

Tony smiled thinly and stepped into the room.

He glanced around, saw another bed against the wall on the opposite side of the room, its covers undisturbed and pulled tightly over the bed. It reminded Tony of an army barracks. "Is your dad home?" Tony asked.

Shaun, still curled in a tight ball at the head of the bed, shook his head. "He's...he's not home right at the moment." The boy's voice sounded small, high, and shaky.

"You mean you're expecting him back?"

Shaun nodded.

Tony pointed to the bed. "Mind if I have a seat?" He didn't wait for Shaun to answer. Tony sat on the edge of the single bed, on the coarse green bedspread. He took a deep breath before asking: "Shaun, do you know what happened? Where is everybody?"

Shaun gazed down at the timber floor, a floor that looked as cold and uninviting as it did hard. Only a single thin, frayed rug in the middle of the room, between the two beds, offered any comfort. Tony shivered, looked around for any heating, saw only a dark fireplace littered with ash.

"Gone," Shaun breathed.

Tony nodded. He reached over and patted Shaun on the arm. The boy's skin was like snow.

Shaun flinched and pulled his arm away.

"It's okay," Tony said. "I know you're scared. But you can trust me. Would you like me to make a fire? It's a little chilly in here."

Tony hopped off the bed, wandered over to the fireplace and picked up the few logs left in the bucket, as well as some kindling. He placed the kindling down, then stacked the logs on top, and after wasting a few matches, finally lit the kindling, which in turn lit the logs. Soon a healthy fire was blazing. Warmth and a smoky aroma filled the room. Tony wandered over to Shaun's bed and sat back down. In the light of the flame the boy looked even more pale, his face too thin.

"So Shaun, do you know what's going on? Where's your dad?"

Shaun looked towards the fire, stared at the licking orange and yellow flames. Finally he opened his mouth and in a soft voice, said. "Daddy told me to wait here until he came back. Told me not to go anywhere. Bluey went with him." The kid looked especially sad after saying that last line.

"Who's Bluey?"

"Our dog. He always went everywhere with dad. He was a good dog, a good sheep herder, and I loved him."

"Where did your dad go Shaun?"

"To see why all the people were crying and screaming."

Tony's heart thudded, like a horse was bucking in his chest. "What were they screaming about?"

Shaun flicked his eyes down. "I don't know," he said. "But I think it had something to do with the lightning."

Tony smacked his lips together. He really could do with a nip of whisky, a swill of gin; hell, he'd settle for a mouthful of cold beer. "Lightning?"

"There was a storm. A funny storm."

"What do you mean by funny?"

"There was no rain or thunder. Just lots of lightning."

"You mean an electrical storm?"

Shaun shrugged.

"So what happened?"

"Well, there were strange lights in the sky, not just the lightning. I was watching from the bedroom window, even though I wasn't supposed to be. I was supposed to be in bed, sleeping, daddy told me so. He…he wasn't very happy with me, he yelled at me, told me I wasn't to watch the storm or anything, just go to bed and sleep."

Tony was careful not to push the kid too much; he was obviously scared and confused, but Tony needed answers.

"Why was your dad angry at you?"

Shaun started picking at his nails. He had a pouty look on his face. "He wouldn't let me go and watch the game on TV. All I wanted was to get us some money. Daddy was always complaining about not having enough money. All I wanted was to make him happy. But he got mad. He didn't like me buying the ticket. And he wouldn't let me go over to Rick's to watch the game on TV."

The storm outside continued to rage and a glance out the window showed Tony an angry sky.

Tony flicked his eyes back to Shaun. "I don't understand, Shaun. He didn't let you watch a footy game on TV?"

"No. The draw. The tatts game."

"The Tattslotto draw? You mean the thirty million dollar draw that was on Saturday night, about a month ago?"

The boy nodded. "We don't have a TV. Daddy doesn't believe in having one. Says it's all just garbage. We have a radio, but that's broken."

Tony shifted on the bed. He wiped cold sweat from his brow. "So let me get this straight. There was an electrical storm on the night of the big Tattslotto draw. You bought a ticket so you and your dad could have lots of money if you won, but your dad got angry, so he sent you to your bedroom. Is that right?"

"Yeah. After he tore up the ticket."

"So you were watching the storm from your bedroom, even though you weren't supposed to be?"

Sheepishly, Shaun nodded.

"What did you see?"

"Well there was this strange buzzing sound in the sky and…" Shaun stopped. "I need to go to the bathroom," he said.

Tony nodded and the boy scampered off the bed and hurried out into the hallway.

Tony hopped up and wandered over to the window. He gazed up at the sky. Thick red and pink tinged storm clouds hovered over the town, instilling Tony with a deep sense of dread. Sparks of light crackled and popped.

This is crazy. I should just take Shaun and drive over to Dover.

But he ached to find out what the boy knew. Maybe Shaun could tell him where everyone had gone, and maybe Tony could help some people—including his wife and daughter.

He didn't hear the toilet flush, it was only when he heard footsteps pattering on the floorboards that he snapped out of his trance and turned around.

Shaun was crouched at the fireplace, hands up to the flames. Tony wandered over and stood beside him. "Shaun, please, if you saw something that night, if you know where everyone went, you need to tell me. I know you're scared. So am I. But if they're in danger, we need to help them."

"All I saw was the light," Shaun said, staring into the fire. "And then the screaming started."

Tony wiped his mouth and took some deep breaths. "What kind of lights were they? Like spotlights?"

Shaun shook his head. "There was a zapping sound, then a small explosion, and then the sky was filled with a thousand bolts of lightning. And not just usual lightning, it stayed in the sky, like the lightning was stuck or something. Then everything was quiet. I hopped back into bed and tried to sleep, but soon I heard the screaming and the crying. People were calling out names. Sometime in the night, the bedroom door opened and daddy came in. He thought I was asleep but I wasn't. I had my eyes closed and he stood over my bed and said, 'Shaun, wake up.' So I opened my eyes. He told me that something had happened in town, and he was going down there to check it out. I told him no, stay here, I was scared, and then I started crying. I didn't want to, but I couldn't help it. He told me to stop crying, that I was being a big baby. There was nothing to be scared about, he said, it was probably just something to do with the storm. Maybe some people had been hit by lightning. He told me not to leave the house, that I would be in big trouble if I did, and that he would be back soon. Then he left. And…and he never came back…"

Shaun squeezed his eyes shut. His chin began to tremble and finally he broke down and started crying.

Tony frowned. Something didn't quite add up. He had pulled up behind Hank's car when he arrived—did Hank have two cars? Not that Tony had ever seen.

Surely he didn't walk into town, Tony thought.

"Shaun…" Tony started, but then a thunderous clap in the sky, like a whip, cut him off, and then rain started pelting the farmhouse.

Tony glanced over his shoulder at the window. "What the hell," he whispered. He moved away from Shaun, and stood over by the window.

Yellow and red streamed down the glass. The off-colored rain oozed down the window like red and yellow snot.

What the hell kind of rain is that?

Tony turned around and said, "Wait here, Shaun."

The boy rose to his feet, wiped his eyes and looked at Tony. "No, you can't leave."

"I'm just going outside."

"I'm coming with you."

"No. Stay here." Tony stepped up to Shaun, put his hands on the boy's bony shoulders. "I won't go anywhere, I promise. I'll be back in a few minutes. You just wait right here, okay?"

Reluctantly, Shaun nodded.

Tony left the bedroom and stormed down the hall. Outside, he stood on the porch and wrinkled his nose at the putrid stench. There was an overwhelming smell of blood and burnt flesh. He stepped forward, outstretched an arm into the muddy rain. The rain felt warm and slimy and when Tony brought his arm back, he stared down at his hand, at the strange liquid that coated his skin like red and yellow paint. He worked his fingers together, feeling the thick gooiness of whatever it was that was falling from the sky.

Whatever it was, it certainly wasn't rain.

He brought his hand to his nose and sniffed. "Christ,"

he choked. The stuff on his hand smelt like rotten meat and blood—a caustic combination of thick saltiness and greasy fat.

He wiped his hand on his jeans, over and over again, but he couldn't get the sticky feeling or the rotten smell off his skin. Tony gazed up at the sky, now the color of raw meat, watched the thick, slimy rain continue to fall, making dirty yellow-brown puddles in the dirt.

Tony thought of what Shaun had told him, about the electrical storm, the small explosion, the lightning stuck in the sky, the screaming and crying afterwards.

And then everyone in town disappearing.

"I hate this smell."

Tony whirled around. Saw the tiny figure of Shaun standing by the broken door. "Huh?" Tony breathed.

Shaun sniffed the air. "This smell, it's like what I smelled that night. It reminded me of the time daddy accidentally burnt himself. He was cooking one night and he wasn't…feeling well, and his arm got caught in the fire on the stove, and his skin and hair got burnt. It smelt kinda like this."

"You smelt this on the night everyone disappeared?" Tony felt numb.

Shaun nodded. "Only, now it's stronger." He frowned as his eyes scanned the falling goo. "What is it?"

"I'm not sure," Tony said. "But I told you to stay inside, so get back in there."

"But…"

"Inside," Tony said and the boy turned and headed back into the house.

Tony turned back to the rain.

What the hell is it?

His head swirled with all kinds of ghoulish ideas, none of them made any sense, but they crashed through his brain nonetheless.

What the hell is going on here!
Amy…Heather…where are you…?

When he felt something wet on his face, he hurriedly

wiped at his cheeks. But when he looked up, he saw that the tin roof wasn't leaking. As more tears rained down his face, he turned and staggered inside.

He stumbled into the lounge room, the need to drink, to douse his fear and confusion, potent. He wanted to forget that his wife and daughter and dear old dad were missing, along with the whole town; that the only remaining survivor was a boy; that whatever happened here a month ago had to do with lightning and an explosion; and that there was now a horrible rain falling over the town, a rain that smelled suspiciously like blood and flesh.

He wanted to forget all those things and instead concentrate on washing his worries away in a flood of amber liquid.

"Come on Hank. I bet you're not a stranger to the drink." He spotted an old cupboard against one wall. When Tony tried to open it, found it was locked. A cold, dark smile broke across his face. "Bingo." Tony couldn't be bothered searching for the key, so he simply continued what he had started with the front door and using a meat tenderiser he found in the kitchen, smashed open the cupboard. Inside he found an assortment of whisky, gin, vodka, rum, cognac, port, sherry…Tony really had his pick. He grabbed the rum, unscrewed the cap, lifted his arm and was about to take a swill, when a small voice said: "Rum was daddy's favorite."

Tony flinched, lowered the bottle.

"He used to get drunk on rum before he…before he punished me."

The bastard beat Shaun? Christ.

Tony closed his eyes.

In his mind he saw Heather and Amy crying, cowering in the corner of the lounge, while he staggered around drunk, yelling. He had never laid a finger on either of them, not in all the years he was drinking and taking drugs, but at that moment, he saw himself as no different than Hank Reynolds.

All that hard work you put into getting yourself clean. All that pain and suffering, and for what? Just to go back to it again?

But without Amy and Heather, what did he have to live for? What was the point? What did it matter if he drank himself into a stupor?

But there must've been a flickering ember of life somewhere inside Tony, because he found himself saying, "Shaun, help me pour these drinks down the sink." He opened his eyes.

Shaun nodded, a smile flitted across his face. Together they dumped the contents of the rum, whisky, port, wine, every bottle of alcohol in the cupboard, down the kitchen sink. Tony watched it all gurgle down the drain with a heavy-heart, but by the time they had finished emptying all the bottles, he felt good, like he had conquered another smaller demon.

"Okay Shaun, we have to get out of here."

There was no way Tony could search the town now, not with that rain. And besides, it really did look like the town was empty.

"But...but daddy said not to leave."

Tony sighed. "I'm sorry to have to say this Shaun, but your daddy's not coming back. I don't really know how it happened, but whatever it was, it..."

Evaporated the town? Incinerated every living creature? Turned them all into flesh and blood rain...?

Tony gritted his teeth at the last thought. He couldn't let himself imagine such a ghastly thing could be true. If he allowed himself to think about it, he'd likely curl up in a ball and go insane.

First, he had to get Shaun to safety. Once that was done, *then* he would go insane.

"...made everyone disappear," he finished. "Including your dad."

"But how? Where'd they all go?"

"I don't know."

"Did it have something to do with the lightning?"

Tony shrugged. "Possibly, I guess."

"Did everyone get hit by the lightning?"

Tony sighed. "I don't know. Maybe. You were here when it happened, not me. You know more about it than I do."

"Did God punish everyone because they lived in sin?"

Tony frowned. "What do you mean by that?"

"Well, daddy used to say that everyone who watched TV or played computer games was lazy. He reckoned that people don't work hard enough anymore, that we've become a bunch of lazy, mindless zombies. Well, according to the bible, laziness is a sin. You know, sloth? Also, the bible says, *'diligent hands will rule, but laziness ends in slave labor'*. So I was thinking, maybe God punished everyone because they were lazy? Because they were all watching too much TV?"

Tony frowned. "Wait a minute. You said that there were hundreds of lightning bolts in the sky that night?"

Shaun nodded.

"And that they were all stuck in the sky, like…"

…like each one was plugged into something?

Tony thought of all the houses he had gone into, each with the television still on, broadcasting nothing but static. And then there were the unmarked Tattslotto tickets everywhere, and the broken windows.

He thought about what Shaun had told him — the lightning, the zapping sound, the small explosion and then the smell of burnt flesh.

Is it possible? Did the lightning somehow plug into all the TV sets, and anyone near the TV was then zapped into the air?

It was a crazy notion, and Tony was no brain. He didn't understand much of anything other than nails and ladders and drills — but it would explain how an entire town could just vanish. It would also explain why Shaun was the only one left alive.

Tony felt short of breath, his head was giddy. He braced his hands on top of the cupboard, lowered his head and took some deep breaths.

"Are you okay Mr. Christopher?"

When the dizzy spell had passed, he straightened,

opened his eyes and looked at Shaun. "Call me Tony," he breathed.

"So were they punished?"

"Let's worry about that later. For now, let's just concentrate on getting out of here."

"We're going out in the rain?"

"I'm afraid so."

"But it smells funny."

"I know. But you can do it. You're a big boy."

"But daddy…"

"Isn't coming back. You have to believe me, Shaun. If you want to be safe, you have to come with me, okay?"

Shaun, looking so small, like a frightened doll, looked up at Tony, and with tears trickling down his lightly freckled face, he nodded. He reached out and took a hold of Tony's hand. The boy's skin was cold and clammy.

"Come on," Tony said.

When they stepped outside, Tony swallowed back bile as the smell of the rain worked its way up his nostrils. "See my truck over there? That's where we're heading."

He felt Shaun's hand tighten. "It's okay, you can do it," Tony said. He started forward. He stepped out into the rain, felt it wash over him. Shaun followed. But the moment the boy was under the warm sludge, he pulled backwards.

"No," Shaun squeaked, and he let go of Tony's hand and raced back up the steps.

"Come on, Shaun," Tony pleaded. "You can do it."

The boy shook his head, spraying yellow and red muck everywhere.

Tony sighed. "Okay, I'll drive the truck over to you, okay? You wait here."

Shaun nodded.

Tony turned and continued towards his car, the rain falling heavily, feeling like warm glue being tipped over him, plastering his hair, slithering down his back. And the smell was like walking through an abattoir at high noon on a summer's day.

Tony stepped around puddles of brown goo as he

trekked towards the Ute. The ground was slippery and Tony almost landed on his arse a couple of times, but he managed to stay on his feet.

When he reached his car, he flung open the door and jumped inside. He had left the keys in the ignition, so he turned them and the engine grumbled to life. He slammed the door shut, switched on the headlights, put the gear in reverse, and pressed down on the accelerator.

The car's engine revved, but the car didn't move. Tony pressed his foot hard on the accelerator, but the car just wouldn't budge.

"Damn it!" Tony grumbled. He jumped out of the car.

He crouched down, was unable to see a whole lot, but enough to see that the tyres were sunken in the muddy dirt. "Great," Tony muttered. He ducked into the car, turned off the headlights, then the engine, then ducked back out and pocketed the keys.

Though Tony's Ute was blocking it, he checked Hank's car anyway; its tires were also half sunken into the ground. He headed back to the farmhouse, to Shaun waiting on the porch.

"Sorry kid, the car's bogged. We ain't getting outta here in my car, or your dad's. Does your dad have any other cars? Maybe one locked away in a shed?"

"Just a ride-on mower way out back in the big shed. But I ain't going in that, no way, not with all the rain falling—it's got no roof."

"Okay." With Shaun leading the way, they headed back inside. "Shaun, why don't you go and have a shower, get cleaned up, and then we'll decide what we're going to do."

Shaun nodded and he traipsed down the hall, his shoes squelching and leaving dirty red footprints on the floorboards.

Once Shaun was inside the bathroom, Tony headed into the lounge, where he stood before the empty liquor cabinet.

He licked his lips, tasted only the foul metallic taste.

With a sigh, he turned around and headed into the kitchen. He found an almost empty bottle of Coke in the fridge. He downed what was left of the soft drink, and though it was flat, it was still sweet and it took away some of the rancid taste of the rain.

When he was finished he threw the empty soft drink bottle into the bin and wandered back into the lounge. His eyes fell on the blackened fireplace.

A fire, that's what we need.

It was getting cool inside, and as the day wore on, it would only get colder. Hopefully they wouldn't be here when night fell, but still, it would be good to get the whole place warmer, just in case.

Tony walked over to the fireplace, saw that the wood basket contained only one log, so he headed for the back door.

He didn't know precisely where Hank kept his pile of wood, but most of the farmers he knew kept it out back, under a tarp, or in a shed, where it would keep dry.

He turned on the back porch light, stepped outside. The smell of the rain assaulted his senses—he doubted he would ever get used to the stench—though it seemed even worse out here.

Surely the rain will stop soon. It has to—doesn't it?

If they couldn't drive out of town, and walking was out of the question, maybe their only option was to wait the rain out, and when it had run its course, then they could leave.

Tony glanced around, he couldn't see Hank's wood stockpile, so he headed to the left. The moment he turned the corner he saw the pile of wood; it bulged under a blue tarp. Tony started towards it.

When he reached the pile of wood, he stopped, turned and gazed out into the darkness.

His gut fluttered. He sensed there was something out there, something wrong, other than the obvious.

Just my imagination.

Still, he couldn't help the way he was feeling. There was a particularly pungent stench, a smell even worse than the rain.

Leaving the wood for the moment, Tony headed back inside. He searched around for a torch; soon found one in a closet. A large, heavy-duty torch, which fortunately still worked. Taking the torch outside, Tony strode around to the side of the house, and standing next to the pile of wood, aimed the torch into the darkness.

The powerful beam cut through the thick blanket of rain, lighting muddy paddocks in the distance. He saw shapes lying all over the place, lying still on the ground.

Hank's beloved sheep. Poor things, they probably died a horrible death.

He thought of Shaun cooped up inside the house for the past month—surely he had heard them crying?

He really took his dad's orders of not leaving the house to heart, didn't he?

Tony moved the light slowly to the left and when he lit a tree stump, most likely Hank's chopping block, he paused. He thought he had glimpsed something odd in the edge of the light. When he moved the torch down, he saw the body of Hank Reynolds sprawled on the ground.

"Oh Christ," Tony breathed.

Shaun's father was lying in a shallow puddle, about six metres away. His bloated head was pointing towards the front of the house, his feet, straight as a razor, towards the dead sheep. The arm closest to the house was splayed, while the other hand rested against his belly. There was an axe lying nearby.

Tony stepped forward. He barely registered the rain as he trod over to the body. The stink was overwhelming. At the body, Tony saw that Hank's eyes were open, staring up into the falling rain, and his mouth was slightly agape. He crouched and scanning the body with the torch, looked for any wounds.

There was a noticeably dark red patch on the man's shirt, almost dead center on his chest, and taking a closer look, Tony saw a small hole in the fabric.

What the hell's going on here? he thought as he straightened and staggered into the house.

He stopped in the kitchen at the sight of the figure standing in the lounge.

"Tony? Um, the shower's free."

Tony looked over at the boy, at the sweet, innocent, boy. He looked clean, his hair was damp, and he wore a fresh, though shabby, change of clothes.

"Shaun," Tony breathed. "I found your daddy outside. He's dead. He has been shot, Shaun. Do you understand?"

Shaun swallowed. A frown creased his round, pale face. "Huh? No, daddy left, and he said he'd come back."

"Tell me the truth," Tony said, dropping the torch onto the kitchen table and stepping into the lounge. "What's going on, Shaun?"

"Daddy left," Shaun said, taking a few steps back. "Daddy left, Daddy left!"

Thunder exploded across the sky.

Tony flinched.

The boy didn't.

"Shaun, you have to tell me the truth. I won't be mad, I just need to know. Did you...murder your father?"

A fearful look came over the boy. "No!" Shaun cried.

Another explosion of thunder, this one rattled the house. Shaun took off running.

"Shaun! Shaun, come back!"

The bedroom door banged shut.

Tony hurried down the hall, to the bedroom door. When he tried the knob, he found the door locked. "Shaun, open up," Tony said. "Please. I just want to talk."

Tony heard sniffling and choking sobs from behind the door. "Daddy..." *Choke.* "...will be back soon."

"Open up, Shaun."

"No." *Sob.* "Daddy will be mad if he sees me talking to you. He'll...he'll get the cane, or the belt and teach me a lesson."

"He can't hurt you now," Tony said. "I promise."

There was silence, then footsteps tapping across the floorboards. The lock clicked, and then faster footsteps, and then the sigh of springs as a body jumped on the bed.

Tony pushed open the door and stepped inside. Shaun looked like he did when Tony found him earlier — curled up at the head of the bed, shivering, looking petrified.

No wonder. On top of everything else, he killed his dad.

Well you don't know that for sure, but Jesus, what other explanation is there?

"Shaun, what happened?"

Shaun started crying. Tony went over, sat on the bed and took the boy in his arms. "Hey, it's gonna be all right. You'll see. Once this is all over, everything'll be all right."

Tony didn't believe that everything would turn out okay, but if he was sitting here consoling Heather, he would've said the same thing.

Tony held Shaun for a while, the boy's wet face dampening his crusty red and yellow shirt.

"He...he tore up my lotto ticket," Shaun said, sniffling, face still buried in Tony's chest. "He yelled at me for wasting my money, and then sent me to my room. He told me he would...would punish me later. After he had made a fire. I was angry, and hurt. I bought the ticket for him. All I wanted was to have a new house, some new clothes, a television. I...I didn't want to be hurt again. I was tired of being hit, over and over. I just wanted to hurt him, the way he hurt me. I waited until he was outside, then I went into the lounge. I knew where daddy kept the key for the ammunition drawer, even though it was supposed to be a secret, so I unlocked it and got one cartridge for the Mauser. I loaded the gun and then went outside. Daddy was in the middle of chopping wood, Bluey was sitting under the porch. I pointed the gun at daddy and told him I didn't want to be hurt anymore, like he hurt mummy, I just wanted to be left alone. He...he just laughed at me, told me to put the gun down, that I couldn't shoot a can I was so soft, and that it wasn't even loaded anyway. He kept laughing and coming towards me. I was scared. All I could think about was how mad he was at me for buying the ticket, and how mad he'd be at me for taking the gun without asking. I...I pulled the trigger. The gun went off. Bluey got scared and ran away.

Daddy looked shocked as he fell backwards. I didn't mean to kill him...I only wanted to hurt him...I...I..."

"It's okay," Tony said.

Oh Christ, Tony thought.

"Tony?" the small voice said.

"Hmm?"

"Will I go to hell?"

"What?" Tony huffed.

"You know, for killing my dad."

Tony squeezed the boy. "I don't think God punishes those who have a good heart."

Tony didn't know if that was true—he wasn't a religious person. But it sounded appropriate, under the circumstances.

Shaun sniffed and then continued, his voice sounding croaky, tired. "So anyway, afterwards, I came into the bedroom and cried, and that's when the lightning started." He paused before adding: "They had never been that bad before. Never lightning. Mostly just clouds and rain."

Tony pulled back. He frowned down at Shaun, at his tear-streaked face and red eyes. "What are you talking about?"

"I guess I must've been really scared and angry, it went out of control this time. When it started lightning, I was even more scared."

"What are you saying?"

"I don't know why it happens," Shaun choked. "It just does. Whenever I get really angry or upset."

"Are you saying that you caused the storm?" Tony gaped at the boy.

Shaun sighed. Then he nodded.

Tony jumped to his feet. "You're the reason everyone in town vanished? My wife and child are dead because of you?"

Crying, Shaun said, "I didn't mean to."

"I don't believe this," Tony muttered. He started pacing around the room. "I don't believe this," he repeated. "A person can't control the weather. They can't create storms out of anger."

"It just happens," Shaun said, voice soft and teary.

Tony stopped, gazed at Shaun. "It just happens, does it? You just get angry and it starts raining?"

Shaun shrugged. "Ever since I was six and got hit by lightning. The doctors reckon I should've been killed, they couldn't believe it when I survived, said it was a miracle. But since then, whenever I get angry or really upset, I go all tingly and my eyes go all dark, but I can see the sky in my head, like I'm outside watching it happen. I can't control it. I can't stop it. Clouds appear in the sky over the town, or it suddenly starts raining. It's usually over pretty fast. When I wake up, I can see again, and I'm really tired. At first, I didn't know I was doing it, but when I started to realize what was happening, I got scared and tried not to get angry. Even when dad was punishing me, I would try and stop it from happening, but it didn't always work. But when daddy tore up my ticket and yelled at me, when I thought of what was to come, I couldn't help it."

"And you got so upset that this time you caused lightning?"

Shaun nodded. "I was so scared. I could see the lightning. Then I heard the screams. I didn't know what was going on. The storm lasted for hours, the screaming lasted for hours, and in my head I could see the lightning, it was like the sky had a thousand electric arms. When the screaming stopped, and I woke up, I was too exhausted to get up. So I lay in bed all night and most of the next day. It was too quiet. I couldn't hear anyone, and nobody came, not even Bluey. I thought someone might come for daddy, but no one did. I started missing him, and that's when I made up the story about him going to see what had happened in town. I told myself he'd be back, soon, even though I knew deep down he never would. But I was scared, and lonely. I wanted to believe it so much that he was still alive. Sometimes, I almost did believe it."

"What about this storm? You caused it, too?"

"I guess," Shaun said. "I was scared when I heard your

car. It meant someone was in town, and I was scared you would find daddy."

"And then the storm started." Tony shook his head. "This is freakin' nuts," he muttered.

"But now I can't stop it. I woke up when you first knocked on the door, but the storm didn't stop. And I didn't mean for it to rain. I don't know why it's raining that...stuff. I'm sorry I didn't tell you about it earlier, but I was scared, scared you'd...leave, or think I was crazy."

I need a drink. Yes, that's what I need.

Tony headed for the bedroom door, mind in a semi-daze.

"Tony, is it...people?"

Tony stopped, turned around. "Huh?"

Shaun looked at Tony with dark eyes, eyes that held so much fear and pain Tony thought they might burst. "The rain, is it blood and flesh? Because that's what it smells like."

Tony wanted to scream at Shaun for what he had done.

But he knew the kid didn't mean for any of this to happen. He didn't intentionally cause the storm that led to everyone in town being vaporized.

Tony nodded and said, "Yes, I think it is people."

The rain is people. Christ.

He thought about how it must've happened. He guessed the valley was like a large bowl, the rising hills surrounding the town acting as a kind of barrier, containing the electrical currents given off by all the TV sets. The lightning from Shaun's electrical storm must've been attracted to those currents, and when the two collided, consequently zapped everyone within the affected area up into the earth's atmosphere over the town. And when Shaun got upset again and started another storm a month later, instead of rain pouring from the sky, blanketing the town, it was the town's inhabitants themselves that spewed forth. Sort of like a vacuum cleaner set on reverse.

Stomach queasy, Tony left the room and staggered down the hall and into the lounge.

The house was cold away from the bedroom. It was dimly lit, depressing, and Tony would've welcomed the warmth of some rum.

He went over to the liquor cabinet, fell to his knees and shoved an arm into the darkness, hoping he had missed a bottle. He slapped his hand around, but all he felt was wood.

"Damn it," he growled and got to his feet.

Why'd I have to go and get all righteous and dump all the alcohol?

His heart was thumping, his palms were sweaty. He searched the room, looking for anywhere there might be more alcohol. He opened drawers, cupboards, throwing out all manner of junk. He flung cushions from sofas, moved furniture around. In the kitchen he checked behind the fridge, under the sink—the kinds of places he used to hide bottles of booze from his wife.

He stormed around the house, kicking things out of the way, flinging objects around, searching for even a drop of liquor.

Come on, Hank. You must have booze stashed somewhere. Don't do this to me!

But after twenty minutes of searching, and finding no alcohol—not even some vanilla essence or mouthwash—he headed for the front door.

Screw this. I need booze. Screw the rain, screw the kid. There's a whole town full of empty houses and pubs. There's enough alcohol down there to last me till Christmas.

He left the house.

Stopped when he saw the lightning in the distance. "Oh no," he breathed. Bolts of electricity were everywhere, lighting the sky in an incandescent orange hue.

Don't tell me it's happened again...

He stepped out into the rain. The warm, gooey feeling on his skin curled his stomach, but he didn't care. He needed to know what had happened to the town—if he could still get down and raid the hotel.

He trudged through thick puddles and soft mushy

ground, keeping his lips tightly closed as the rain rolled down his face. He blinked thick strands from his eyes.

When he came to the crossroads of Wickes and Camp Street, which overlooked the town, he stopped at the edge of the hill and gaped at the sight below him.

Rain seemed to be everywhere — pooling on rooftops, dripping from signs, clogging up the trees. The streets below were running red and yellow.

But that wasn't the worst of it. Lightning had speared nearly every house, making it look like a giant thousand-fingered electric claw was gripping the town. He could hear the air hissing and crackling with electricity. There was no way Tony could get down there, not unless he wanted to be vaporized.

And no way to get to Dover, either. Dover was Gainesville's closest neighbor — the next town was double the distance away — but you could only get there via the main road that wound through town.

As he stood watching his town being assailed by human rain, Tony noticed the occasional spark of electricity coursing through the rivers of flesh and blood that littered the streets and surrounding countryside.

Jesus. And then a thought occurred to him: *Could the town flood? Is that possible?*

The town *was* nestled in a valley. But Christ he hoped it wasn't possible. Because if the rain did continue to fall and the lightning continued to sizzle, then the entire town would become one great big sea of electricity. And if they were still stuck in that farmhouse with the waters rising, then they would well and truly be trapped.

If he could at least make the lightning disappear, then they could get to Dover (*or the pub*), rain be damned. But how on earth could he manage that?

If his assumption was correct, then the lightning was getting power from all the active TV sets. If he could somehow switch them all off...

But that was no good. No way to go into the houses now without being turned into human rain.

Turn off the power to the town? Yeah, that could work. Only problem is…

Tony had no idea how to do such a thing. He was just a simple hardware salesman; he didn't have the slightest clue where the town's power source was located. And even if he did know, he wouldn't know what to do once he got there. He'd likely get electrocuted for his efforts.

Shit. Scrap that idea.

Wiping sticky rain from his eyes, Tony gazed around at the town below. His eyes fell on a large puddle near the intersection of Main and Camp. There was a dip in the road, so the rain had pooled to a puddle the size of a small car.

Yep, if this rain keeps up, the town might very well go under…

Chills bumped over his skin.

Suddenly an object rose from the puddle. Well, it was more like the puddle *itself* rose, as a glob of the muddy brown puddle shot upwards, like a tree branch was rising from deep below the water's surface. The brown glob reached towards the sky, straining like it was searching for something, and then collapsed back into the puddle with a gooey splash.

"Ugh," Tony gasped.

What the fuck was that?

Tony stared at the puddle, a bewildered frown plastered across his face.

Another movement caught his attention, and snapping his head to the right, he saw more puddles stretch and curl. It was almost as if…

As if they were…alive.

The notion was ridiculous, but then he only had to remember what he had seen and heard these past few hours to know that anything was possible.

As electricity continued to crackle throughout the town, Tony turned around. He had to get back to Shaun, take the boy away from here, away from this madness, this hell on earth.

Wait a minute. Shaun's the cause of the rain, the lightning.

If he started it, he can finish it.

Tony started forward. He slipped. His heart seemed to fly from his chest as he fell to the ground. He landed face first, his head was knocked backwards, and flashes danced before his eyes.

He lay dazed for a bit, and then attempted to get to his feet.

But his shoes found only the slickness of the flesh and blood mélange, and this time he slipped backwards, towards the hill.

Oh shit!

He clawed at the ground, but it was no use. It was like he was on a slippery slide and there was no way he was going to stop himself from going down.

He started sliding down the grass. He saw the road quickly vanish, and then the world above turned to red and brown. He grabbed at the grass, but all he got was handfuls of dirty blades covered with goo. He hazarded a glance back, saw only the sloping hill, and he was sure that this was it.

The hill was about ten metres to the edge, and then there was a five-meter drop to Camp Street. He was going to land on hard asphalt, and if the fall didn't break his neck, then he was sure the electricity would zap him the moment he was within the affected area.

His only hope was that the section of road below was out of range of the electrical field, much like the Reynolds farmhouse was.

He continued to slide, hands gripping at anything, trying to stop his descent by digging his feet into the ground, but it was hopeless.

The end of the hill came up much too quickly, and Tony barely had enough time to realize he was falling in mid-air before he smacked onto the road.

The wind was torn out of his body as he landed on his left side. He felt something snap, a fireball of pain shot through his body, and he would've screamed if he had anything left in his lungs to scream with.

He ended up on his back, the rain splashing down on his face. He remained conscious, though dazed. He clutched at his left arm, and when he tried to move it, more pain jolted through his body. He gritted his teeth and tried not to think about the pain, or that his left arm was most certainly broken—but that was easier said than done.

He sat up, biting through the pain.

Tony thought he was going to faint, but he closed his eyes, swallowed, tasted blood, and fought through it.

It took him longer than it should have to realize he was still alive, that he hadn't been zapped by the lightning. It seemed this section of town was out of range too, but it was definitely closer, because the buzzing of electricity was stronger and he could feel the heat.

He opened his eyes and turned his head. He was on a lower platform now, still above the town, but from this position, he could see only the roofs of buildings. Except for St. Augustine, the Catholic Church, which stood stony and silent over to his left.

Tony struggled to his feet. He kept a hold on his left arm and once he was standing, he turned fully around, stepped over to the edge of the road and gazed down.

He saw a house just below with a bolt of lightning plugged into it, its inside glowing. Another house slightly farther down also had lightning spearing through a smashed window. There was a third stream of electricity coursing between the two—which seemed to be the pattern throughout the town.

Tony swallowed.

If he had fallen just a bit farther, he would've been a goner.

Suddenly a muddy blob, like a reddish-brown hand, reached up from the ground below and grabbed him around the ankle.

Tony shrieked, felt a mild electric shock.

He pulled back, but the long thin glob held tight. His leg burning, Tony almost toppled over, but he managed to stay on his feet. He scanned the road for a weapon; spotted a jagged rock sitting in a nearby ditch. Reaching down, he picked up the palm-sized rock and smashed one of its sharp ragged edges against the blob. The rock ripped a chunk of the thing away, mud-like stuff splattered on the road. Tony felt the thing loosen its hold and with a few more bashes, the puddle-thing finally released its hold and drew back quickly.

"Fucker," Tony spat. Keeping hold of the rock, he turned and started up the road.

It was tough going. His feet skidded a few times and he almost tripped over, but fortunately he didn't. When he reached flatland, he headed right, towards the Reynolds farm.

He ventured some glances back, saw more mutant puddles taking shape, and, like the thing that had grabbed his ankle, they too were starting to look more like parts of the human body.

He quickened his pace, all the while clutching at his throbbing left arm.

He staggered down the dark, lonely road towards the farmhouse. He heard sucking, slurping noises behind him, but this time he didn't turn around.

What the fuck is going on? What are they?

When he reached the driveway, he turned left, and when he spotted the distant porch light, he headed towards it.

At the house, he threw the rock away, stumbled up the steps and crashed inside. "Shaun," he cried. He headed down the hall and into the bedroom.

Shaun was still curled up on the bed.

Tony staggered over to the other bed—Hank's bed, he assumed—and collapsed onto its hard mattress. The springs underneath creaked. "The town," Tony breathed. "There's lightning everywhere. And the rain, it's..." Tony stopped to catch his breath. "It's alive."

Shaun's face turned ice-cold white. "Alive?"

Tony nodded.

Shaun looked down at Tony's left arm. "Y...you're hurt.

I'll get some bandages and make a sling." Shaun hopped off the bed.

"You know how to do that?"

Shaun cast his gaze down, nodded once, and as he left the room, Tony called, "Can you get a towel and a glass of water too?"

A few minutes later, Shaun came back carrying a large bucket with both hands. Water sloshed onto the floorboards. He set the bucket down, then he left again and next time he appeared he was holding a glass of water and a towel. He placed the towel on the bed, handed the glass to Tony, then vanished once again out the bedroom door.

Tony downed the water in three gulps, wishing it was vodka, or scotch (any liquor would do) instead of water.

I need booze now more than I think I ever have.

He wet the towel and with his one good arm washed his face clean of the rain, beginning with his eyes and mouth.

He had washed most of the gunk off his face, the towel now looking like it belonged to an ER trauma room, when Shaun came hurrying back. "Here, I got you some bandages, and this sheet can be the sling. I'll help you get your shirt off."

Tony managed to get half his shirt off without much trouble, but it was the other side, his left side, that proved difficult. Hot pain ripped through his arm, down his body, as the kid took the rest of the shirt off. Tony gritted his teeth and once the shirt was off, he said, blinking tears away, "Fuck me sideways that hurt." He looked down at his arm. There was a large graze and red mark on his shoulder and across his ribs. "Place your arm like this," Shaun said, and gently moved it so Tony's wrist was resting against his stomach, parallel with his chin. Shaun then wrapped bandages around his shoulder and tied the sheet around his wrist and shoulder.

The sling was good and tight. "You could be a doctor when you grow up," Tony said and forced out a smile.

Shaun shrugged. "Yeah, maybe." Shaun sat back on his bed, and hung his head low. "I thought you'd left," he said.

"I thought you hated me and didn't..."

"Well I'm here now," Tony said, trying not to think what would've happened if he had been able to get into the town.

No use thinking about that now. We've got bigger problems to deal with.

"Shaun, can you stop the rain?"

The boy didn't answer.

"Shaun, please. I know you're scared. But listen to me. We can't stay here and I need to get to a hospital. There's no way we can get to Dover, not with the whole town electrified, and Daylesford is too far for me to walk in my condition. If we could get into town, maybe we'd be in luck and find a car still with the keys in the ignition. But first, Shaun, you have to stop the storm."

"I can't," Shaun whispered.

"Yes you can. You said so yourself, it happens when you become upset. So I guess it stops whenever the anger or hurt or pain is over, or at least subsided."

"But I can't control this storm. It's too big. I'm awake and it's still happening. That's never happened before."

"Shaun, please." Tony sighed. "We can't stay here. The rain, it's...I don't know, it's getting power from the lightning or something. The rain it...it attacked me."

"It attacked you?"

Tony reached down and with his right hand lifted the pants on his left leg. There was a small red welt on his ankle, the skin around it was blistered. "The thing gave me an electric shock. Do you understand? The lightning is causing the flesh and blood to become active, and if I didn't know any better..." Tony stopped. "Well anyway, we either have to leave right away and hope we can score a lift to Daylesford or Hepburn Springs. Or you need to stop this rain and make the lightning disappear."

"I can't go out in the rain," Shaun said.

"Then stop this storm!" Tony cried. His head went dizzy, his whole body felt weak. "Shaun, please, you have to try," he said, softer.

"But I don't know how to."

"Try."

Shaun closed his eyes. He pinched his face. After a short time, Shaun's eyes flashed open and he whimpered, "I can't, it's no use. I'm useless."

"Hey, don't say that," Tony said. "You're not useless, Shaun. You wanna talk about useless, you're looking at the definition right here."

"What are you talking about?"

Tony smiled crookedly. "Forget it, kid. You don't want to hear about it. Let's just say that I let my family down. I wasn't there for them when they needed me. I gave them nothing but pain and heartache, I was a royal fuck-up, and what happens? They're gone and I'm left behind. I'm the world's biggest screw-up, and I'm spared. I don't believe in God, but if He does exist, He must have some sick sense of humor."

"I always talk to God," Shaun said, sounding ashamed, like he had just confessed to a grave sin. "Daddy doesn't believe in God either, says religion is a bunch of bull, but I still pray to God. I don't know, it makes me feel better. It helps whenever he…well, I don't feel so lonely. Mummy used to pray with me. It made her feel better, too. She also used to read me the bible. Daddy didn't like it when she did, but she read it anyway — she had a secret hiding spot for it. And then she died, and daddy found the bible and threw it away, said I should be ashamed of myself, reading nonsense like that."

"That's nothing to be ashamed of," Tony said. "Just because your daddy doesn't believe, doesn't mean you have to follow in his every footstep."

"Daddy punishes me when he catches me praying. He once caught me praying at mummy's grave, he really got mad that day. Said that if I wanted to be with her so much, then he would gladly arrange it. I still go to mummy's grave, even though daddy doesn't like it."

"Well he can't hurt you anymore."

"But I deserve punishment. It's all my fault."

"You didn't mean to cause this."

They both heard the noise at the same time. Tony knew straight away what it was, but Shaun frowned and, looking terrified, said, "What's that?"

Tony hopped off the bed and staggered over to the window. Through the sheet of rain, he saw maybe fifty strange shapes approaching. They sucked and sloshed their way towards the farmhouse, muddy red and yellow things that resembled melted human beings, the occasional spark of electricity coursing through their gooey forms. "Holy shit," Tony muttered.

Tony flinched when he felt the body press against his. He looked down and saw Shaun staring out the window, eyes wide, face creased with terror. "What are those?" he breathed. "Are they people? People from the town?"

"I don't know," Tony said. "I think it's just..." he said the first word that came to mind. "An abomination."

"What does that mean?"

"A freak of nature, unnatural." He turned to Shaun. "We can't stay here. Those things will electrocute us if they get close enough. And who knows how many more there'll be. I mean, if the rain keeps falling and there's still lightning..."

"What do they want? Why are they coming here?"

Tony opened his mouth, but what came out wasn't what he was truly thinking. "I don't know, but come on." He gripped Shaun on the arm.

The boy turned around. His face was dark, intense. "They're coming for me, aren't they?"

Tony blinked. He sure was a bright kid. Tony nodded, figured Shaun didn't need anymore lies. "Yeah, I think so," he said.

"Because of what I did to them?"

"But it wasn't your fault. You didn't do this on purpose."

"But I'm still responsible."

Tony clenched his fists. "Doesn't matter now. All that matters is getting you to safety."

"And you," Shaun added.

"Right. And me."

Suddenly there was a loud crash in the lounge. "What was that?" Shaun gasped.

Heart thumping, Tony said, "Wait here." He left the bedroom, dashed into the lounge room and stopped in his tracks. "Holy Christ on a crutch," he murmured.

Half the roof had caved in. There was now a pile of plaster, tiles and wood lying in a heap on the floor—all covered in slick flesh and blood. The rain continued to pour in through the sizable hole in the roof. Tony turned and hurried back into the bedroom.

Shaun was pressed against the window. When he heard Tony enter, he turned around. "There's more of 'em, and they're getting closer."

"Part of the roof in your lounge has caved in. We have to get outta here, now, before the whole house collapses."

Shaun looked at Tony like he had just been told his favorite dog had been run over by a car. "My house is collapsing?"

Tony nodded. "'Fraid so. This old place just can't handle the rain." Tony looked up, sighed heavily as he imagined the bedroom roof caving in, crushing him and Shaun. "Come on," Tony said, looking back down.

"But..."

"No buts, come on!" Tony gripped Shaun on the arm.

There was a thud at the window. Tony turned and saw one of the creatures pressing itself against the glass, looking like a mass of yellow and red puss. The thing at the window had black eyes and a red, oily mouth, and it gazed right at Tony and smiled at him.

"Mildred," the thing at the window said. "Mildred, I'll have my coffee now..."

"Holy Jesus," Tony muttered and he pulled Shaun out of the bedroom. When they reached the lounge, Shaun stopped and stared at the pile on the floor. Shaun gazed up at Tony, tears in his eyes. "But I don't like the rain, or those things."

Tony thought of what was waiting for them outside.

"Shaun, go and get some cartridges and load the Mauser. I would, but with only one arm in use, I don't think I'd be much good using a bolt action."

Shaun sighed. "I can't," he said, softly.

Tony turned and looked at the boy. "I know it's painful for you. You can use the other gun, if you'd prefer."

"No, it's not that. I...I threw the key for the ammunition drawer away."

"What?"

"Afterwards, I was so upset, I threw the key as hard as I could into the paddock. I didn't want to hurt anyone like I hurt daddy, so I threw the key away. I had already locked the drawer after I loaded the gun—daddy always kept the drawer locked, after mummy...after her accident, so that's what I did."

"Damn," Tony muttered. "Okay, forget it, doesn't matter. Let's just get outta here, those things will be in here soon. Bullets probably wouldn't have worked anyway. I don't think those things can be killed, at least, not with weapons."

He turned, gazed at the mess on the floor, figured he may as well be armed with something—it helped him having the rock before. So he sorted quickly through the rubble, found a wooden beam, about five inches in width and around two feet long. Gripping the beam in his hand, he said to Shaun, "Come on."

Outside, they stopped under the porch. Stretching out in front of them were about a hundred of the gloopy creatures, all crackling with electricity. They slopped closer, blobs resembling human form, some bigger than others.

"I'm scared," Shaun whispered.

"It's gonna be all right," Tony said.

Shaun nodded.

And then, through the noise of the rain and the creatures, came the cry: "Shhaaaaauuuun." The voice was muddy, but it was clear what had been said.

Shaun gasped; his eyes widened. "Daddy?" he breathed.

Tony stood momentarily shocked at what he had heard.

"Shaaaaaauuuun..." came the wolfish call again and then a figure lurched from around the side of the farmhouse.

This figure was different than the others; it moved stiffly, with a slow shuffle, and when it stepped into the path of the porch light, its full hideous person was revealed.

Tony felt the blood drain from his face; he blinked once, twice, and then gaped in revulsion as the corpse of Hank Reynolds ambled towards them.

"Daddy?" Shaun whispered again.

Hank's slimy, bloated body trudged through the muddy ground.

Tony swallowed something foul and he choked out, "How?"

And that's when he noticed the other figures behind Hank, their slimy flesh and blood bodies charged with the giver of life, and he figured, as incredible as the idea seemed, that these rain creatures must have been able to revive Hank's long-dead body with electricity.

"Shaun, come to me, son," the Hank creature burbled. "I forgive you. Come to daddy. Bluey's here and he wants to lick your face."

A smaller, elongated blob beside Hank gave a weird, watery bark.

Tony stared in abject horror at Hank. He heard Shaun crying and saying, "Daddy, oh daddy, I'm so sorry, daddy..." and when he saw the tiny figure of Shaun hurrying down the porch steps, into the heavy rain, he broke from his daze and cried, "No Shaun! Come back!"

But it was too late. The boy was running towards his dead father and nothing Tony could say would bring him back.

"Damn it," Tony muttered and he took off after the boy.

The rain creatures were everywhere, flesh and blood humans full of electricity, and they were all intent on stopping him from getting to Shaun. Or maybe they wanted Tony, too. Maybe they didn't care who they killed, maybe they just wanted to cause pain, make others suffer as they did.

Tony's gut sank when Shaun reached his dead father. "Shaun! Stop!" Tony wailed, but it was no use. The boy either couldn't hear him over the noise of the rain, or didn't want to hear him. Because when Shaun arrived at his dad, he stretched out his arms and wrapped them around his old man—didn't matter that the kid had killed him a month ago because he was tired of the beatings, the abuse, the pain, the hurt. Shaun hugged his father like he was welcoming him home after his father had been away for a long time.

Tony saw a wicked smile curl on the dead man's face and looking down at his son, Hank said, "You dumb little shit. You're just like your mother. Weak as piss. Only difference was, she turned the gun on herself, instead of on me, like you did."

Shaun gazed up at his father. "W…what?"

"That's right, the same gun you used to shoot me, your beloved mummy used to blow her brains out. Shit, her death was no accident. Bitch just couldn't hack it. Like I said, weak, just like her son. And now you're gonna pay for what you did to me. To us. To all of us!" He grabbed Shaun around the waist and pulled him tight. The boy screamed, struggled in his father's hold, but the dead man wouldn't let him go.

"Tony! Help!" Shaun cried.

Bluey jumped and barked, clearly excited.

Tony dodged rain creatures as he raced towards Shaun, swinging the wooden beam, ripping through the creatures like they were made of jelly.

He didn't know what Hank and the rain creatures had planned for the boy, but whatever it was, Tony wasn't about to let them carry it out. Not if he could help it.

Tony was within two meters of Hank, the dead man clutching his son hard against his decayed body, grinning at Tony, waiting for him, when Tony heard a familiar voice. It sounded like the person was talking through a mouthful of mud and gravel, but there was no mistaking who the voice belonged to. "You left us," his wife said. "You weren't there for us and now look what's happened."

Tony stopped, turned to the direction of the voice.

And stared at the rain creature shambling towards him. The thing didn't look much like Amy, except for its eyes. Tony stared into the creature's reddish-yellow face and saw two familiar round eyes, the green of the pupils distorted due to the rain. "A…Amy?" Tony breathed and he knew it couldn't be. And yet…

"I thought you loved us," Amy continued, voice like booze gurgling down the sink. "But you abandoned us."

"No!" Tony cried. "I do love you. I'm sorry. I should have been there, I should have…" Tony shook his head.

What are you saying? That's not Amy. Not really. Don't fall for their tricks, you have to help Shaun.

"All you cared about was the alcohol and the drugs," the Amy-creature said.

"But I'm clean," Tony told her — *it*. "I went through hell, but I made it. I'm back and I'm better now."

The Amy-creature grinned, a black slit curling through the slime. "Are you?"

"Yes," Tony said, an unwanted wavering in his voice.

"Daddy," said another voice somewhere nearby, this one younger, higher-pitched. "Daddy, why did you let this happen?" Heather sounded sad.

It's not Heather. Ignore her…ignore it…

Tony fought the urge to turn and look at the thing that used to be his daughter. He turned and faced Hank. The corpse was holding onto Shaun, a wicked grin cocked on his slickly bloated face.

The stench of Hank up close made Tony's head spin. He fought hard not to puke.

"You can't take him," Hank said. "We won't let you. I'm his father, you can't have him."

"You stopped being his father a long time ago," Tony said. "The first time you laid your hands on him, you gave up that right."

Hank laughed — it was a harsh, strange burbling noise. "You can talk, Tony. Think you were father of the year?"

"Fuck you," Tony said and took a step forward.

He was grabbed from behind by one of the rain creatures. Electricity shocked his body. The wooden beam dropped from his hand. After a few seconds, the electricity went away, leaving Tony hurting and weak.

"Think you could take my boy away?" Hank said. "Sorry Tony, but we can't let that happen — we can't let sins go unpunished, can we? But you know, I'm surprised you want to save him. After what he did to your family."

Tony looked up through stinging, bleary eyes. "Leave..." he began, but another jolt of electricity sent him buckling to his knees. Lights sparked behind his eyes.

The pain was intense, like hot oil was running through his veins, and the last thing he remembered before his body shut down was feeling sick at the smell of singed hair and cooking flesh.

* * *

Tony awoke to foul rain splashing against his face.

He lay on the ground for a few disorientated seconds and then felt the nausea build and then explode. He sat up, turned to the side and vomited.

When he was done, he sat there, wiped his eyes and gazed around. He was alone. The light from the porch behind him lit the wide area in front of the Reynolds farmhouse, and all he saw were the two bogged cars over to his right and the expanse of rain-soaked land. No rain creatures, no Hank, and no Shaun.

Shit, Tony thought.

He had fucked up. He had let those creatures take the boy to be punished. For all Tony knew, the punishment had already been carried out.

No, the rain's still falling. Shaun must still be alive.

He struggled to his feet, the feeling of fire bursting through his body.

He looked to his clothes, saw they were singed. Patches of skin on his arms and shoulders were scalded, and by the feel of his back, areas there had been burnt, too.

On his feet, he looked towards town, saw lightning still crisscrossing the orange-tinged sky in the distance.

Shaun was definitely still alive.

But for how long?

And where had they taken him?

And why the fuck did they leave me alive? Why not go all the way and electrocute me to death?

It didn't make sense.

With a shake of the head Tony glanced back at the house.

He froze, a gasp stuck in his throat.

What in God's name…?

Was he dreaming?

Hallucinating?

Had the jolt from the electricity scrambled the circuits in his brain?

He stepped forward, sloshed through mud, trod up the porch steps and reached down and picked up one of the bottles. It was real all right. The bottle was heavy in his hand, 700 ml of pure Bundaberg rum.

And if that was real, then so were the dozen or so other bottles sitting on the porch like bowling pins waiting to be knocked over.

Tony swallowed, felt his heart quicken.

Where the hell did these come from?

Maybe there was a god, after all.

He smiled, a crazy, "I've struck gold but I'm not gonna share it with anyone" kind of a smile.

He walked around the assortment of bottles, saw there was everything from whisky, to gin, vodka, tequila, port, sherry, even wine—both kinds. Everything a guy needed to get totally wasted.

He stepped on some rain that had gotten onto the porch, but when he looked down, saw words written on the wooden boards.

Frowning, Tony stepped back, until he was nearly at the edge of the porch.

He felt his heart sink.

Written beside the bottles, in dirty red paint (*that's not paint, buddy boy*), was:

A gift from us, to you. Think of it as a welcome home present. Don't worry about Shaun, he's safe with us. Enjoy – I know you will.

Tony read the message three times, feeling his chest getting tighter and tighter. He knew who had written it, he recognized that handwriting anywhere — it was the same hand that wrote hundreds of love letters a long time ago, back in another world. It was the same hand that wrote little reminders on the white board magnetized to the fridge at home, things like — *don't forget to buy some milk*; or, *I won't be home 'til late*; or, *I love you, darling*.

It was a gift all right, and it was clear to Tony the idea behind it.

They were fucking with him.

They were playing with him, toying with him, teasing him — *daring* him.

They could easily have killed him on Hank's front lawn. But instead, they wanted to keep him alive, to show him who was in charge around here. Also, it seemed Amy wanted to pay him back for what he had done to her and Heather — to all his friends. This was her revenge — or maybe it was a test.

They all thought he was weak, that he would take one look at all that alcohol and forget about trying to save Shaun.

He surveyed the dozen or so bottles sitting in front of him, begging to be opened, waiting to be drunk.

He had to admit — he was more than a little tempted.

He gazed down at the bottle of rum clenched in his hand. He longed to taste its sweet fire.

Perhaps they were right — he was weak.

Tony closed his eyes, eased out a shaky breath.

I mean Jesus, after everything that's happened today. Fuck, I'm in so much pain. What harm would one small nip do? Just to dull the pain?

A lot of harm — he knew what would inevitably happen. One nip would lead to another, which would lead to a longer drink, and pretty soon he'd discover with dumb surprise that half the bottle was empty, and damn he was feeling bloody good.

And that would be the end of Tony Christopher, at least for the next few hours, maybe days, even weeks. That would be the end for little Shaun, probably scared, wondering what was going on, where was Tony?

Well Jesus, what does he want me to do? How can I save him now? I don't know where they've taken him, and even if I did, I can't take on hundreds of those rain creatures. And shit, he was responsible for all this. If it wasn't for him, Amy and Heather...

He caught himself, felt ashamed for thinking such thoughts.

But all those bottles *were* mighty inviting. All it would take was one twist of the cap and he'd be in a drunkard's paradise.

He could forget that he had lost his family, his town; he could wash away the horrible visage of his beloved Amy having been turned into one of those...*things*; he could even forget there was a boy out there, somewhere, in grave danger, probably desperately crying out for Tony to come and help him...

He could drown all of those problems away, all he had to do was admit defeat and surrender to temptation.

So easy. So damn easy...

It's what they want you to do, a voice said. *They want you to accept their gift and in doing so they'd win.*

Well shit, and how do I make them lose? Me? One man? One weak, easily-tempted man?

You throw that bottle down, that's what. And then you turn around and walk in the opposite direction. Forget about the booze. They're chains, remember? Do you really want to go back to being bound to such a heavy burden?

Tony opened his eyes, blinked away cold tears.

With great effort he tossed the bottle of rum down. It smacked right into the heart of the pack, knocking most of them over—almost a strike. Glass and liquid coated the porch.

Tony turned around and stepped off the porch, landing on the soft, muddy ground with a barely contained sob.

Well done. You did the right thing.

Yeah? Well tell me, what the hell am I supposed to do now?

He knew the answer to that question, and fear like tiny pinpricks ran up and down his body.

But he killed Amy and Heather and dad and all my friends…

He didn't mean to. You told him that yourself.

Still, he was responsible…

He needs you. Do something right for once in your life. Think of someone else for a change. Make things right. No matter what the cost…

No matter what the cost.

The phrase rang over in Tony's head like a church bell tolling at midnight.

No matter what the cost…

He trudged towards Wickes Road, still feeling the bottle of rum in his hand, still smelling the amalgamation of the booze that was now seeping into the wood and dripping through the cracks, splashing the dirt underneath.

When he reached the road, he stopped.

Where to now?

Clearly they hadn't gone into town—there was no way they could've taken Shaun down there without the boy being vaporized.

Wherever they had taken him, it had to be somewhere on the outskirts of town, away from the lightning.

The church?

Tony looked to the left, down to where St. Augustine stood, somewhere in the distance, hidden by clumps of trees.

No, by Shaun's own admission Hank wasn't religious.

The guy knew Shaun gained solace in religion, so Tony doubted they would've taken the boy there.

Something Shaun said earlier sprang to Tony's mind. He looked right, towards the cemetery that sat on the very edge of Gainesville's limits, past Burt Hammond's farm.

He saw a glow hovering in the dark sky, like the glow of floodlights.

Tony heaved a deep, shaky breath.

What the hell are they doing in the cemetery?

He wasn't sure he wanted to find out the answer to that question.

He started down the road.

As he made the journey towards Gainesville Cemetery, he wondered what, if anything, he was going to do when he arrived.

He was outnumbered by about a hundred to one, and he was sure those rain creatures couldn't be killed in any conventional way.

What the hell am I doing, he thought as he trudged along, fear pecking away at his gut. *I must be crazy.*

He passed the Hammond farm, and then the night seemed to swallow him up as he neared the cemetery.

When he arrived at Cemetery Road, he turned right.

The radiant light seemed to grow in intensity as he neared the entrance, and when he arrived at Gainesville's one and only cemetery, stopped at the gate. He could see patches of white light between the trees, deep within the cemetery grounds.

He could hear the distant murmur of voices; muddy and cold.

Tony walked through the open gate, heading in the direction of the light.

He tread softy, carefully, staying close to trees where possible, winding his way around the knee-high metal fences that surrounded many of the grave sites, and the many different sized and shaped head stones.

Soon he was close enough to the congregation of rain creatures to both see and hear what was going on. He stopped behind a tall obelisk gravestone about eight meters from the nearest rain creature.

"...all be over soon," Hank Reynolds was saying. "So stop your crying. Come on, stop being such a wimp and take your punishment like a man."

Tony peered around the gravestone. Saw around a hundred rain creatures milling about; some were talking, laughing, others were quiet, staring at something happening in the middle of the rough circle. Through gaps in the circle, Tony saw what they were looking at. His heart sank, his mind reeled.

Oh no...

Three rain creatures were busy digging at one of the graves. Already there was a large pile of dirt to one side. Tony was too far away to be able to read the inscription on the arched and slightly askew gravestone, but he bet he knew which grave they were digging up. Standing off to one side, opposite the ever-growing pile of soil, was Hank, one arm wrapped around Shaun's neck. Shaun looked in shock; his wide eyes were staring into the pit, his face contorted, obviously trying not to cry as per his father's instructions. Tony wondered how tight Hank was holding onto his son.

Bastard...that bloody bastard. They're all bastards. Jesus Christ, what are they going to do?

"You hit the fuckin' coffin yet?"

"No," answered one of the rain creatures.

"Dig faster," Hank growled, and Bluey, sitting beside his master, growled too. "It's going to take long enough for this to end, and I don't want to be in here any longer than I have to." Looking down at Shaun, Hank smiled. It looked like some kid had drawn a squiggly black line on a balloon. "You'll be with your mummy soon, Shaun. You'll like that, won't you? You can pray all you fuckin' well want, then."

"No," Shaun squeaked out, shut his eyes and choked on some sobs.

"What's that? You don't want to pray, or you don't want to be with your mummy?"

"I don't want to…go down there," Shaun sobbed.

"Well too bad. You don't have a choice. Your mate Tony ain't going to save you. He's too busy drinking his life away. So there's not much you can do to stop it from happening. Ain't that right, Amy?"

"Right," a rain creature standing near the grave said, joy and malice in its voice.

"We've both had to live with failures. Christ, I had two of 'em. You know what it's like to live with disappointment and regret, don't you?"

"Fucking arsehole was always drunk or high. Shit, I hope he chokes on his own vomit."

It's not Amy. It's not her talking. Ignore it.

"Kinda funny, ain't it?" Hank said. "Both of 'em will die a slow, painful death. Tony by choice, but he'll probably be totally unaware of what's happening, whereas Shaun, who's here by force, will be all too aware of every terrifying moment. What do ya reckon everyone, wanna place bets on who'll die first? I say give 'em both around two, three days. But who will croak first? The drunk, or the kid buried alive?"

A chorus of wet, cruel laughter burbled from the group clustered around Doris Reynolds's grave.

Holy fucking shit, Tony thought, mind whirling with shock and disbelief.

They were going to bury Shaun alive? With his long-dead mother?

And then what, wait around, listening to the boy begging and pleading to be let out? Listen to him slowly suffocate to death?

This is some seriously fucked up shit.

Tony couldn't let that happen. He would rather it be him in that coffin than the boy. Just the thought of the kid being put through such torture curdled his stomach. Christ, he was so young, had so much life still to live. He had already faced death once before—it was a miracle he survived, according to the doctors. Well maybe he had been spared for a reason. And now maybe it was up to Tony to make sure the boy continued to live on.

Tony remained behind the gravestone, mouth dry, body wet, wracking his brain, trying to think of a way to save this poor boy.

There was no way he could run in and snatch Shaun. Not with one broken arm, and not with all those rain creatures around. He'd be electrocuted before he could ever get near the boy.

He could try bargaining with them—ask them to let Shaun go in exchange for Tony. But would they go for that? No, almost certainly not. They wanted to punish the person responsible for their demise and then unholy resurrection. Tony was just a diversion to them, a plaything, a petty pest. They didn't care about him, not unless he proved a direct threat to them carrying out their punishment on Shaun. No, if he went out there and tried to reason with them, they would laugh in his face and probably place them *both* in the coffin.

Shit, shit, shit, shit...think, think, think, think...

Of course, there was one sure way of stopping this madness.

There was one way Hank and the rain creatures could be defeated; there was one person who had the power to bring this all to an end.

But that person was too scared, too unsure of himself. He had the power, of that there was no question, but he needed to be reminded of that. He needed to put an end to his fear and pain and anger at his dad, his guilt over what had happened a month ago, in order to stop this storm. Shaun was convinced that he had no control over the storm—Tony had to convince him otherwise.

But how could Tony even get to Shaun to try and get him to end this storm? He'd be stopped by the rain creatures the moment they heard him speak.

Tony's head pounded with worry and confusion over what to do.

The sound of shovels stabbing into the dirt was like a ticking time bomb—soon they would get to the coffin, and when they did, they were going to place Shaun inside with a bunch of bones that used to be his mum, and then close the lid and begin filling in the hole.

If only he could talk to Shaun long enough to make the boy see he had the power.

When the idea struck Tony, it was like gray clouds parting, revealing a clear blue sky.

The idea was insane, fear gushed through his being at the thought of it, but it seemed to Tony the only solution.

Jesus, could I even go through with it?

Would it even work?

He had to at least try.

No matter what the cost…

What did Hank say? That he had a choice of how he was going to die, but that he would be unaware when it happened?

Wrong.

It was true, he did have a choice. Only it wasn't the one they all thought he would make. But most importantly, he *would* be aware of his death; of that, he was now certain.

He would make the correct decision, for once in his life. After all the pain he had caused others, it was the least he could do.

He hated leaving Shaun, but as he turned around and headed back the way he had come, he knew he would be back soon enough.

He just hoped he wouldn't be too late.

Tony hurried through the cemetery, and once he was out of the boneyard, he hurried along Cemetery Road.

When he arrived at Wickes, he turned left and started jogging.

No time to lose.

He bounded down the road, not registering the pain in his arm as it jostled, thinking only about one thing—saving Shaun.

Finally he reached the intersection of Wickes and Camp. He stood at the top of the hill, breathing harshly, sweating like a hog on a spit, and gazed at the town below.

He saw more puddles forming; watched as rain creatures sloshed about the town, looking like a bunch of drunks after a big night at the pub.

Tony closed his eyes.

Thought about Amy—the *real* Amy—and imagined what she would say to what he was about to do.

He heard her voice, as plainly as he could hear the rain slapping Gainesville: *You have to, darling. It's the right thing to do.*

When he opened his eyes, a smile had spread thinly across his face.

Tony started forward.

* * *

The thing that sloshed through the cemetery didn't look much like a human. Its matter had been vaporized, sucked up into the great beyond, churned, and then spat out like a kid spitting out vegetables. It had two extremities on its upper portion, two on its lower, and a gooey, slimy head. It looked like a human that had been melted, or a person made from gelatine.

But it had emotions and feelings like a human.

It thought like a human. And those thoughts concentrated on only a few things.

Namely getting to the boy in time.

The thing that used to be Anthony Christopher—still was, in a manner of speaking—knew where they were keeping the boy. It remembered, just like it remembered the pain, the hotness, the suffocating burning like it had swallowed a forest fire. It remembered a feeling of being torn apart, of floating through a lake of fire; of being suspended in agony. It remembered hearing screaming, lots of screaming, and not just its own, but others, all around, but like they were a radio that wasn't quite tuned in properly, and lots of static.

It remembered thinking but not thinking, feeling but not feeling.

It also remembered the rebirth, the coming together of thought and feeling. Of darkness, and then light, slowly at first, like swimming up from the darkest depths of the ocean, towards the surface, until finally breaking the water.

It remembered these things, but mostly it remembered its purpose, the sole reason for it being here.

It didn't feel hatred like the others. Unlike them, it had chosen its current situation. It hadn't been thrust into pain and death for seemingly no reason. It knew what the others were feeling and thinking, but it didn't share their murderous impulse.

It wanted nothing more than to end the pain and suffering.

The thing neared its brethren.

None of them took any notice as the thing that used to be Tony Christopher joined their group. They all thought it was another one of them, coming to watch the one they all hated be punished.

It wasn't too late.

They had stopped digging, but they hadn't yet placed Shaun down into the ground. The boy was struggling against his father, who was attempting to drag him towards the grave.

"No, I don't want to," the boy cried. "Daddy, please, no…"

"Come on, in you get. Say hi to mummy…"

"Shaun," the thing—Tony—said, still getting used to hearing his distorted voice.

Hundreds of dark, watery eyes flicked towards him.

"Who is that?" Hank Reynolds barked, halting his efforts of trying to get his son down into the coffin.

"Tony?" Amy said, her round eyes holding surprise.

"That's right," he said.

"Daddy!" Heather cried, but Amy held her daughter close.

She could sense her husband wasn't like them.

Hank smirked. "What happened? You stumble into the town, drunk?"

Tony sensed suspicion, unease in the dead man. Beside him, Bluey also seemed to sense that something was amiss; the dog growled under its breath.

"T...Tony?" Shaun breathed, staring at the thing in front of him.

"It's okay, Shaun. I'm here."

"You come to watch the boy face his punishment?" Hank asked.

Ignoring the question, Tony looked at Shaun through flesh and blood clouded eyes and said, "Shaun, you can stop this."

Hank snarled. "The hell he can. Who do you think you are? Grab him!"

Two of the rain creatures moved in and grabbed Tony on both arms — one was Tony's dad. Instead of zapping him, the electricity that coursed through the creatures acted as a kind of sizzling bone, so they were able to hold onto Tony.

"Take him away," Hank ordered. "He just came here to make trouble."

Tony struggled, but their grip was too tight.

"Come now," his dad said. "Don't fight."

The two rain creatures started pulling Tony away.

"Tony, I'm scared," Shaun whimpered, bucking against his father.

"I know you are," Tony said, his strange form fighting against his captors, "but listen to me, Shaun. You have to stop this storm...now!" He knew his time was limited — he predicted they would try and stop him, take him away from Shaun the moment they heard Tony speak. Tony just hoped he could get through to Shaun before he was dragged right away and out of the cemetery.

"I can't," Shaun cried. "I already tried, it's no use. I told you, I'm useless."

"No you're not!" Tony bellowed. "Listen to me, Shaun. You have the power to stop this. You know you do."

"He has to be punished!" Various rain creatures cried.

"Yes, the boy has to be punished," Hank said. "Get that

mutinous drunk out of here!"

"Yes, come now Anthony, you're spoiling all the fun," his dad said, continuing to drag Tony away along with the other rain creature.

"Shaun," Tony continued. "Shaun, listen to me. It was your anger and pain against your father that caused this. It's your anger at yourself for what you did that has carried it on, and the guilt that caused this storm now. That's why it's gotten so big and out of control. But you can stop it. I know you can."

"Enough!" Hank bellowed. "Time has come for Shaun to meet his fate."

Now on the outer fringes of the circle of blood-hungry creatures, Tony watched as Hank lifted Shaun up, Bluey, the ever-faithful mutt, jumping around excitedly. "No! Shaun, listen to me!"

But Tony feared it was too late. In just a matter of seconds, Hank would put his son down into the grave, and Tony was powerless to do anything about it.

But then it happened.

Shaun stopped fighting and went limp in his father's hold. Tony sensed a change in the boy—a change in the air.

All the rain creatures seemed to sense the shift in the atmosphere at the same time.

And they felt a change in themselves, too—it was like someone was turning down the gas on a stove.

Hank froze and let out a quiet whimper.

"What's going on," Amy cried. "Tony, you're screwing things up again, just like you always do."

Tony felt his dad's and the other creature's grips loosen. He broke free from their hold and shambled back up towards the open grave. He stopped and stared hard at the thing that used to be his dear wife. "This time, I'm doing what's right," he said as rain creatures panicked all around him.

"You're upsetting your daughter," Amy said.

Heather was weeping—blood tears ran down her slippery face.

"Heather died a month ago yesterday," Tony said, finding great relief in admitting that fact. "And so did you." He turned to Hank, still trying to lift the boy into the grave, but struggling as his strength diminished.

"Shaun," Tony said, feeling his own power quickly fading. "Shaun, it wasn't your fault. Your dad abused you, just like he abused your mother; you were only protecting yourself. That's all. Do you understand?"

"Yes," Shaun whispered, barely audible. "I understand."

"You killed me, boy!" Hank cried. "That's a sin, right? You think your God will forgive you for that?"

Again, even softer, Shaun answered, "Yes."

Thunder cracked in the sky.

Hank gasped, released Shaun from his hold. The boy collapsed to the ground next to his mother's grave. The bloated figure of Hank Reynolds gazed up at the sky, fear on his face.

Rain creatures, including Bluey, scattered, most towards the entrance, probably heading towards town, hoping to find sanctuary within the electrical field.

Tony looked down at the boy. Shaun, eyes closed, looked intense, but strangely calm.

"Shaun, if you can hear me, know this—what happened to the town wasn't your fault. I don't blame you. And you shouldn't blame yourself. So stop this storm. Stop it now!"

Tony watched the boy start to quiver, the intense concentration on his face never faltering.

Hank edged back slowly, away from his son, away from the giver—and taker—of life. "You ruined everything," he muttered, though Tony wasn't sure who he was talking to.

There was another crack of thunder, one so loud it seemed to rattle the very fabric of time and space.

Tony felt his energy leave him, like a great big vacuum cleaner was sucking away his power.

"No," Hank breathed, sounding weak. "No, you need to be punished, boy. You can't do this, you can't do this!"

The electricity that was crackling through all the creatures sizzled out.

Tony managed a flicker of a smile within his flesh and blood features before the light was switched off and his last thought was: *You did it, Shaun.*

And then the thing that used to be Tony Christopher was no more.

* * *

When the boy awoke, he felt the overwhelming tiredness that always afflicted him after one of his episodes.

So he lay on the ground for a while, enjoying the blue skies and the round fireball of a sun, thinking about how he had ended the storm.

Listening to Tony talking was like taking medicine when he had a cold. Suddenly things made sense and he realized that, while he was the cause of it, he wasn't to blame. And that it wasn't up to himself, or daddy, or anyone, except God, to judge him. He had remembered something Tony said to him—God doesn't punish those with a good heart—and that had led to an inner calmness. In his mind, he had reached out and grabbed the bolts of lightning, crushing them. Then he had pushed all the rain back up into the sky. He then wished for sun and happiness, and soon after, he had awakened.

When the boy felt strong enough to move, he got to his feet.

Sadness swept over him as he gazed at the puddles of rain all over the cemetery grounds. He wondered which puddle Tony was.

I can't believe he did that. Just for me. He saved me.

The boy wiped his eyes and turned to the grave.

He stepped to the edge of the hole, squeezed his eyes shut, reached down and fumbled around for the lid. When he found it, he slammed it shut. Then he opened his eyes.

He didn't want to see what was inside; he couldn't bear to see mummy lying in there. He wanted to remember her *his* way, the way she looked when she used to read him the bible—beautiful, warm, like an angel from heaven.

He never truly believed her death was an accident—deep in his heart, where dark secrets were kept, he knew the truth. "It's okay, mummy," he said. "I forgive you."

He turned to his dad, lying dead on the ground.

"Oh daddy," the boy said, and he felt his chin tremble and tears spill down his cheeks, despite everything that had happened—or maybe because of them.

He walked around behind his daddy and bending low, started rolling his body towards the hole in the ground.

It was hard work, his daddy was a big man, but eventually he got the body to the hole and with one final push, his daddy flopped down into the grave, his body landing on the wood with a wet thud.

The boy was aching and covered with dirt by the time he left the cemetery.

He started down the road, which was covered in that red and yellow paste and it was slippery to walk on—but the boy was used to it now.

On the trek back home, he thought mostly about Tony, and what it must've felt like to become one of those things. The boy was going to miss the man he once knew only as Mr. Christopher. He knew Tony didn't believe, but the boy said a prayer for him anyway, and he was certain that Tony was now up in Heaven, and that made him feel better.

He wasn't so sure about the rest of 'em...

When he arrived home, he trudged up to the house, but didn't go inside. He frowned at the smashed bottles on the porch, wondered what they were doing there, and then stood looking at the old dilapidated farmhouse, at its worn paint, droopy drains, grubby windows, and felt a sense of loss, of sadness—but also freedom.

He felt a change in the air.

With one last goodbye, he turned and headed towards town, swiping at the tears in his eyes.

At the intersection of Wickes and Camp, he stopped and gazed down over the town.

The houses and shops stood empty, sheathed in the

flesh and blood of its inhabitants. The streets were ankle deep with thick, gloopy rain.

He stood looking over Gainesville for a long time before heading off.

The boy didn't know how to drive, so he didn't bother checking to see if any cars had keys poking out of their ignition. He would have to hike it, though where he was hiking to, he hadn't yet made up his mind.

When he started through the center of town, along the road that led out of Gainesville and towards Dover, the boy said a silent goodbye to the town he had lived in for nine whole years, to all the people he had known: mummy, daddy, Bluey, Tony, Rick, and all the kids at school.

He waded through the foul smelling muck, the sun shining nice, but mocking in its purity.

He had left the town behind — including all the TVs and radios continuing to speak to ghosts — had started up the hill, muddy pastures opening up on either side, when the boy had a thought: What if it was everywhere?

What if what happened in his town had happened all over the country? Surely there were others like him, who possessed the same power.

He noticed then how deathly quiet the world was.

No birds sang, no dogs barked.

And were those storm clouds gathering in the distance?

The boy couldn't be sure.

He guessed he would find out soon enough.

ELIMINATE THE IMPROBABLE
Nick Mamatas

ONE

You watch mysteries on TV and if the script is hard-boiled enough and the lead actor has a chin like a big ol' shoe or at least trench coat shoulders you'll see this scene. A door opens in the dark. Maybe it's a cellar; maybe it's the trunk of a car, or a manhole cover. Fog and dust swirls about as the sleuth holds up a great big flashlight and peers into the nothingness.

But he's not peering into the nothingness, is he? Hell, that joker's not even looking at some secretary, all tied up in nylons and a short skirt, a gag in her mouth so sexy. Not some corpse with a map or amulet clutched in its stiff hand. He's looking at you. And you stare on back, into the light, wondering what it is he sees.

I try telling this to Paulo but the words don't come out right. My jaw is bloated, like I was a cartoon, and Paulo is way too high to speak to. He's singing to himself in Spanish; he gets nostalgic for the cliffs and shade trees of La Hispaniola, an island he's never even been to, when he's high. It's four in the morning and it's been the first of the month for just that many hours. We're waiting till six, when our landlady and her husband will show up and stomp and shriek their way up the steps, banging on doors and demanding rent checks. I don't have mine. Paulo has his, and he put it in the mail slot hammered to the door three stories below. Usually, I sneak out onto the fire escape, lower myself down the ladder and with one quick breath let myself drop onto the pile of garbage bags right under my window, then strike out to pick up cans and bottles all the way across Houston and up to Sixth Avenue. I cash 'em in before the homeless people and crackheads clog up the machines at the Food Emporium, get myself an egg sandwich at Gray's Papaya and then head down to the Barnes & Noble to read free magazines till noon. Then back home through the crazy streets.

You know why? Fuck the rent. Fuck the goddamn landlady who doesn't do shit for this apartment, who lies to the city about the number of units so she won't have to hire a janitor, whose only phone number connects to an answering machine sitting in the middle of the basement—it's always a laugh when some NYU bitch rents here, gets locked out and calls the landlady for help; she gets to hear the phone ringing in one ear via her cell phone and the same bell, distant and muffled under a few slabs of concrete—who wants our checks waiting for her in a mail drop hammered to the inside of the front entrance where anyone can just drop trou' and leave a big ol' shit. Fuck the rats climbing the walls and pushing through cracks to eat my pasta, brave as cops, fuck paying $1010 a month for a room with a tub and a gas oven less than a foot apart, a "two-room studio" where I smack my knees against the bottom of my sink whenever I sit on the toilet, where I have to plug in a space heater just to keep from dying, fuck it fuck it fuck it all.

"Shut up, I'm tryin' to watch," Paulo says finally. I didn't even know I was talking. I haven't always been like this. Recently though, I've been agitated. A fire in the brain and gut. Paulo too. That's why we're actually here, together, bats on our laps, on this particular morning, while during all our yesterdays we'd just bullshit about taking up cudgels to the man and then fall asleep to pizza grease and the National Anthem.

I glance at the screen. There's no mud on the ankles of the just-rescued legal secretary with the feathered 1980s hair and her nails are perfect. Other than that, the production values of the show—whatever the hell show we're watching—are pretty high (on location, not a sound stage, some fresh sound effects for gun shots rather than the canned stuff) so I guess it's an implied plot point and not just coke-addled Hollywood laziness. "This character wasn't kidnapped and held for ransom," I tell Paulo. "She set herself up as a victim, knowing that her disappearance would send ConHugeCo or whatevertherfuck company she's supposed to be working for in disarray, and thus the CEO—undoubtedly her secret yet strangely and recently disinterested lover—would summon this best-in-the-business detective to find her. But in the course of doing so he would also surely discover that the CEO is having an affair on his mistress...with his own wife!"

"And then she'd have her revenge," says Paulo. He took a giant toke from his Red Bull can and Krazy Straw bong. He'd offered it to me two hours ago, and I declined as I need all my senses sharp. Paulo never offers twice, so he sucks deep, his sinuses almost trilling.

"Except that the detective will see through the deception, and also thwart the secretary's attempt to frame the CEO and kill the wife."

"Yeah."

"Yeah."

"Man, you just spoiled this show for me," Paulo says, but he doesn't turn off the TV. We watch the drama play out. No, not even watch. We just look. If Paulo had an aquarium, we'd be sitting in front of that. We're waiting for the landlady and her scarecrow of a husband and we're gonna come running out of Paulo's apartment and storm across the hall, ball bats in hand, and give them a goddamn beating. Fuck them and fuck the rent. It's still New York City; it's still almost impossible to evict anygoddamnbody.

Paulo has an old digital clock from back in the day when the numbers were flippy clicky plastic. All three numbers click when the hour turns: four to five, five to zero, nine to zero. Without thinking, I suck in my breath, waiting for the doors to swing open below, for the shouting and the stomping to begin, but the landlord doesn't show. They're always on time on rent day, like traffic lights or the subway in novels, but they don't show.

"It's snowing," Paulo says. He knows, even though he has cardboard boxes taped with black gaffer's tape to the windows, he knows. It's so easy to tell, from the smells, the sounds. "They're late. That's all."

But they're not. They never show up at all. At 7, when the canaries come out into the hallways to marvel at the rent day silence, we get all smug. Maybe they took a spill on the way down from New Rochelle, the fat landlady unbalancing their pickup and sending it rolling over a patch of black ice and into a tree. At 9, when the old ladies surface and call out to one another in Spanish and Chinese, we wake up from the stupor we'd fallen into. At 11 AM, when the sun seeps in through the cardboard we actually start to get worried. The devil we know is gone for real.

"Yo," says Paulo, "we got a case."

TWO

Paulo and I, we don't talk to anybody. Canaries especially.

What's a canary?

A canary is from Cleveland, or Ypsilanti, or sometimes even the rich parts of Mexico City. You can tell the last because they're always blonde, with thick lips, like an actress on a Swedish soap opera. They come here to New York and sit and starve as a joke, lifting their shirts and counting their own ribs and laughing. Oh ho, I'm poor! What a great story this will make one day, once grandpa dies and my trust comes in. And they buy from Paulo and close themselves off, wrists crossed and over their chests, when I'm around. And I'm always around.

Sometimes a canary takes a three count. One OD…must have been some bad smack, cut with baby powder or Splenda. Two ODs. Life on the edge. Get some backbeats on the Mac and write a song about it. Three ODs. I get a free bookcase.

She's a canary, the girl in front of us. We're outside Paulo's door. I lean, Paulo stands tall, a big smile on his flat face. She's thin, black, with tasty cornrows, but she sounds white like Martha Stewart.

"Uhm…hello guys." Paulo and I, we don't talk to anybody. I smile wide and nod, the way an elevator operator would to a pretty girl if they still had elevator operators. Paulo and I still have our bats. Mine's against my leg. Paulo's got his slung over both shoulders, his hands flapped over either end. I want to tell him he doesn't look like Jesus. Paulo stares at the canary; she's a real pork chop.

"Do either of you…have a number for the landlord?" We look at one another, Paulo and I. She's a tough chick though. Arms drop. Chin points. That flirt evaporates, like they do. "Well? Or are you guys just the softball team now?"

"There's a number down in the entrance—"

"I know about that one. It's fake."

"Yeah," says Paulo.

"How long have you guys been living here?"

"Eight years," I tell her, and Paulo says he's been living here for most his whole life except that when he was a kid he lived in a very similar shithole in Washington Heights, which is true. She tilts her head toward Paulo, leans in, hoping that tall and thin will impress roly-poly, but she doesn't know Paulo like I know Paulo.

"How long you've been here?" I ask and Paulo says "Yeah."

She shrugs. "Three months."

"Why you so eager to contact the landlord?" Paulo asks. "Huh?"

"Yeah," I say.

"Listen, I don't want any trouble."

"F.I.T."

She stops there, mouth open but her words forgotten. Then she says, "How did you know?"

"Your papa co-signed the lease," Paulo adds. "He didn't want you living here—"

"—or wasting four years studying fashion. It's not like he can tell the difference between being a designer or bending over a sewing machine for fifteen hours a day."

"Yeah, no girl of his is gonna work in a sweatshop," Paulo added. "And then there are the *maricon*."

I nod. "The homo*sexuals*."

Hands on her hips, tongue clicks. "Like you two?"

"Ouch," I say but Paulo doesn't play. He steps. She doesn't back down. "Easy baby," I say and they both think I'm talking to the other.

"Listen, you're not smart," Paulo says. "Think about it. Maybe they're dead in a ditch somewhere. What if the landlady got up early this morning to make eggs and bacon for her man—the way he likes it is baked and chewy, not fried and crunchy, see—so she puts the strips on grates and fixes them in the oven, and there's this gas leak so instead of bacon the man gets two lungs of CO_2, and so does she, and they're up in New Rochelle right now, just drifting off on hazy dreams to their deaths. You know what this means? Do they have kids? A will? There could be months, maybe years of court cases, of fights over who is going to pay the taxes? In the meantime, they can't throw us out, not whatever anyone wants."

"Rent free."

"Years," Paulo says.

"So...New Rochelle. Okay. Thanks guys," she says and turns and walks away, heels clicking down the hall and up the steps.

"Man, why are we even standing out here again?" I ask, mostly myself.

"She wants me," Paulo says, his face a big pumpkin smirk.

"Yeah, she does. I can tell."

"You cock-blocked me, brother."

I nod. "Right now, you could be on your way up there to the fifth floor, having been led up there all the way by her fingernail under your chin, half-hook half-stroke. She has a leopard-pattern duvet on her futon. Candles on the side of the tub. Maybe some of those Chinese screens in bisecting the room so she won't have to see her fridge when she dresses each morning."

"Little lace panties dripping off the sides of the open top drawer of her bureau..." Paulo says.

"And a little wooden box with condoms, lube, and a tasteful pocket rocket—"

"Hello Kitty vibe."

"Definitely Hello Kitty," I agree, "the whole place smelling of sage and citrus."

"No TV."

"Not the kind of girl who watches TV, but she'll come down to visit you sometimes—"

"When something *special* is on..."

We trail off after that and wait in the hallway for another witness to come by; the only one who does is the old hunchbacked lady and her two-wheeled shopping cart full of canned goods. She grunts each step of the way up the first flight of steps, then skitters in the hallway, cursing it, her wagon, and us in Lithuanian or something as she passes us by. She moves up the second flight of stairs, each stair a thump of wheels and another hacking cough of a swear, and then out of our sight. There's a fine roll of wheels across the hallway over our heads, then the thumping begins again.

It stops. Then there's a crash and in the gap between banisters it begins to rain cans of sardines and kitty litter.

THREE

The old lady's cart is on the steps, bags spilled everywhere, leaving a delta of broken glass and glop — gefilte fish, sturdy pickles, applesauce — by the landing. She's gone. It's impossible, but I peek over the gap between stair and hall anyway to see if she fell to the first floor.

"You think we missed her?" Paulo asks, the asshole. He scratches his chin with the wide end of the bat.

"What's it look like?"

He stares at the scene for a second. "She's too slow to have gotten to her apartment."

"And not the type to just abandon her groceries. She'd be shoving pickles into her cleavage if she could."

"Yeah, so the Gestapo won't get 'em," says Paulo.

"Could it have been adrenaline? She loses the cart, the crash gets her fight-or-flight sparked, and she's off?"

"Nah, we would have heard her feet stomping, then a door slamming. Besides, that old lady lives two stories up."

We climb the flight of stairs, careful not to slip on any of the ort, and check out the other landing. Dusty, as usual. Of course, had she run there would have been less distinct prints. Balls of the feet, plus those old house slippers. She didn't run though, and she sure as hell didn't jump. That old lady is shaped like a pumpkin balanced on two popsicle sticks.

"Okay, I got it," says Paulo. He gestures with his bat up to the door of 3R. "She's in there. Someone was standing on the landing, shocked her. Maybe he whipped it out and waggled it at her. She gasps, let's go of the cart. He reaches out, grabs her quick and drags her onto the landing, then into his apartment. Then," he says, "he very quietly closed the door."

"The tenant in 3R kidnapped an old lady for no reason?"

"Who knows what diabolical reason he may have?"

Paulo says. "Maybe it's the toxo?"

"I thought you didn't believe in the toxo. I thought you said it was hysteria because a couple of white people got killed for a change."

"*Racist* hysteria," Paulo corrects me. "It's all racist hysteria. Whoever heard of a rat who wants to be eaten by a cat."

"Who ever heard of an old, old lady quietly being killed by an old, old man? Nobody, so long as it's quiet enough, I guess," I say.

"Who knows what he's doing to that old lady now?"

"Whatever it is," Paulo says, "he's doing it quiet." Paulo has tinnitus. His ear is dead to so many sounds, but to make up for it, the brain has turned up the volume. "Dog ears," he calls the effect. He can hear what's going on thirty feet away better than anything I say when standing right next to him. Forget the chicken wire and glue walls of this tenement, if an old lady was being ass-raped in a bank vault Paulo would hear every thrust. Sphincters squeak like old shoes.

"Let's do it," I say and we rush. It ain't like TV. I plant a front kick right in the middle of the door and feel a shiv of pain right up my leg and through my back. I nearly fall down the steps, but Paulo is there to catch me, except that he's got his bat his hands, so I smack hard against it. We stumble, grab on to one another, nod, and rush the door as one. Then bounce off again. Paulo hefts his bat and starts smacking away at the doorknob. I'm taller and sneak in some low kicks. We start shouting. Paulo in Spanish, me in Spanish-sounding gibberish. I can't even help myself.

Then we hear rattling and shouting from the other side. "You stupid motherfuckers!" the guy in 3R shouts, distant and muffled like a kid in winter clothes. "You fucked up the door. I can't open it now, even if I wanted to."

"Where's the old lady!" I demand.

"My old lady's working, like you two fucking bitches should be." He starts banging on the door. "C'mon, open this shit! I'll put a fucking hole in you!"

"Man, good thing we fucked up the door," I say to Paulo.

Paulo says, "That bitch doesn't have a gun." Then, to the door, which is rattling and getting plashy from dust. "You don't even have a gun, bitch!" Then the rattling stops.

"Is he getting his gun?"

"He getting something," Paulo says.

We skootch over to the side of the door. Paulo extends his arm and keeps smacking the door with the bat. A shot fires, taking out the crumpled door knob. Then two more thick *ponks* smack into and through the door, bullets flying over the expanse of space over the steps and probably into the living room of 3F on the other side of the hall. I groan dramatically. Paulo does too, in Spanish. *Aiiiiiie.*

The door slides open heavily, its corner dragging across the floor of the hallway. I squat, and meet the wrist holding the pistol with a hard grip and *yank*, pulling the guy out. Paulo swings the bat again, but there's not much room and the guy just smacks into me. We pretzel and sprawl across the floor, scratching and grabbing for the gun. Paulo hefts the bat like a spear and jabs at the guy, nailing me a few times. Finally, I find the corner of his mouth with two fingers and fish hook him for the win with a solid rip. He howls, then Paulo plants the big round end of the bat between his eyes. I grab the gun from his half-dead hand.

The guy isn't much after all. A thick older wop. Maybe semi-connected back in the day when the Mafia mattered, maybe just a dick who jerked off to *The Sopranos* and got a pistol because his brother-in-law's a cop out in Nassau County. 3R is a shithole. Clothes on the floor, plastic dinner table covered in old newspapers and DVD porn with hard-edged older women on the covers. Paulo slips one down his pants. I hand him the gun too, since he has those big jeans black dudes and retarded people who get clothes from the church like to wear. Anyway, there's no old lady in here, or even any traces of old lady. No smell of lavender, just feet and Chinese takeout. The crap on the floor—wrinkled shirts and loose wire from the TV and satellite dishes—hadn't been disturbed. Paulo pulls back the curtain on the tub: no old lady. It doesn't take long to search a two-room studio. She's not in the fridge either. Just an onion, a mostly empty jar of Hellman's, and a friggin' sock. Even I'm not that bad.

"So much for that theory," I say.

"Yeah," says Paulo. In the hallway, the guy groans.

"Now what?"

"Where's the old lady?"

"She's not here," I say.

"No shit," Paulo says. He sits, rests his chin on the bottom of the ball bat. "Gotta be somewhere."

"Does she?" I ask, mostly to myself. "Does she?"

"People just don't disappear," Paulo says. I don't bother to contradict him, to feed him a line, because he knows what time it is. "Except that they've been doing that today."

"What do they have in common?" I say. "The landlady and that old lady."

"Old ladies."

"Fat ladies."

"Head wraps," he says.

"Yeah, the old lady had a babushka. The landlady wears one of those Africa things." I make the universal hand sign for African head wrap by lifting my arms and shaking my palms over the top of my head.

"*Mami*," says Paulo.

Yeah. An old fat lady with a handkerchief on her head. That does sound like Paulo's mama.

He looks up at me with sad eyes. I hate leaving the building. I know he can't go without me though, not all the way up the long snake of a town, to Washington Heights. "Yeah. We should go check on your mama."

FOUR

Paulo doesn't like to leave his apartment and he certainly doesn't like schlepping all the way up to Inwood, where his mama lives, on the friggin' subway. Nobody does. Inwood doesn't even feel like Manhattan, though it's on the swollen glans of this cock of an island. There are houses there, not just housing blocks and high-rises and little postage stamp-sized front yards. It's also a barbaric shithole. They only have a handful of canaries.

Paulo had been sent down to the Lower East Side by his brother and cousins a couple of years ago. One of them comes by every Friday to pick up a brick of bills he puts in a Ziploc baggie. "I'm the downtown franchise," Paulo told me once. He doesn't say why he doesn't live in Inwood (or nearby Washington Heights) anymore, even though his mama was one of the laundry-doing, ass-wiping totally doting types.

"I ain't even seen her since Easter," is all he says. Neither of us even have a MetroCard, because we never go anymore, so we buy a bunch of one-way tickets so we can't be tracked later. Not that we'll be tracked later. We got our bats though, wiped clean. I dig up my old mitt and stick it on the end of mine so I look like someone on my way to Central Park for softball. Paulo's with me, so the cops won't hassle him too much about bringing a bat on the subway either, unless it's one of those days where they randomly search everyone who might have a grudge. Well, that would be everyone, just people who look like they might be half-sandnigger.

It's a long ride up to the tip of Manhattan, and we've got nothing to talk about, nothing to do but count the number of fat old ladies we pass on the streets down to the 1 train, and note them waddling up and down the platforms and across the length of the train cars, and wonder if there are somehow fewer of these heifers than there should be.

It's a dumb-ass theory really—*The fat ladies are vanish-*

ing!—but it's what we have so far. Plus we didn't want to be in the apartment when someone found the guy we fucked up. Or if he woke up and called the cops, or the Sopranos.

I turn to Paulo. He's green and nervous, already sick from the subway, even though it's just past noon and we have plenty of room and air in the train car. "Yo, I don't feel too good. It's like I'm sick, you know. That kind of sick where even taking a shit doesn't feel good no more." Paulo wasn't even talking to me, but instead muttering to his belly, his chin. He sleeps. We ride. I wonder if he even remembers where his mother lives. Why we didn't just call her, or one of his brothers?

It's a long ride. We could have gone out to Long Island, or the Jersey shore, instead of spending an hour under bedrock. When we hit the West 90s the Great Race Force Field activates and all the whites in the car leave but me, replaced by their opposite numbers in black—the same baggy pants, ragged shoes, business suits, and stringy iPod earbuds. Some Black Israeli guy dressed like a glowering genie instead of the Hassidic Jew.

Go far enough north and the subway becomes an elevated track. The train car bursts with sepia sunlight and we travel along the rooftops, old TV aerial antennas with spindly appendages wide open like a cast of skinny thousands in an old musical. Paulo stirs next to me and looks up, not at me but past me. "Holy shit," he says on the wrong side of still lips. "Lookit." His eyebrows twitch. I turn around to look at what he wants and see nothing but another row of empty plastic seats, but I know enough to trust him. It's been a few minutes since our last stop and it's by no means hot. I get up, walk over to the seat, its bottom molded to some Platonic ideal of a New Yorker fatass and touch it with my palm. Still warm. I try the one next to it too, to make sure it's not the angle of the sun through the windows, and that seat is still cold.

"What did it look like?"

"Like blinking back a tear," he says, almost crying himself.

"Was she—"

He shakes his head. "Just a dude in a hoodie."

It could be any of us now. Unless Paulo is just sick. "What stop are we coming to?" I quiz him. He says 125th Street, right on the Viaduct. Then we go back down underground, down into the hills of Washington Heights. He's got his act together. And then the train tilts and I stumble, the lights flicker, we're back in the dark. For a second, I'm lost.

"Paulo?" I call out, but there is no answer.

FIVE

Paulo? Is the last thing I can hear myself say. After that, it's like talking into a wall, except there is no wall there and I cannot feel my jaw or tongue or teeth either. I am in the dark, but I don't think I'm paralyzed. Lucid. *Far too lucid.* Air must be coming into my brain somehow, though I feel no breeze, no heat or cold. Can I see the train, or Paulo? I cannot tell the difference anymore, between picturing something in my mind's eye and actually seeing it.

Can you? Think of someone you love or—fuck it—hate. Picture them, sick and pathetic, eyes glassed over, skin a greenish brown. Smell 'em, that weird funk that reminds you of them, or the swampy burp from his stomach. The flexing rise of your wife's tits in bed, or the snot bubbling out the nose of somebody else's kid. Yeah, you can see it but you can feel it too, almost. Heat in your crotch or a twitch in your own gut. The powder of their skin on your tongue. A whole body strains and tingles when a brain remembers. A universe of phantom limbs, and houses, and cars, and oceans, all in the bag of chemicals we keep in our skulls.

I don't even get those sensations, now, here, like now and here mean anything.

Wherever the fat ladies are, I'm here. Now. In that moment in the middle of the night when you wake up and forget where you're living these days. The sense that your head is where your feet usually rest. What city is this? Is mama in the next room, breathing? Then you go through your life.

I was born in Youngstown, Ohio. I shat my pants in third grade once, and spent the afternoon bottomless in the boys' bathroom, stained briefs soaking in the long trough sinks and then hung over the side of the stall in which I was hiding. Why didn't they dry?

I almost went to college, but left after a semester of the local junior joint. Almost joined the Navy. But I had a job, pulling starters out of junk cars and selling them to a factory. Two bucks a starter. Sometimes I ran low on junkers. Not worth the risk to steal a whole car though, or even one owned by somebody. Those damn Ford dealers on the interstate though, with their oily promises and that new car smell primed to cloud men's minds, fuck 'em. One-way trip to the Port Authority and $100 in my shoe was all I needed way back when.

Where do I sleep? In the can in the Port Authority at first, following the cocksuckers who knew to stay one step ahead of the stooped janitors and the one cop who didn't want to feed his dick to a hustler for free. During the daytime, Barnes & Noble on 23rd and 6th. Keep washed, keep shaved, don't look homeless. Read a novel a day, the *Village Voice*. I got a button-down shirt and a blazer from the Salvation Army. I look haggard, but like a worker. I jerk off at the urinal, shave in the park. People ask me if I'm an artist. Two old Germans with knees like piano keys ask me to take a photo with them, my face half-smooth, and then press a wrinkled ten-dollar bill into my hand. I eat dollar hot dogs at Grey's Papaya on 12th Street and 6th. In the East Village there are still community gardens. I eat tomatoes at midnight, nibbling small bits like a squirrel.

I get an idea in the pit of my stomach. At the Key Food on Avenue A I try to keep myself fed on purloined grapes and Fun Size Milky Ways sneaked from a bag whose corner I tear oh-so-casually. Fall. Fill a cart, reach for the Ragu, and fall. Jars of sauce drop like bombs around me. I twist my own leg, now thin as a finger in my oversized pants, just to the brink. I see stars and for a second I think I'm here, where the fat ladies go, then I uncross my eyes and stock boys, mouths open and smocks, a wall around me stirs.

A social studies teacher told me this once: fall in a supermarket and they'll settle, sometimes right then and there. He's right. I'm helped up. They lead me to the back. Water. Yeah? Glass? A tiny whisk broom. For an hour I wait. I have bad teeth, inflamed gums. I suck on my molars till I come up with a convincing mouthful of blood and drool on command and curse to myself, really angry too because it's taking too long. A manager comes, with a clipboard and a cell phone. The sun is down now. I can smell the night, cool and smoky. They cut me a check for $2500. It comes with what looks like a pay stub, since it was spit out of the same machine.

I spend a sleepless night wandering downtown, looking to see which check cashing place opens first. I camp out there, so hungry. I want silver dollar pancakes and the twenty-four hour diner, a ptomaine palace, is bright and warm. The guy shows up late, with two friends and obvious bulges on their right side. I take a long walk and then walk back so I don't seem suspicious, and I pray to God oh you motherfucking cunt of a bitch God that they just cash the check. They take my picture. They dial a phone number, photocopy everything, fax the check to some distant place. My stomach feels ready to snake out my asshole and crawl away. Finally, God, finally, they do it. Twenty Franklins, twenty-five twenties. The diner, oh God the diner. Pancakes. Bacon. Cake of the day. Two danishes to go. Then down to Chinatown and the cheap Holiday Inn. A real fucking shower. A goddamn bed I sleep in for the whole day. Porn on the tube. I'd call for a whore but they're all whores. I come so hard I nearly hit the ceiling. Steaks three times in the dingy lounge. Screwdrivers with every meal and a plate of baby spinach for strength. Fucking toothpaste; the concierge gives me a travel tube for free. For *fucking free*. I buy shirts and pants. Three days and six hundred dollars later I get my ass to a bank and my shit to a SRO way down on Avenue D.

A week later I take a bus out to Staten Island, find a Food Emporium and slip on a cracked egg. I checked on the Internet in the public library first. They have a different insurer.

Three thousand fucking dollars.

I recall it all, every second, but can't taste the salty sweet of the pancakes, not the nervous twitch marching over my mouth at the check cashing place, not even the warm dip into oblivion of my first night in a bed in three weeks. Hell, they say, is the absence of God. I'm the absence of me.

Paulo, help me!

SIX

I keep thinking. My mind's always spun like a top and it's a good thing as in my state to not think is to wink out of existence. There's nothing to see or hear or smell, not even my own blood in my ears, or the stink from my underarms, or my tongue over my teeth. *What's Paulo doing?* I wonder.

The kid in the hoodie vanishes. I vanish. Paulo is sick from his agoraphobia and his massive weed habit. I can see him doing what everyone who was ever a kid in the city would do: stand up and stagger across the car to pull the thick red handle of the emergency brake. The fucking thing works too, and the train jerks to a stop hard, sending Paulo onto his ass. The train's in a tunnel again, under the hills of Washington Heights, with nowhere to go.

You know, Paulo and I always used to argue about the brake, even though we didn't disagree. I thought it should be a signal to the conductor to stop the train; he kept calling me a shithead and telling me it was a real brake that anyone could use in case some kid or old lady got caught in the closing doors and was being dragged along by the train across the platform to the mouth of the tunnel. And I'd tell him that I knew that, but that it was really fucking stupid to give a tube full of assholes free access to the brakes, and that I bet a lot of people just pulled the brake when they felt sick or saw a fight or were about to get mugged and that wouldn't help them at all since they'd be stuck in a tunnel far between stops for half an hour with a puddle of their own puke or a knife in their belly anyway. But he never got the is-ought distinction I was trying make, mainly because we were mostly way too high to make much sense to anyone but ourselves.

But Paulo would pull the cord and end up on his round ass. The lights would flicker on and off, then buzz to a sullen yellow, only half-charged from the third rail. And Paulo would start to figure. Yeah, he's ill, but in the dark of the train car, in the tunnel between stations, he'd start to feel a little better as there was no big wide forever looking to eat him up anymore. Paulo even likes his shitty Rivington Street studio apartment, and put up cardboard over the one window to keep out the sky. In the half-dark, Paulo is a Viking.

Paulo would think that either people are really disappearing—and we're not just talking the fat old broads who nobody ever notices because they don't drip sex like younger bitches (even the heifers, if you're Paulo) do—or he's crazy. So he'd test himself. Why is he on the subway, when he hates the subway? Because the landlady never showed up (a good thing). Because the old lady vanished halfway up the steps of his building (neutral). Because he checked out the only place that second old lady could have gone with his best friend, me, and ended up beating the shit out of some wop who may already be on the phone to Brooklyn, calling on twenty Benzes worth of bat-wielding semi-connected Guidos for a house party (that's a bad thing). And his mother, he misses his mother (a good thing).

Plenty of reasons to leave the house, and at least one of them—the guy whose shit we wrecked—perfectly reasonable. Paulo would have blown forty bucks on a cab if he'd been alone too; he would never take the subway by himself. So I must have been with him. He was sick to his stomach for the whole ride, unlike those dreams he has of taking the subway to naked terrifying eighth grade geometry, so he must really be on the train as well. So it's real, not a sticky-bud dream.

So he starts looking around, Paulo does, from car to car, hoping for clues or maybe even another sudden disappearance. There are only a few other riders, this far uptown and headed north at this time of day, and they're mostly eager for an authority to lead them. Paulo could be an MTA employee, even without the uniform, since he's got a paunch and dark skin and most people aren't very observant. Plus, he's crossing from one car to another with such seeming purpose. Some white guy with a military haircut gone to seed, shaken up in his seat, asked Paulo what was going on. Paulo lied and told him someone jumped on the tracks and the guy and everyone else in the train car reacted as expected—gasps, muttering about the assholes who ruin it for everybody, facial ticks, the usual. All real, and nobody disappeared like hot breath in cold air the second after an exhalation either.

It's a long wait, but Paulo has plenty of time to check all the cars. He reads the signs, in Spanish and English, in every car. Reads and closes his eyes and remembers them. Can you do that in a dream? Never. There's still that nagging feeling though, in his fingertips and the base of his spine. In the last dark car, where the window leads out only to the dark, maybe Paulo sees a light bobbing along in the depths of the tunnel. Like on a TV show Paulo lifts his palm to the glass, tilts his head, and squints into the light. He sees a chin like an old gibbous moon and a flash of orange and yellow—an MTA employee in the tunnel, marching over the tracks toward the train. Paulo stays still, not waving, not trying to open the door. He just watches.

The MTA worker, an older guy, keeps the beam of his flashlight trained on the back of the car. Paulo's eyelids flicker, but he doesn't hold up his hand to shade his eyes.

Paulo knows MTA guys, knows this kind of work. When an emergency brake gets pulled, and the calls go out along the switches, a whole set of lines back up: the 1, the 2, the 3, the A, C, and E too a bit at the stations shared. There's always that adrenalin spike; the quick desire to find a wayward thread and pull the knot to pieces with one quick jerk. It's almost never that easy, though, and the dunning buzz of standard operating procedures take over. Paulo stares into the light and doesn't even see the guy anymore; he sees himself. He gets what's happening.

The light falls to the tracks. The man is gone. Paulo knows he cannot ever ever stop thinking, or let things go on automatic pilot again. One blink in the dark and he'll be gone like me.

SEVEN

What's Paulo's mother like? Beats the shit out of me. Maybe she's a fat old stereotype: Paulo in a dress with a big bowl of refried beans carried in her elephant trunk arms. Or maybe she's a hot little number with crow's feet and a big smear of red lipstick and tight gray-black curls and a nice waist for the mama of four kids and she credits it all to salsa-dancing in the living room every night after the news. Paulo doesn't keep pictures of his family around, but he's a damn mama's boy all right, and he's thinking of his mother now. Like me, he needs to think of something and keep thinking, and it's hard in that dark subway tunnel. But Paulo has the squeaking and hollow echoes of distant trains pulling up to far-off stations, a whiff of piss, crumpled newspapers, a glimpse of the curve of graffiti, while I have noth —

Can't think about that. Can't think about *can't*. Paulo.

Paulo takes his bat and pounds his way through the door of the train, then carefully steps down. Sweat streaks down his back as he steps tiny Chinese girl steps along the tracks to the flashlight. He's so afraid of the third rail. Everyone in New York is except for assholes and dead people. The third rail is the great leveler—it can be Bloomberg or Giuliani, some prissy bitch being pushed onto the tracks by a crazy, an MTA guy, whoever. We're all helpless before that iron.

And then there are the rats. Fearless motherfuckers, they are. Rats don't sweat like men do. Paulo is afraid of them; his head spins at the thought of one running over his foot, of eyes and teeth in the dark, of a tail stroked against his cheek. Just like what happened in the shithole apartment he grew up in, in the tiny doomed room he shared with his brothers, once mama would turn off the light and shut the door. But now Paulo's a man—he watches 50+ porn on DVD because it's "realistic," what with the cottage-cheese thighs and the saggy tits. Paulo has to pay bills and buy presents, not just make birthday cards with glitter and crayons. He goes to the doctor and takes a finger up the ass every year so he won't die on the can like his grandfather did, shitting blood and crying for the Virgin Mary to save him. Paulo is a man, but he's sweating so hard his eyes are full of salt, and he wants his mama.

It takes a minute of shuffling and sniffling to get to the flashlight, and to realize that not everything in the tunnel is out to kill him. The A Train isn't going to silently round a corner and run him down. The third rail won't appear under his heel. The rats have no fear, but the swooping beam of the flashlight scatters them. Nothing to fear but fading away into the nothingness.

Mama!

It takes only a second, I imagine, I dream, I hope, of Paulo poking around in the dark to find a door, but that one is locked. The rumbles of subway cars are rare now. Are so many people vanishing that the conductors, switch-operators, and even the early crests of the rush hour wave just blinking out, leaving the subway system jammed with steaming, empty, subway cars? Stumbling in the dark, he comes across a ghost train, idling and settling like a sleeping snake. It's either cross it or walk back south, down a couple of miles to the platform. Paulo takes his bat and swings at the door, denting it, but it remains locked tight. He whoops and hammers away at it again, banging the shit out of the locking mechanism until it's totally fucked up. He sighs and drops the bat and thinks back to the time he heard about that guy who fell onto the tracks, and who got saved by another guy who jumped down after him. A train was roaring up to the platform, but the hero guy just pulled the other one down low and held his breath and the train passed right over them. This train isn't even moving. So Paulo gets on his back and winces as the coals lining the track bite into the back of his head. And then he begins to shrimp and squirm, his belly soaking with grease, a million tiny edges slicing into his denim jacket and fatboy jeans, and the smell of soot and steel setting his tongue aflame.

 He passes under the first car and is already exhausted. It's hard to walk on your shoulder blades and ass cheeks, especially when you have twenty pounds of gut balanced atop your bones like a Jell-O mold made out of McDonald's and ramen noodles. He gulps the tainted air and starts squirming again, pausing for breath and to lick the sweat off his lips every few feet. He hopes, God, he hopes, it's a four-car train. It should be, since it's only midday. Under the third car, Paulo just stops and screams, English and Spanish, "Why me!" and "Fuck fuck fuck!" Also, God is a cocksucker and the Virgin Mary takes it up the ass like a whore. And then he moves on. It's a six-car train.

 Finally he breaks through and drags himself to his knees—they're bloody and sticking to the interior of his fouled jeans—and then to his feet. Paulo tries to wipe his face on his shirt, which is just as filthy and encrusted with perspiration and piss-limned soot as his skin is. He digs into a pocket and finds a receipt from a burger place that isn't entirely blackened, and uses that instead, for all the good it does. It's still a block or two to the next platform, but he trudges along, not even thinking of mama anymore, really, but just about seeing some sky, finding a bottle of water. Maybe Paulo thinks of empty streets, some horrid movie or dream, or maybe he dreams of me, alone in the dark with my thoughts, thinking of him.

And Paulo finds a door, and he doesn't even have the strength to run for it. He staggers over, more than anything else, and leans on the bar handle, knowing that it'll be locked, just like the last one was. In his grimy hand, the lever moves and a puff of cool air issues forth and Paulo opens the door and the universe on the other side is empty except for me, suspended like in the ink of night.

And then I'm back here. And I think of it all again, Paulo, the door opening in a slicing square of light, some goddamn sensory input in this bit of numb black, and then it vanishes and I'm back to the nothing. And I do it again, and then another scenario. Ever wake up from a dream and try to turn off the clock radio, only to find that you cannot, even if you unplug it, and maybe even swing the damn thing around by the cord and smash it against the wall, and it's still playing, and your mother comes in to wake you up for school and her mouth opens and it's Howard Stern's voice going on about the protein content of semen and you feel a spasm in your leg and then the clock radio is back where it belongs and it's some lame summertime song with no guitars and you reach for it again to turn it off but you're in some other room, like the really nice bedroom in Brooklyn with the French doors that you lucked into one time when that skinny blond with the too-long nose and green eyes took you home for a fuck and she had a silk robe and the whole place smelled like lavender and cats and you reach for the radio and you cannot wake up and you want to turn off the music and you do but you cannot wake up so the music keeps playing and you dream of waking up but the music keeps going and a rock star is in the corner of your room, in black and white like in the video and you reach for the little folded up instructions to the radio in the drawer of a dresser you don't even own and you spread it out on your lap and stare down at the paper but it's all lines and strange characters because you can't read in dreams and then finally, finally, you wake up?

It's like that, but I don't wake up.

EIGHT

Paulo cannot save me. There's no dream of him I can dream that will lead to his brown hand coming out of the darkness. He may just be sitting on the damn molded plastic butt-bucket, on his way to his mother's house. Or maybe he vanished too, into his own private shithole. Or it could be anything—twenty million years could have passed, for all I know. Humanity dead, or evolved into nose-less, slithering, snake-men. The sun a burnt out match hanging in the night. And right next to me in this limbo could be ten billion screaming souls—Hitler and Mother Teresa babbling to themselves, your grandmother and those little girls who were drowned in the tub by whatshername with nothing to hang on to but that last press in their chests before it all went black. I could be buried in them all, but I can't feel a thing.

And if I stop talking, I'm gone. It's like turning the switch on a lamp with no bulb.

I need something. Not some dream memory, or fantasies of what might be going on in a world without me. A squiggle of phlegm on my tongue, if I had a tongue. Something other than the black that isn't even black—it's just the buzz of static, or the black of daydreams. Forget it, start small. Find something. A bit of pressure, a fluctuation or eye floater in the dark. The memory of an inhalation. How it felt to cross my eyes.

And then I see it. Glowing eyes in the dark, tiny, like the rat what don't fear cats. Why does this come to mind...stuff I don't even know that I ever knew: *Toxoplasma gondii*. A parasite in the brain, the thing that drives a rat to seek out the piss-stench of a cat, just to be eaten all up in service of the bug. And in the cat, the squirming little bastards actually fuck, reproducing sexually — *sexually!* — till they get shit out. Then the cycle starts again. I can feel them, in my brain. They're not fucking, they only fuck in cats, but they are there. I can feel them. I feel them and I'm real again, real as the red rat-eyes squaring off with mine as I blink my way back to the universe. Then the rat lunges and bites at me, teeth like little razors. I twist away and the sting and tearing never comes. I look up and see the world from my back. Filling it, crushing a rat in her hand: Paulo's mama.

NINE

Paulo's mother doesn't look like either of my visions of her, but rather a combination of both. She's well-dressed, and with that smear of lipstick, but has a bucket chin and flat face like Paulo, and hands like a man, which was handy given that she had just crushed a life in her fingers.

"What did you do with my boy?" she asks, her voice harsh in that way a dashboard is to a forehead. I lift my head and see that I'm on a carpet in the middle of small living room in a railroad apartment; there are only two walls, and I spy the kitchen behind Paulo's mother's shoulder, can smell the Latin spices. Paulo sleeps heavily on a sunken couch next to me. There's no coffee table. Paulo was always so proud of the coffee table he found on the street that time right before the case of The Bloodied Woman. He wakes and stretches an arm. A small dog, some kind of terrier, emerges from the other room and sniffs at my head before sitting down in front of Paulo's mother and whining for the rat. She doesn't drop the rat, or even lower her arm. Instead the corpse begins to drip down toward the dog, as if it was boneless and melting, like molasses. It's then that I realize that something is wrong. I am extremely high.

"You—" Paulo's mama says to me, "you and Paulo were down in the streets, giggling and screaming and crawling along the sidewalks like you were sliding off the Earth." I try to raise my head, but it feels as though the whole floor was coming with it, so heavy. Paulo doesn't turn to look to me; his face slides around to the side of his head to preserve precious neck-muscle energy. He says, in a voice that sounds like wind, "Yo man, my mama's all right. Half of her is anyway." And I look up at mama, who has turned away in disgust, and see that her back half is missing. For a moment it's all hollowed out, like a chocolate Easter bunny sliced down the middle, and then she's gone.

The world jerks to a stop and I feel an elbow in my side. The train. Paulo next to me. "Come on," he says, and I forget why we ever left the apartment. Is this another dream in a dream? I decide not to ask, but just observe. Paulo shuffles off the train and me right behind him. Is everything normal? What do I feel? My heels in my shoes, check. The hoodie around my head, I feel that even when I'm *not* thinking about it. Am I high? Did we smoke up and try something new this morning while waiting for the landlady with our baseball bats. I still got mine, Paulo has his. Consistency of reality—that's a good thing, right? Did we beat the shit out of that guy? Are we looking for Paulo's mama or do we have someone else to brain with these bats? So I ask "Is it much farther, Papa Smurf?" and Paulo says, "Not much farther my little smurf," and now I know this is "teh r3a1" as the kids say. We always talk to one another like smurfs, except we mostly say fuck.

There's a shift in the mood, and not just my own. This part of town is still run-down, covered in a fine layer of exhaust and snot, but it's alive like the Lower East Side used to be. No banks, no cafes, just storefronts selling fruit from cardboard boxes, old men too thin to be alive sitting on folding chairs in front of tenements, and kids shrieking in the streets like they're playing with machetes. I have to ask.

"Paulo, when you were growing up, were there rats in

your apartment?"

"Yeah," he says. "Lots. Fucking scary, they are. We got a cat, but these were the rats what don't fear cats." He says *what*, not *that*, just like that wayward thought I'd had in my…whatever the hell it was. *Was* I think, as if I know for sure that this "is" *is* anything other than a continuation of that fugue of blackness and memory. "We had a cat too; she was afraid of them," he says. "We'd put Brillo pads in the cracks in the walls to try to keep them out. That's the one thing rats can't chew through, but the walls were weak and they can squeeze in anywhere, those little motherfuckers. Where the pipe meets the hole, under the sink, or through the drain in the tub, they were all over the place."

He stops, turns to me, and puts a hand on my shoulder. "Listen, you have to know something. My mother was clean. She's very clean. We were a clean family. It wasn't us. It's like our shithole building; the landlord leaves the garbage to pile up in the vacant lot and rats climb up the walls, no matter what you do or how clean you are." Nervousness ripples across Paulo's face, like a slow twitch. He cares what I think, and whatever is happening, isn't interested enough in the machismo façade anymore to hide it. It's unnerving, actually.

"Yeah, I know. It's my apartment they crawl into, remember?" They do. I'm in 2R, the rear apartment. I was so happy to get the place too, and went hog wild down at the C-Town, a place I hadn't even thought to do a slip-n-fall in because I was sure they didn't have a lawyer on retainer to cut checks. I bought all sorts of stuff I normally only stare at on the shelves: Froot Loops, big piles of pork chops wrapped in cling-film, tons of dollar bags of linguini, Hershey's Kisses, five kinds of apples. I took it all home and, exhausted, took a nap. I woke up to rustling on the other side of the wall—you know, the wall on the edge of the tub in the kitchen, the wall that makes just enough empty space for a twin bed, just enough space to call my dump a "two-room studio" and get three digits a month for it. That wall. So I got up and went to the kitchen and there was my spaghetti, all over my little curbside table, the bags torn open and the edges of the pasta nibbled. The cereal box was eaten through too, and the bag within it ripped; Froot Loops piled up colorfully by the damaged corner, like a Viennese table for a gay wedding.

I made the mistake of going down to the bodega and buying the cheapest rat trap I could find, glue pads. I stuffed all my pasta and bread and whatnot in the fridge, laid out the traps and waited. It didn't take long. At three that morning—I knew the time because all the windows in the apartment are in the kitchen; behind the wall it's nothing but dark (that inky black, and, thank God...) the glowing light of my clock radio. Screeching. A rat was in a trap screeching. I had some Percocets thanks to one of my spills and an indulgent clinic and chewed them till I got back to sleep.

In the morning the rat was still there and still screaming. I smacked it with a broom, and that was useless. I got my Docs and threw them at the rat. It squealed and the glue trap slid across the floor, and I managed to stun it. I couldn't look. I took a towel and wrapped it around my hand, and my neck twisted and staring at the ceiling grabbed at the rat. I got the corner of the trap and with my free hand opened the window, then threw it all out, towel (which got stuck to the glue) and everything. I watched the rat and trap hit the ground hard and the towel flutter after it, to the garbage-strewn vacant lot (the remnants of a community garden from the days before crack and five-dollar cocksuckers, actually) below. Then I saw the cat. *Fuck it*, I thought, *cats are smart. She won't mess with the rat.* I hoped there was enough Percocet powder on my pillowcase to get me another good nod, then I heard the yowling.

I met Paulo a few minutes later. I was in the lot behind the house, arms and face bleeding from long slashes, tiny bits of a rendered glue trap sticking to my palms and hands, my towel soiled with blood and dirt. The cat was gone, and so was the rat, though it was minus a leg and half its viscera, which had dragged after it like toilet paper on a pant leg. Paulo stopped and shook his head and laughed, and then we became friends.

* * *

"Hey," he says, "stop muttering to yourself. We're here." We're right in front of an old row house with new glass security doors on both sides of the vestibule and dusty buzzers with blank spaces where the resident names should be. My arms tingle with phantom cat scratches and my head swims as I think of that shitty old song. For a long moment we wait. I still can't bring myself to ask if we're here for Paulo's mama, if this is really the case of the disappearing fat ladies. Behind us, a sock hits the cement with a solid-sounding *chock*. Keys. Somebody's home. "They broke the buzzer when they replaced the door," Paulo tells me as he goes for the sock, but I had figured that out already.

TEN

It's the real apartment this time, I'm sure, because it is tiny and cramped. Apartments in dreams are never so tiny. They're deep like minds. If Paulo's mother's apartment was a mind, it would be that of some kind of obsessive compulsive retard. The key word is Palo, the crazy voodoo religion of the Dominican Republic. Three rooms, but smaller altogether than my dump on Rivington Street. Candles everywhere with gaudy wide-eyed saints painted on the jars, leaning on awkward shelving units of cinder blocks and milk crates. A statue of another hanging upside down, by long chains of garlic and bushes of dried herbs. No tub at all, but a shower stall in the corner of the kitchen, its base filled with dirty dishes and pans. Paulo's mother, looking nothing at all like anything I'd previously envisioned—she's black, and small, nearly a midget, with thick glasses—

sits at the small kitchen table. She has a bundle of feathers in front of her, it's a chicken, still under a firm left hand, and atop a white sheet. A statuette of the Virgin Mary looks on.

I speak: "Are we having chicken soup?" The room smells of old blood, like the shelves of a butcher shop. I know that we're not, or at least that if we are gonna get some soup it's going to be after some crazy spirit-medium stuff, but I know that a naïve-sounding question will spark a monologue from Paulo.

"We are calling up Tiembla Tierra, the spirit of mind and thought, peace and wisdom," Paulo's mother says, matter-of-factly.

"It's okay," says Paulo, "only the chicken gets it." The chicken looks at me with one eye.

"Paulo, what the hell—"

"You got problems, friend," Paulo says. "Big problems. Wandering the halls, moaning and screaming. I find you wrapped up in a tiny ball in your tub, gloves on, a cap pulled over your head like a hood. You freaked out on the train on the way up."

"Bullshit," I say. "Prove it."

Paulo pulls out his iPhone and shows me. I'm on the train, or at least it's someone who dressed like I do and has my belly—my shirt is pulled over my head and my arms are outstretched like I'm playing Marco Polo with the world.

"Well, that might be me," I say. My throat goes dry. "How do I know this is real?"

"The video?"

"Any of this! I thought we were coming to check up on your mother because fat ladies were disappearing." And with that Paulo's mother cuts off the chicken's head with a big cleaver, spraying me and Paulo both in blood and screaming feathers.

I get up. "This is fucking crazy!"

"No, you are fucking crazy," says Paulo's mother, pointing the blood-splashed cleaver at me. "Or something within you is crazy, yes. Paulo, hold him." Paulo's a big guy, though it's mostly fat. Bigger than me, he grabs me by the arms with thick hands and says, "Listen, just try it."

"If any of this is true, why did you bring me here? Why not to a doctor?"

"You think I didn't? The clinic down on Stanton Street wanted nothing to do with you. You were in Bellevue for two nights and they let you go. Budget cuts, plus they said you were totally normal."

"I *am* totally normal."

Paulo's mother whips the white sheet out from under the carcass and holds it up to the light. She starts muttering a chant to herself in a language that doesn't quite sound like Spanish. Paulo says, "Yeah, you talked your way out of there. Look, maybe you're possessed."

"I don't believe that shit," I say, though my attention is captured by the Rorschach design of the blood on the sheet. "I'd rather be crazy. Hell, for that matter, the easiest answer that explains everything is that you and your mother are crazy, and..." I want to believe that, but my heart isn't in it. I let the sentence die in the air.

"Eliminate the impossible, and only the improbable remains, dude," Paulo says. Paulo's mother hmphs at that and folds up the sheet in quarters, then turns over the Virgin statuette. It's hollow. She shoves the sheet in, and then takes the cleaver and cuts off the feet as well. They go inside the Virgin, too. Then she hands it, upside-down so the stuff within won't fall out, to me.

"Am I going to have to bury this somewhere stupid?" I ask.

"Yes," she says. "Very stupid, like you." She wipes her hands together and says "Hang it in your closet. When the sheet is white again, then the spirit that bothers you will be gone."

Paulo and I share a look. "Uhm, mami," he says. "He doesn't have a closet."

"Yeah. I don't have a closet. Can I hang it like that one?" I ask, pointing to the statuette in the kitchen with my chin. The Virgin is surprisingly heavy in my hands, and warm like a rat. *Like a rat! Why did I think that?*

"You'd better get a closet," Paulo's mother says, and she turns away, done with us. The apartment is too small for her to leave the room, and we have no place to go, so we just all three of us stand there like morons for several minutes. I look to Paulo, but he holds his fingers to his lips. Paulo's mother clears out the sink, which is full of potted herbs, and then goes to the shower stall and drags out some of the dishes and a saucepan.

"Are we going to watch her wash dishes?" I ask, and Paulo asks her something in Spanish. "We gotta stay for dinner," he reports to me. "Mami's not had one of her sons over in a long time." She says something else in Spanish. Paulo translates: "Because we all hate her and want her to die."

"Is there a place we can talk in private?" I ask him and he nods and steps around the table and over an empty birdcage on the floor to the soot-smudged window, opens it, and steps out onto the fire escape. I nod to his mama, who snorts at me while putting on some rice to boil, and clamber outside as well, into the wind. Mama shuts it behind me with a trace of menace.

We're twelve stories up and the fire escape is all rusted bars, though artfully curved and spiraled, and flat slats leading to the gaping hole from where one might descend all the way down to the eight-foot drop that finally leads to the sidewalk. My head spins lightly. If there was a fire, I think I'd rather burn. I almost drop the statuette. We are alone out here, except for plants and dead toys littering the surrounding fire escapes, and clothes hanging on lines stretched across the cement courtyards between buildings.

"Tsup?" Paulo says.

"I have questions. I just want yes or no answers. Okay?"

"Yes." He's so good.

"Were we waiting up all night to beat the shit out of the landlords today?"

"Yes." Paulo smiles.

"Did they not come?"

"No."

"So they *did* come?"

"Wait, I mean yes they did not come," Paulo says. "If you want yes or no answers, you have to ask your questions better, okay?"

"Yes," I say, and now I smile. "Anyway. Did we meet a girl?"

"She was hot," says Paulo. "Bitch though. Stuck-up bitches everywhere."

"And then was there an old lady, and we thought the wop on my floor kidnapped her so we beat the shit out of him with ball bats?"

"Yes."

"Then why did we come up here to do—" I hold up the statuette, careful to keep it upside down so the handkerchief doesn't flutter away.

Paulo looks at me. "Why do you think?"

What didn't I ask? "Was the old lady real?"

Paulo shrugs. "What do you think, detective?"

"I thought I was asking the questions here," I say, "and you were just going to say yes or no."

"Yes," he says.

"Did I actually get that book on Plato and Socrates from the street hawker on St. Mark's the other day when I thought it was your birthday but you were actually just happy about how some soccer game went, and you read it anyway and now you're trying out the Socratic method on me?"

"...yes."

I'm starting to get comfortable out on the fire escape, but also hungry, and make the mistake of turning my head to check out what Paulo's mama is doing. I shudder when I catch a glimpse of the curve of the world in the corner of my eye and almost fall to my knees, almost drop the statue. Paulo seems so far away, like the fire escape is a ring stretched around the planet. I take a step and hear a squeak—rust or rat!—and nearly jump out of my skin. I want to push myself back through the window, let the teeth

of glass shred me alive, just to be on a floor again. I catch a look at my reflection; I'm fat, wild-eyed, unshaven, like I'd stuck my thumb in my mouth and puffed out my cheeks till on the verge of unconsciousness. Paulo looms behind me now, a fleshy mountain. Whatever is happening to me is motherfucking happening
   to
   me
   right
   the fuck
   now.

ELEVEN

Palo means stick. It's a faith of slaves and former slaves. When the Portuguese and Spanish came to Africa, they brought with them Christ and Mary and a phalanx of saints. It's a syncretism, a stew. It's a lot like the stew Paulo's mother is feeding me now, from a clay pot. It tastes like chicken, and cocoanut, and ash and feet. You'd think she might have a kind look on her face, or maybe a hint of a smile, but no. She's about as expressive as the Virgin Mary statuette, which I still hold on to. And the stick, I feel like I've been with one hard, my brains scooped off the floor and then poured back into the top of my hollow, open head. Paulo's on his cell phone, going on about something in Spanish.

"Listen..." I say, then forget what I was going to say. Paulo's mama has the magic. She knows what I forgot. "You're not the only one. It's happening to lots of people. You're all getting sick." Paulo snaps his phone shut and walks over to me. I'm on the floor, except that my head and feet are elevated by moldy old laundry. Boy clothes. Paulo's brothers. Cigarettes and sour musk.

"Listen..." he tells me, and he doesn't forget what he

has to say. "You're schizophrenic, okay? What happened is that the summer's been hot, remember. Global warming, you know?"

"It's not global warming..." I hate when people assume that one hot summer means global warming.

"Yeah, anyway, the summer was hot. Hot summer, warm winter, you know what that means?"

I do. "More mosquitoes, more rats."

"The rats what don't fear cats," Paulo says. "I've been observing them. There are plenty of strays around, you know. And the rats have been almost shoving themselves down the throats of the stray cats. That's how it spreads."

"That's why pregnant women shouldn't have cats," Paulo's mother says, mostly to herself. "Leads to madness."

I try to sit up more, but Paulo's mother has a hand like the thick roots of the trees that buckle concrete. She puts me back down. "Toxoplasmosis. I had a vision of it. But that's a common thing. Millions of people have it, but it doesn't cause symptoms or problems unless the person has—" and I don't finish the sentence: *AIDS or something like that.*

"Something has changed in the world," Paulo's mama says. "The news, it is everywhere. People who have this parasite are being driven to attack their families, or to sink into the darkness—"

"Like you hiding your face all the time, craving the dark," Paulo says.

I take another spoonful of the stew. I'm surprisingly hungry. Maybe not surprising—psychotic episodes take a lot out of a body, I suppose. "What does this have to do with magic?"

"AIDS, maybe it is. Maybe it has no cure," Paulo says, "and the virus mutated, or *something* mutated. There's no possible answer, it seems like." He scoots down into a squat and moves some stuff—a garbage bag full of stuff that probably isn't garbage, a dusty fan—and finds a TV, then turns it on. There's no cable here, and no rabbit ears, so the picture is snowy, the sound tinny and distant, and the TV show *The People's Court*. Some fat guy is standing behind a podium and shouting while next to him, a younger girl (Daughter? Girlfriend with no taste?) cringes.

"Pfft, what were you expecting?" I ask. "To turn on the TV just in time to tune in to a Special Report about crazies rioting in the streets? We could have another 9/11 and they'd only break in to programming for five minutes. This isn't the movies." Paulo's mother pushes me back down onto the floor and pillow of clothes, her hands on my shoulders. "Try a car radio next! Maybe a squeal of static and some hollowed-out AM announcer going on about Revelations, then you find a 'real' radio news station and the generic Biff Talkey newsreader there is desperately trying not to say 'People are turning into insane zombies and running through the streets'?"

"It's three o'clock. Mami's stories are on," Paulo says. He reaches for the second knob, the UHF one, and finds Telemundo. Mama doesn't pay too much attention to the TV, though the low-key hysterics of a woman standing by a iron wrought staircase keeps us all company for a while, as Paulo tries to explain.

Something happened out there, or, really, down there. In the sewers. Rats carry toxoplasmosis. It makes them fearless. Rats are usually runners, that's how they survive. The little brain-germ makes them chargers. Into the needly mouths of cats. Then into the world, one turd at a time. It's almost poetic, really. There've been studies—Paulo read this in the paper—that men get the teensiest bit more aggressive (Paulo really said "teensiest"; he cracks me up sometimes) and women a bit more extroverted, when infected. But something changed. After countless generations of breeding in cat shit, *Toxoplasma gondii* got tough. A random mutation, radiation from some toxic waste dumped in the sewers, sunspots? Nobody knew. A few professors already managed to get on TV by claiming that all of human history—the fall of Rome, China's Warring States, the French Revolution, the Holocaust—were caused by mutant strains. Once the bodies piled up so high that the parasites have no vector for transmission, they die out, and everyone calms the fuck down to the level of everyday wars and atrocities for another fifty or two hundred years.

"Cure?"

"Nothing, really. Generally, it doesn't even hurt people. Millions are infected and live their lives without even knowing it." Paulo says. From the corner of my eye, I see an actress on the *telenovella*, all tits and a big bushel of curls, lean dramatically across a wrought iron spiral staircase and heave. Is she infected or just a bad actor?

"So why this and why now?" I say.

Paulo's mother says, "Spirits. *Nfuri*. They wander the world, causing mischief—"

"—like that mischievous little Holocaust?" I say. Paulo fumes over me. "Listen, didn't you come up here thinking that we had to check on my mother because fat ladies were mysteriously disappearing? Why is it so hard to believe?"

"I'm also schizophrenic due to germs found in cat shit. You can't trust a word I say," I say, but then I see the trap I set for myself now, "except in my lucid moments, of which this is one. I mean, did we look for the old lady out on the old wop's fire escape? Or maybe he just rolled the body out the window and it hit the lot behind the building with a dusty thump, like cinder blocks wrapped in rags?" Paulo blanches. We didn't.

"We should go," he says. "That was my brothers on the phone, and I don't want to be here, not with you, when they come by."

"That's fine," I say, and I start to get up. Then I ask, "Maybe I'm not the only infected person. How do I know that you weren't just talking into the phone, pretending to hear the conversation?" He tosses me the phone, and it flies through my hands and lands on my belly. Paulo's mama snorts. I check out the phone, finding the Recent Received calls item on the menu, and click.

It's my landline number. And it was a call made just a few moments ago.

Who the hell was this, in my apartment? I want to ask, but the question makes no sense. I look up at Paulo, but Paulo has no tells. Did I see the number wrong, or is Paulo sick too now, or are his brothers really at my apartment, making calls and eating my Easy Mac and pissing in my tub like it was the trough at Yankee Stadium? I hit redial and put the phone to my ear.

It rings four times and then connects. "Hello?" I say, nervously, into the phone.

"Hello," I say, back at my apartment, to myself. "Who is this?"

TWELVE

I'd been ill, shivering in bed for three days, when I got a phone call from myself. Paulo hadn't been by—nobody ever comes by. I always met him in the hallway, or watched TV in his apartment, inviting myself in when the sticky sweet smell of KB wafted across the length of the building and seeped under my door. Until he called, but only to jabber away in Spanish at me—the only words I picked out were *hermano* and *maricon*—I didn't even realize that he realized I hadn't been around.

Even the landlord hadn't come by today. There was shouting, and I think a gun went off in the hallway before. Could have been anything; the asshole on the other side of the wall could have bought a plasma TV with awesome speakers, or maybe he just got one that fell off a truck. A truck backfiring, an oven exploding. I'm the kind of sick where it all blends in, where the fever is on my skin and the cold in my bones, where even taking a shit is a trial instead of a relief.

That sounds like something Paulo would say. I decided to go next door to see what he's up to, but my body didn't move. Even the idea of slithering out of bed and getting out of the dirty sweatpants I use for pajamas and into some jeans feels like it would be painful. Denim encasing raw skin, ugh. Sitting up is a trauma. Even when I go to the water closet, I just roll, slowly and taking breaths between, to the end of the bed, then slide off. For once I'm glad that the water closet — a room so tiny that my knees brush the bottom of the porcelain sink when I'm on the commode — is built into the wall of my room, and that the room is just big enough for the bed. I can practically fall into the crapper, and I've managed it once a day for the past three days. I drink tap water. I don't eat. How could I possibly manage to make it across the hallway? I'd call an ambulance, but I have no health insurance, and think the trip on a gurney down two flights of steps might kill me.

Plus, if I nap a bit more, if I wet my lips and turn over the pillow to rest my head against the cool side, maybe I'll feel better when I wake up. That's what I thought anyway, when I closed my burning eyes. The phone rang, I thought, then it stopped. I woke up when the phone rang again; it was so insistent. I tugged on the line and dragged the phone out from under the bed where I'd kicked it, and fumbled for the phone.

"Hello?" I say, nervously, into the phone.

"Hello," I say, back at my apartment, to myself. "Who is this?"

"It's me," I say. "Calling from Paulo's phone." I think of what to ask and hear the answer in my tinny voice before I can even state the question.

"Anyone can tell you your social security number. In these days of easy credit, even someone like you, with a checking account all of three months old, with seven dollars in it, is all over the grid. Phone bills, utilities, state non-driver ID. So I won't bother with that.

"You're a walker. Every night you take a jaunt, with an umbrella and an old suit jacket. A real-life East Village eccentric, cutting down the same streets. Rivington, west to Allen, then up to Houston and then north to Lafayette, and back. Dangerous habit, when you think about, but that's part of why you do it. Amateur sleuths have their quirks. And you keep a journal too, a little Moleskin on you at all times and a shoebox full over your fridge. The rats nibble on the corners, but that's just another little decorative detail in the architecture of your life. But the long and short of it is that I'm not going to tell you anything from your recent past to prove who I am, who you are, because you'd just jump to the conclusion that someone had been tracking your night-jaunts and slipping in to the apartment to read your old diaries for a telling, embarrassing anecdote.

"Don't be so cocky. If there's anyone after you, he's in your head. Probably literally. But I'll prove myself to you, I'll prove you to myself. If only you had a scar this would be easier, eh?"

That's what I was thinking, so I laughed.

"There's no mirror over the sink in the WC. Right before you got sick—this isn't in the journal because you've been too out of it to write—you came home from one of your walks in the rain and went to the toaster and peered at the chrome side, touching and poking your neck to feel how inflamed your lymph nodes were. And when you did that you thought back to something you hadn't remembered. A dumb little conversation with fat Christine from high school, and a book she'd read once about a girl who crawls through a mirror and gets married to the dark prince on the other side. You don't even like fantasy crap like that, but it just bubbled up out of the slow-boil of your brain. You didn't even remember that the girl's name was Christine till you were in bed that night and on the clock radio you heard the first few bars of a Pretenders song."

"Right," I say. "So, how is this conversation happening? Are you the me in the mirror, or did I record a monologue when I was high one night and hanging out with Paulo, and he's just playing it back to me now somehow?"

"I dunno," the me on the phone says. "But I hope you can figure it out. I'm as sick as you. I've spent my day in black holes. The world is vanishing around me. Scenarios slide off like rotting snakeskins. Save me. Fuck, save yourself."

Real or unreal, good or ill, *Fuck, save yourself* is always good advice.

THIRTEEN

Step one to saving myself is getting dressed. I keep the T-shirt I'm wearing, even if it is stiff with sweat and spittle. I can't go outside in these sweatpants though. It's chilly probably, and I look enough like a homeless person or someone who just wandered out of a psych ward as it is. I grit my teeth and try for the jeans, sliding off my sweats. I sit on the edge of the bed for a while before slipping my feet into the jeans, then laying back down onto my mattress and pulling-slash-sliding the jeans up my legs. Not as bad as I'd imagined, but pretty shitty anyway. I just want to go back to sleep, but then I remember who I just talked to. *Me!*

Gee-whillikers, it's a mystery! I make it into the other room. Never had it seemed so big, not even when it was empty of everything but stove and tub when I moved in years ago. I lurch over to the window and crack it open. Brisk air with a hint of a chill, like a single ice cube in a warm summer Coke, that's what I need. Plus, the whole apartment smells yellow and sick. I stick my head out the window and through the slats of the fire escape see the cats and rats and little black birds. There is usually a little wildlife outside in the lot that used to be a community garden back when there was a community here, thanks to the trash piled ten feet under my window, but this is Tippi Hedren territory.

There's a moment you see in TV shows, or read about in *The Daily News*. Someone looks down at a bundle and thinks it is just some garbage. Not me, I just wonder whose body it is. I put my foot on the windowsill, but get the shakes and decide I can't handle the fire escape, or the ladder and that last seven-foot drop to the ground today. I can make it out to the hallway and walk down the steps, I'm sure. I get halfway down the flight when my knees give out, and scoot down the rest of the dusty steps on my ass. There's nobody around, thankfully, and in the daytime nobody puts their face to the window cut into the door to the building. That's only for night-stalkers and crack-heads and college kids from Long Island who think it would be fun to live in The City and peer in just to give a bit of substance to their daydreams of love and squalor.

I make my way out the back door and kick a brick toward the animals. A few of the pigeons and other birds flutter away, but even the cats just glare and stand. She's pretty chewed up, the old lady, and not quite split open, though her jaw is about three inches higher than it should be. I've seen her around. She lives in the building, way up on the fifth floor.

She didn't fall from the fifth floor though; the body is too close to the side of the building, and the way she shuffled and dragged her old-lady grocery cart I doubt she's been out on her fire escape in a decade. Plus, she lives—lived—in the front of the building, not in one of the rear apartments. All the fire escapes look fine from down here. The only one I can eliminate as a staging point for her swan dive is mine.

But then I remember that I'm out of bed, and standing by a body, all because I got a phone call before, from Paulo's number, and the man on the other end of the line was me. Even on the Lower East Side, someone is gonna call the cops, even if it is just some other old lady stepping out onto the fire escape to hang her horrible nylons and tarpaulin muumuus.

Back in the building the big clue is too obvious. When I look up at my nemesis, the steps again, I can see past my landing and up to the third and fourth floors. The door to 3R is totally wrecked. I don't want to climb an extra flight of steps, I don't want to do anything but go back to bed and chug Nyquil like it's vodka till I sleep and float on a green and dreamless sea, but I have to know. I walk up to the second floor, nearly doubled from the bubbling taffy in my lungs, and then make it up to the third after a rest.

The door's pounded in. Baseball bat, looks like. A bullet hole too. Quiet now though, no moaning, no TV, no breathing. I slide my hand under my T-shirt (fingerprints, you know) and nudge the door open. The old wop who lives there is on the floor, looking like a bag of garbage stuffed into a pair of jeans, but he's not dead like the old lady is. He is still breathing, barely, and whistling too, a gurgling wheeze thanks to his torn cheek.

His place is no bigger than mine, but he has some nicer shit, and an open window. The curtains sway in the breeze, expectantly. It's cold in here, and smells like cigarettes and rotten fruit and, yes, a whiff of old lady. Acrid piss and mothballs. I go to the window and see what I thought I would. It's open. The windowsill, dusty and smoky, is spotted with semen. I check the Italian guy. His fly is still half open, no underwear, his wang is crumpled up like a blue sausage. Case closed: Italian guy gets off on killing old ladies by throwing them out like so much garbage. After his last escapade, someone beat down the door and managed to overpower him, even though he had a gun. The bullet hole on the door tells me it was fired in here, and the guy's crooked, broken finger, tells me that the gun was his.

What I don't expect is the clearing of a feminine throat and the canary in the doorway, looking more put out than outraged or terrified. "What are you doing here?" she asks, as I turn around.

"What are *you* doing here?" I ask. But I'm not talking to her. I'm talking to Paulo, and to some guy I almost don't recognize for a second, but then I remember. It's me. And I'm holding a little statue.

FOURTEEN

I started wearing glasses when I was eight years old. I was in second grade and terrified that the other kids would make fun of me, and they did, and I probably deserved it on some level. I remember going to the eye doctor, his fingers cold, smoke on the breath, a roll-top desk full of glasses frames, but I could only choose from among the three—thick and nerdy, this was two decades before the Buddy Holly look became a cultural signifier for underfed hipster chic—black, red, and tortoise shell. I can remember myself looking in the full-length mirror, with my tight pants and thick belt and plaid button-down shirt, and I didn't want to look anymore. I wore my glasses every day, and lost them a few times like kids do, and got them slapped off my face a few times like kids do, and ate dirt and had to leap and whine to get them back from a kid two heads taller than I like kids do, and I never, ever imagined or pictured myself as wearing glasses, till I was in high school and daydreamed about fucking Alyssa with the tight heart-shaped ass and a big Jewish nose that made her seem accessible. In those wanky dreams, glasses were all I was wearing.

So when I see the husky guy behind Paulo, the guy with a few bruises and glasses and scraggly hair and a cheap shave, he looks familiar but I don't realize that he's the ass at the bottom of my glass seven nights a week. He's me. The canary gets it. "You got a brother?" she asks.

"No," the me behind Paulo's shoulder says. "He doesn't." I peer at Paulo and can't help but smile. He smiles too. It's like TV. Then hallway-me smiles too. We look at one another meaningfully, and get ready to say the same thing:

"Grow a Vandyke!"

And we laugh and the guy on the floor stirs and grumbles and Paulo suddenly blanches and the canary's bracelets rattle on her thin black arms and we all decide at once to get the fuck out of here. "Your place," the he-who-is-me says, but he doesn't mean me, he means the canary. "I need to hang this in your closet," he says,

"My apartment doesn't have a closet," I say.

"Mine neither," says Paulo.

"How do you guys know that I have a closet?" the canary wants to know.

I open my mouth to start to explain but I beat myself to

it. "You wear too many clothes for you not to have a closet, plus you live in a front apartment and they're a little larger, so there is room for a closet—"

"And you moved in three months ago, and four months ago the previous tenant in your apartment didn't pay rent for two months, but he also wasn't dragged out by a fist up his asshole by the landlady on the first of the month, and he had a union card, so he probably traded some carpentry for rent—" I say, interrupting.

"And you pay a grand a month in rent," says Paulo, "so your apartment is better."

"What do you guys pay?" she asks.

"Five seventy-five," we all tell her as one, and now she is really pissed.

*   *   *

The canary's apartment is nicer. Her hardwood floors are thin and tasteful planks, not big slabs of red-painted and warped boards. She has a newer tub, with claw feet, and a full-size oven. Her two-room studio really has two rooms and not just a space behind the tub for a bed. Her closet used to be the water closet. There are two new walls on the far end of her kitchen; probably the new toilet and sink sit behind them. And her closet is full of sparkling thongs on hangers, and plastic tubs of clothes. Canary is stripping her way through school, except that there isn't a book in the house, not even under the bed, so she's not in school anymore. I hang up the statue Paulo's mother gave me, and go back to sit at the table with Paulo and the me who never left the apartment last night.

"It's the toxoplasmosis," the canary was saying. "That's why Galluzzi killed Mama S."

"Galluzzi? Mama S.? You knew them? You talk to people and learn their names," I say. Not me, the dirty, sick me. Hair like a batch of leaves. Crust on his lips and around his eyes. His knee jiggles and his voice is hollow. He's not drinking his tea, because he doesn't like tea, but the canary insisted on serving him because he's sick.

"I know everyone's name here," she says, "except for you." And she looks at me, sitting down, when she says that. We're all around her little plastic table now. She has three chairs, for us, and she sits on the radiator, over a towel so she won't burn her ass.

"Good," I say, and the guy who looks just like me nods. Paulo keeps his lips shut too.

"Thanks for having us," the other guy says, between sips of tea. "Let's just try to figure out what happened."

"With who?" asks Paulo. "The old lady? The wop? You two."

"Or everyone in the city who is going so crazy?" says the canary.

"That much we know, I think. *Toxoplasma gondii*, a new breed of parasite driving people crazy. 'Stay in your homes, stay away from cats or vermin,'" I say, doing a pretty good impression of that generic newscaster voice, sonorous yet empty, for that last bit.

"I don't have a twin," says the other me. "Neither do I," I tell him. "But I have an alibi. Witnesses. Paulo." The other me looks at Paulo hungrily, but Paulo remains inscrutable. Finally Paulo says, "We can work this out, or not. If not, it's the work of the spirits, like my mother said. Souls separated from their bodies, ridden by the gods, from the world beyond—"

"Okay, let's work it out," says the other me quickly. I kind of like him after all, despite his fatness and sniveling and the way he keeps glancing over at the canary and then when she makes eye contact quickly shifts his gaze to the high ceilings or the boring art—a white canvas with a crooked black circle and a stripe of orange—on the wall.

"Oh, should I be the secretary?" says the canary. She's dripping with sarcasm, but isn't so brave after all, as she hustles to the fridge and grabs the little whiteboard and marker anyway, wiping it clean with her forearm of all things. She's into it, really. "Where were you guys on the night of the thirty-first?"

"With Paulo, watching TV."

"And you guys had baseball bats," she says.

"So?"

"So you were looking to beat the shit out of somebody," the other me says, "and you guys did. Galluzzi, the wop. You must be infected."

"No, we were planning on hitting the landlady hard," Paulo explains. The canary jerks like the heat from the radiator finally ate through the towel. The other me says, "Heh, we always talked about doing that. Funny though that only last night you—" he looks at me, "— or should I say *we* actually tried to carry it out." Back to Paulo, "Whose idea was it to finally do it?"

"Yours. I mean, uh his," Paulo says, nodding toward me.

He is silent for a minute, thinking. I can read his mind, I'm sure of it. Yeah, obviously he thinks I'm the fake, the guy from the mirror universe with the beard and the sexy spaceship. "Doesn't sound like me," he says. "Sounds like work." The canary snorts at that. "How's this for a theory?"

And he explains that maybe *toxoplasma gondii*, which is after all mutating in some horrific ways—the murder right downstairs, the chaos in the streets (albeit magnified immensely by the screeching TV and the diabolical *New York Post*, with its controversial headline of BUGF***!) show that to be the case—could be mutating in some other way as well. Nucleic exchange, infecting the DNA, not only changing the behavior of an individual, but perhaps his appearance as well. I am, *he is* ill. Perhaps an infection with the little buggers gone horribly wrong, and he's been sick for a few days with only the fever dreams and news radio soundtrack to keep him comfortable.

But maybe he coughed something up. Maybe some guy was rooting through the trash down below and came across a plastic bag from the grocery store, but filled with soiled TP instead of discarded food or anything that might be saleable for crack. And that guy had an open sore, or maybe he was immunosuppressed from AIDS or just hard living in the chilly winter and pissed-up subway tunnels of downtown, and he got infected too. But somehow, in some hideous black box of a way, the infection didn't just change some of the chemicals in his brain, but almost all of them, creating a new past, maybe even a new face. Skin cells shed and are reformed differently; there's a fire in the belly and the guy goes crazy eating anything he can get his hands on — garbage, crescents of Big Macs, slow rats and dying birds — for a protein to fuel his metamorphosis into a doppelganger of the man with whose genetic material he had come into contact. This new man, in a face he never knew, swimming in the memories and desires of a life he never lived, sought out his home. Paulo couldn't know that this old friend was a few days before some hobo or street kid with a broadly similar facial structure and a habit of dumpster-diving, so of course he'd go undetected.

"Oh yeah," Paulo says. "How did he get your clothes?"

"He's wearing a black sweatshirt and black jeans. Half the people in town dress just like him," says the canary. We all look at her. "What, do you think you lot are the only ones who notice the things around them, who take little mental notes? Especially about clothes." She says to me, not to *him* but to me, "You always dressed like you wanted to be unseen, anonymous. Camouflage for neighborhood strolls, and your little kiddie spy games." The sick guy coughs. The canary snorts, "You don't even know the names of everyone in the building."

Paulo speaks for the first time in a while. "Okay, let's say that the story is right. How do we know that the guy with me on my couch this morning is the infected one, especially if the other guy is sick. And who *was* the first guy, before this inexplicable metamorphosis?"

"Someone in the building, I'd think," says the other me. "Someone picking around the garbage would probably have to live here. There's no easy way to the back lot, except through the building, and, let's face it, 157 Rivington's garbage heap is no prize. Not worth it to break into, or to find access to some other roof, stroll across the tar beach, and then chute-and-ladder one's way down the fire escapes."

"Who's missing?" asks the canary. "Amongst the tenants?"

"Nobody," I say. "All the rent checks were still in the mail drop nailed to the interior to the door in the vestibule downstairs. If my little double was in my apartment all night sweating off some sick, then there would be one fewer rent check down there."

"Is everyone in the building living alone? No roommates, no kids? Anyone could send down a rent check in some kid's hand."

"No kids," Paulo said. "And lazy roommates, if there are any—and there aren't—aren't going to be taking down the garbage."

"I don't remember anyone doubling up recently. I'm on the second floor," the guy says. "I hear everyone and everything."

"So do I," I say. He makes a face at me. My face. "Anyway, I have another concept. It's not the toxo; that doesn't even make any sense. I'm sure it breaks some laws of physics or something. That's not science, that's late-late-movie crap. Maybe we're not identical. Maybe we just kind of look alike, and you came across me somehow. When I was in community college, I had other kids coming up to me all the time to ask me biology questions. I looked just like some adjunct instructor. It happens. So, who are you, where are you from?"

"Good questions," he says. "You answer them."

I'm about to, and he's about to say something fucking obnoxious—Christ, how do people stand me?—when the lights go out.

FIFTEEN

He opens his mouth—*Is that what I look like when I talk, jowly and reedy at the same time?*—just as I'm about to say one more thing, and somebody cuts the lights. His name, my name, is strangled by his yawp of surprise. It's dark, but not pitch. I can smell Paulo, sweating pot smoke and agitated, and the canary's heels start clicking. She goes to the stove and turns on a burner; I hear the clicking, but there's nothing. Paulo's cell phone glows in the dark too. "No service," he says.

"No lights, no gas, no cell phone," I say. "Major blackout."

"Oh God, terrorists," says the canary, then she goes diving into the dark, looking for something, probably a transistor radio.

"Or toxoplasmodic lunatics," he says. I don't know if toxoplasmodic is a word, but I get a charge out of hearing it.

The canary has a radio, but it just shuff-shuffs with static. "Nothing! Why would all the stations get knocked out?"

"Try AM," says Paulo. "Even if the local stations are knocked out, you would still get distant stations from Boston, even from Florida."

"Could be the big antenna atop the Empire State Building," I tell her. "Lots of FM and broadcast TV stations use it to beam their signals downtown, and into Brooklyn. If that got knocked out—"

"Terrorists hit the Empire State Building!" she concludes, a bit too readily.

"A major blackout could cause all of these things," my voice says from across the table. "Or even a single loony with an axe. I wonder if they got the Internet too." About a decade ago, I was obsessed with an idea of heading down to the meatpacking district and finding that thick trunk of fiber optics that some guy who used to live here piped into the whole of the 'net onto the island of Manhattan. I'm sure a decade on, there are many more points of entry, and wireless. An invisible world, buzzing all around us. Maybe...

Toxoplasmosis. It's a dumb theory. Nothing in evolution could make a parasite make such a leap from the bad craziness to vat-free cloning. But what else could it be? A twin wouldn't know any of the shit I know, not even someone who broke into my home and read my journal, or who spent months watching me. No FBI profiler could have come up with "toxoplasmoid." He's me.

There is an invisible world, and it is all around us. Paulo was right. Spirits. Somehow, in my fever I summoned up this man, this me. What does he want? In mythology, doubles are never good news. Changelings replacing babies, the Jungian shadow always on the edge of consciousness, prodding the self toward destruction. There's only one thing to do. Eliminate the impossible and only the improbable remains. Eliminate the improbable and the impossible remains. He is that which remains.

A light comes on, white and frosty, from a flashlight. He's holding it. No, I'm holding it. I remember now, it was on the fridge, held there by a magnet. Even the canary had forgotten about it, panicked as she is—she's muttering at the radio now, and shaking it in her hands as though she can make some talk radio fascist in Ohio hang up on his latest caller and get to the national news. He swings the light away from her and points it at me.

You watch mysteries on TV and if the script is hardboiled enough and the lead actor has a chin like a big ol' shoe or at least trench coat shoulders you'll see this scene. A door opens in the dark. Maybe it's a cellar; maybe it's the trunk of a car, or a manhole cover. Fog and dust swirls about as the sleuth holds up a great big flashlight and peers into the nothingness.

But he's not peering into the nothingness, is he? Hell, that joker's not even looking at some secretary, all tied up in nylons and a short skirt, a gag in her mouth so sexy. Not some corpse with a map or amulet clutched in its stiff hand.

He's looking at you. And you stare on back, into the light, wondering what it is he sees.

Paulo stands up and looms large over us.

SIXTEEN

"Oh my God!"

"I had to do it," Paulo says.

The lights are on again, down on the Lower East Side and on the Manhattan and Brooklyn bridges. Most of midtown is still dark, as is Jersey. We're on the roof. The canary is shivering, her face a rictus of rage and confusion. I'm covered in blood. My own blood, though it's not from my body. The other is at my feet, wrapped in what used to be the canary's favorite set of sheets, I'm sure. Egyptian cotton.

"Oh my God!" she says again, but this time a deflated balloon. She's a broken woman now, this canary. Tell the coalminers she's dead and that they'd all better stay on the north side of Houston Street. But she's not dead, I am.

"How did you know to kill...this one?"

Paulo says, "What makes you think I knew? I just had to eliminate the impossible. It didn't really matter which of you it was, as long as you both knew the same exact things and lived in the same exact way." He's messing with the statue. It's bloody, like the man in the sheet.

"Oh my God," said the canary again.

"So, what do we do with the body?"

"Leave it here," says the canary. "Oh my God, I can't believe this. Just fucking leave it up here. Let it get snowed on all winter, get all soggy and bloated. Nobody ever comes up here. There aren't even any TV aerials up here anymore. Nobody will tan in a lawn chair up here in the summertime." Then she says "Oh my God," again, because the Empire State Building, a middle finger in the dark city, has just lit up.

"Not bad," Paulo says, stepping up to her, the statue now in both hands but behind his back like a surprise bouquet of flowers, or a hammer. "It looks nice." Paulo isn't slick; he still tries to get chicks the way a twelve-year-old kid might. But there's something different about him. The statue, the blood.

Paulo, *my* Paulo isn't like that. He's a sweet guy. He likes his weed and his TV and loves his mama and when it snows he tells the same story about being so jealous of the kids upstate and on Long Island where they closed the schools, because they never close here in the city. "Ed Koch," he says every single time, "he was more like Ed Cock." The snow up here on the roof is white as noon except for where we three stepped, and where my double was dragged. There it's a snake of red and black.

Toxoplasma gondii, it must have gotten to him. That's why he had that urge to kill, and that's why he's with the canary now. Killing and fucking are so much alike, all flailing and screams and sometimes blood. And sometimes something new. A baby, or a new world born on the billion bodies that make up the rotten earth of the old world.

That's when I realize—*I can't do this anymore*. And I don't have to. I was gone for so long, in the blackness of my head, or the fevers of my bed. Nothing needs eliminating. I can pick and choose where I want to go, who I want to be. Like that man who dreamed he was a butterfly, only to one day be struck by the realization that he was really a butterfly who once dreamt he was a man. Can I wake up and be thrilled that this was all just a dream? The sweet relief of losing your teeth, even feeling them on your tongue, but then jerking awake and you've got them back. Counting them in the dark. The canary is crying. Paulo stands close to her, looming as he did in her kitchen, when he painted her little plastic table like it was a Jackson Pollock original.

I can do it. I stare at the silhouette under the blanket. The mountain range of me. The crying stops. Paulo is shuffling his feet; I can hear the snow crunching under his Timberlands. I inhale, exhale, and then feel the sheets wrapped around me, the draft of winter in the hole in my head. Organs dead in my meat.

The canary says "Oh my God," one more time. It doesn't matter how many people he brains with his mother's statue, there's a fact that cannot be smashed here. There's me, standing here, and me, the same exact me, on the ground, dead. Whatever we thought we knew about the world, we didn't. You can eliminate the improbable all you want, but you can never kill the impossible. The corpse at my feet moans and shudders, hot gas meeting cold city. Paulo turns at the noise and I look up at him. The girl does too, unaware of how close she came to hitting the streets.

And then I turn into white moths and fly away.

BOREALIS
Ronald Damien Malfi

ONE

Twelve years ago, a man named Bodine checked into a Las Vegas motel under the name Thomas Hudson with a young girl who was of no relation to him. She was a pretty little thing, perhaps eight or nine years of age, dressed plainly in a simple cotton dress embroidered with tiny red strawberries around the waist. To glance casually upon the pair, one would assume they were father and daughter. But on closer inspection, anyone with a knack for detail would see that the man was no one's father. Tall, gaunt, haunted — looking at him was like staring infinity in the face. With his black, hopeless eyes recessed into deep pockets and an air of chronic fatigue surrounding him like a cloud of Midwestern dust, this man was no one's father.

"What's wrong?" the girl said. "Why did we stop?"

Bodine's grip tightened on the Bronco's steering wheel. The sodium lights from the motel fell against the Bronco's windshield. A light rain had begun to fall.

"We're getting a room here," he said, his voice low. "We're staying here for the night."

The girl leaned toward the dashboard to peer out the

windshield. She wasn't wearing her seat belt. "Looks dirty," she said, sizing up the motel.

It was one of a million nameless joints he'd passed on the drive from the mountains of Colorado and across the equally anonymous desert highways. There was nothing distinguishable about it. After a while, on the road, everything started to look the same.

"We call this comfortable digs," he said.

"What's that mean?"

"Means we stay here tonight." He shut the car down and popped open the door. Paused. "You wait here," he said, an afterthought.

"Can I play the radio?"

He didn't think there was any harm leaving the keys in the ignition. Unless she'd been lying, judging by her simple questions about what the pedals on the floor were for and why he had to turn a key in order to start the "growling," as she called it, he didn't think she knew how to start the vehicle let alone drive away in it. Bodine turned the switch over until the door chimes sounded. The girl, whose name Bodine did not know, smiled and switched on the radio. One tiny white hand ran through the dials until she located an oldies station while Bodine watched.

"How come you need to turn the key to play the radio?" she asked now.

"Because it runs off the car's battery. I need to turn it on to use the battery."

"Cars have batteries?" She sounded almost incredulous.

"Yes."

"Is that how they drive?"

"They drive on gasoline."

"Like from the last time we stopped," she said. "How you put it into the gas tank, like you said."

"Yes." He suddenly felt like an imbecile. What the hell was he doing talking to her like this, anyway?

"Are you going to shoot somebody?" the girl asked before he could step out of the Bronco. The statement caused him to freeze, caused the fingers of his left hand to tighten on the door handle.

"Why would you say something like that?"

"Because you have a gun in your pants."

His throat was lined with sandpaper. "How do you know that?"

The girl didn't answer.

"How do you know that?" he repeated, one foot out on the blacktop, his fingers still strangling the door handle.

The girl just smiled and stared straight ahead out the windshield. She swung her legs to the rhythm of the music, her face radiating a sickly glow beneath the wash of sodium lights. "I like this song," she said after a bit.

The motel lobby was rundown, filthy, and haunted by cigarette smoke. A flickering black-and-white television was mounted to the wall on brackets behind the night counter.

"One room," Bodine said at the counter. "One night."

"Just you?" said the grizzled cowboy behind the counter. No stranger to midnight characters of peculiar design, the cowboy did not give Bodine a second glance. And that was just fine by Bodine.

"Just me," Bodine said.

"Name?"

"Thomas Hudson," said Bodine.

"Credit card?"

"Cash," he told the cowboy, who did not raise an eyebrow.

The room was tomblike. Peeling alabaster walls and an oatmeal-colored carpet, the single bed, wide as a coffin, was dressed in a fleur-de-lis spread, heavily starched. The bathroom reeked of mildew, the shower curtain itself curled at one end of the shower into a filthy plastic sleeve. In the tub, a bristling brown spider did pushups by the drain.

"It smells bad in here," said the girl, wrinkling her nose. "Gross." She stood clutching the empty cardboard cylinder that had moments ago contained a milkshake.

"Go turn down the bed," he told her, carrying his nylon

duffel bag into the bathroom. He sat it beside the sink and unzipped it. Inside: fresh sneakers and a change of clothes. Brand spanking new. The sneakers were too bright and the clothes still had the tags hanging from them.

The girl did not move. She watched him through the open bathroom doorway. When he turned and saw her staring at him he nearly jumped out of his skin.

"Thought I told you to go turn down the bed," he said, his voice quiet and level. Nearly monotone.

The girl shrugged and stepped away. A moment later, he heard the mattress springs creak.

A skeleton stared back at him from the mirror. *Jesus Christ, is that me? Is that really me?* He grimaced, inspecting the way his purplish gums had begun to recede from his teeth, the teeth themselves discolored and patchy with calcium deposits.

Bodine peered out into the room. The girl had turned down one corner of the bed and was now sitting on the edge, staring directly at him. She'd set her empty cup down on the nightstand.

"Did you want another milkshake?" he said. His voice shook. *Stop it,* he thought. *Stop it, stop it, stop it.*

"Why did you tell the man at the counter your name was Thomas Hudson?"

Sweat stung his eyes. "There's a soda machine down the hall. Do you want a Coke?"

"Your name's not Thomas Hudson," she said, swinging her legs.

"I don't like playing these games."

"What games?"

"These games where you ask all these questions and expect me to answer."

The girl shrugged her small shoulders. "Your name's Frank Bodine," she said.

Bodine swallowed a hard lump of spit. Seconds ticked by. His own heartbeat was like a drum in his ears. "How do you know my name?" he said finally. He'd never told her.

Again, the girl shrugged.

"Yes," he said after a moment, blinking the sweat from his eyes. "Yes, my name's Bodine. Frank Bodine." Sour, shaky exhalation. "You think you're ready to tell me your name yet?"

The girl shook her head. Grinned.

"Why not?"

"I told you," she said simply. "I don't have a name."

"Yes you do. Everyone's got a name."

"Nope. Not me."

"Sure you do. You just don't want to tell it."

"You're silly," said the girl.

"What about your parents? Didn't they give you a name?"

"I don't have any parents."

"You don't have a mom or a dad?"

"No."

"Everyone does."

"No, silly." She giggled.

Withdrawing back into the bathroom, Bodine toed the bathroom door shut. He lifted his pullover up, which stank of perspiration. The butt of the 9mm protruded from his waistband.

Can you do this? a voice spoke up toward the back of his head. It was the same voice that had followed him all the way from Durango. *Are you really sure you can do this?*

He plucked the 9mm from his waistband, set it down beside the duffel bag, and turned the water on in the sink. Just the hot water. He waited as the entire bathroom steamed up before shutting the water off. With one hand he carved an arc through the condensation on the mirror before him. Dead eyes stared back.

Can you do this?

Bodine removed his pullover and tossed it on the floor. Took a deep breath. A chill accosted him, pimpling his flesh with goose bumps. Grabbing the handgun, he eased open the bathroom door and stepped out into the room.

The girl hadn't moved. She grinned at him as he took a single step toward the bed. His nostrils flared with each inhalation of breath. He stood unmoving no more than ten feet from her, peripherally aware that the digital clock on the night stand counted through several minutes while he simply stood there.

"You're skinny," she said after a while. "Your chest has red marks on it." She said, "I can see your ribs." As if this was funny, she giggled. Said, "Your bellybutton looks funny." Legs still swinging.

"Tell me who you are," he breathed. Leveled the gun at her. His hand shook. His whole fucking arm shook. "Tell me."

"Your hair," she said, wrinkling up her nose as if she suddenly smelled something awful—the room itself, perhaps. "It's too long. Like a girl's."

He lowered his arm. The 9mm suddenly weighed fifty pounds. Without a word, he turned and retreated back into the bathroom. He felt cold, clammy, made of vulcanized rubber. The soles of his work boots creaked with each step.

In the bathroom, he set the gun down in the sink basin, which was still streaked with water. Staring up at his reflection, he thought the girl was right—that somewhere along the way, his hair *had* gotten too long. Like a girl's.

Wearily, Bodine grinned at himself. Skeleton-faced, too-big teeth protruding from retreating purple gums...

Can you—

Grinned.

Next morning, a Puerto Rican housekeeper would discover Bodine's body in the bathtub, a dried spray of blood on the tiled shower stall behind his head. Bodine's hand, still limply holding the 9mm, was nestled into the thatch of black pubic hair between his legs.

The woman's screams would bring the grizzled cowboy who would in turn alert the local sheriff. Suicide, the sheriff would say, and the grizzled cowboy would nod while he chewed on an unlit cigar stub no longer than a grown man's thumb and greenish in color, and would recall nothing special about the man from the night before. There were all breeds of stranger that passed through his place, after all—all species of outlaw and lummox and daft buffoon—and who could remember one from the other?

"Name's Hudson," the cowboy would tell the sheriff, handing over the log from last night where the man had signed in. The sheriff, a grizzled old cowboy in his own right, took the log without so much as a grunt while fishing out a pack of menthols from his nylon coat with the faux fur at the collar.

There was no sign of the little girl. But, of course, no one had seen her come in with the man and therefore never knew to look for her.

Anyway, that was twelve years ago, and in a whole other part of the country.

TWO

After seven days of futility—

"So fucking cold my goddamn lighter's giving up the ghost," Charlie Mears said, chasing the tip of his cigarette with a tarnished Zippo. His cold, gray eyes leveled out over the vast nothingness of charcoal waters and icy strata from over the bow of the trawler. The air was cold and sharp, only vaguely scented by the trawler's diesel exhaust. Each inhalation burned his nostrils.

Beside him, hugging himself in his bright orange slicker with the hood up, "Dynamo" Joe Darling offered nothing but a grunt.

"What's your vibe on *el capitán?*" Charlie said, exhaling smoke out over the bow. The trawler was at a crawl now yet the wind still stung his chapped face.

"Think he's got a good eye for snailfish, is what I think," muttered Joe. Charlie could tell he was shivering in his orange slicker without looking at his face.

"The rest of the guys are getting restless, too," Charlie said, though it didn't need to be said. He was a big, broad-shouldered guy, square-jawed with a salt and pepper beard tinged with copper strands. Creases splayed from the corners of his black eyes: years spent wincing through the glare of the sun off the water. "Look at that," he added, nodding toward the bleed over pastels beyond the horizon as the sun dipped into the Bearing Sea. "Something, eh?"

"I got bills to pay," Joe went on, unimpressed. "I got two mortgages, Charlie."

The crew hadn't seen a single blue since disembarking from Saint Paul Island one week ago. The captain was Mike Fenty, fairly new to the red circuit, though he'd carved out a name for himself going after walleye and sablefish. Crabs, however, were a different story. While he wouldn't say so to anyone on board, it was Charlie's distinct impression that *el capitán* was in over his head.

"You think you'd get used to seeing the sun go down out here," Charlie said. "But I never do. It's fine in the daytime, but at night it's like God and the rest of the world forgets about you. Left behind, like some kid in a grocery store."

"Got three kids at home, Charlie, countin' on me." There was no shaking "Dynamo" Joe. Anyway, he was right.

"Christ," Charlie grunted, flipping his half-smoked cigarette over the bow. "We'll give him two more days before suggesting we reassign coordinates."

"There's nothing out here," Joe said. "There's us and God and nothing else."

"Not God, either. He's somewhere else at the moment. Too damn cold for him."

"The blues are laughin' at us."

"Two more days," Charlie repeated, hugging himself now as night fell over frozen arctic wastes.

THREE

But it wouldn't take two days: early the next morning, while the sky was still black and the stars as bright as fireworks, the crew of the *Borealis* struck gold. What they called space-spiders. Moon-bugs.

During the night, Captain Fenty had wound the trawler through a section of black water alongside the Kula Plate, the wind so harsh and unforgiving the sea spray kicked up by the trawler would freeze in under a second. The giant steel pots were lowered by the great hydraulic arm, which seemingly grunted in protest, and a breakfast of warm oatmeal and watery coffee was served below deck. Each of them still half-asleep, they ate their oatmeal and sipped their coffee like zombies, undedicated to their roles, their broad and heavy bodies swaddled in long johns and flannel underwear. Pulling on their gear after breakfast, the sun still brightening some other part of the world, they climbed topside and set the arm to work again, this time hoisting the pots, which were giant steel cages that weighed 800 pounds each. The first pot ascended from the black waters alive with bristling, clattering crabs, scores of them, nearly to the top of the cage. There sounded a united cheer from the deck. The pot was hoisted over the side and onto the deck where Billy McEwan and a young greenhorn named Sammy Walper each grabbed one side to stabilize it.

"Jesus Lord!" Joe shouted, clapping his rubberized gloves together. "Jesus in a propeller hat!"

Charlie shot a glance at the pilothouse windows, which were beaded with ice and grimy with diesel sludge. He raised one hand to Fenty and Fenty raised one in return.

"They're reds! All of 'em!" shouted McEwan. "A pretty fucking penny better'n blues!"

Charlie and another deckhand, Bryan Falmouth, bent and grabbed the handles of the tank lid that was impressed into the trawler's deck. Each of them grasping a wrought-iron ring, Charlie said, "Ready?"

Falmouth nodded. "Do it."

"One…two…three!"

The lid was hoisted on angry, squealing joints.

"Ha ha!" Joe was still stomping and clapping on the deck.

The pot was opened and the crabs were dumped across the deck. Immediately, the sound of the bone-thick, segmented legs chattering along the planking was like a wave of applause, their enormous, grotesque bodies clambering over one another, abbreviated pincers raised and snapping, biting at the freezing air and, more often, at one another.

They set to work sizing the crabs and examining their sexes, mostly by sight—a quick glance of appraisal, no more than a second and a half long—though occasionally one would have to be lifted and examined and judged before tossing it either into the under-deck holding tank or over the trawler's side back into the sea.

"This ugly bastard's a new pair o' bowling shoes," Joe shouted, holding one of the giant reds with two hands. He was grinning from ear to ear—Joe, not the crab. Bending down and planting a kiss on the top of the creature's carapace, Joe flung it down into the tank and quickly scooped up another. "And this 'ere one's a flat-screen TV!" To the crab, which was raising and lowering its legs with a mechanical, hydraulic quality, Joe muttered, "How you gonna like that, you ugly son of a bitch?"

Sammy Walper the greenhorn laughed and kicked one of the crabs down into the hatch soccer-style.

Most were keepers; they threw back very few. And once they'd finished, Captain Fenty brought the trawler around to another buoy and they repeated the process over again. This went on until lunchtime.

Nearing dusk, they reran the circuit and dumped the traps overboard, scattering a trail of neon buoys in the ship's wake. Having worked up monstrous appetites, the rest of the crew descended below deck to the galley quarter where Walper the greenhorn would be coerced into whipping up fried eggs and ham while everyone got drunk on

"Dynamo" Joe's vodka. Blood-caked lips, splitting and chapped, with eyes like black pools…everyone stinking of codfish guts and dense with perspiration…

Charlie did not join them right away. He remained topside, his joints and muscles aching pleasantly, digging out a pack of menthols from within his overcoat.

"Whatcha smokin'?" Mike Fenty said, coming up behind him. He was a distinguished-looking guy, particularly for out here in this ungodly void — of good height and symmetrically-featured, his close-cropped hair silvered at the temples. His eyes were lucid and a shade of blue that recalled Caribbean waters. Had that George Clooney appeal with the ladies back in Anchorage.

"Hey, Mike."

"Here," Mike said, extending him a cigar as black as demitasse. "Try this. Helps you settle down."

"Thanks."

Mike produced a second cigar for himself and together they bit off the tips and spat them into the water. The trawler was idling down a chasm of banded gray sea, bookended on either side by thin crusts of ice. Off to the north, the silhouette of an iceberg loomed like the spinal column of some giant prehistoric skeleton. Even in the oncoming darkness Charlie could make out the black specks of seal pups nesting along the rookeries.

Mike lit Charlie's cigar for him and Charlie pulled on it a number of times, working up good passage. It was strong like coffee and tasted good. Charlie exhaled a jet of cigar smoke into the air. "Nice," he said.

Mike leaned over the ship's rail. His lucid eyes watched the sun sink down beyond the backbone ridge of the iceberg. "Listen, Charlie," he said. "I want to thank you."

"For what?"

"I'm not an idiot and I'm not deaf. I know there's been talk all week. Was starting to prep myself for mutiny."

"Don't be ridiculous."

"Nothing ridiculous about it." Mike squeezed one of his shoulders. "You're a good friend, man. I appreciate you keeping the wolves at bay, giving me a chance." Mike turned and stared at the glow of the lamps coming through the pilothouse windows. His face partially masked in shadows and outlined in the glow of the sunset, he said, "They're all good guys, all of 'em. I'm glad today was a good day. We needed a good day." Mike plucked the cigar from his mouth and examined the glowing ember at its tip. "Anyway, I wanted to thank you for sticking up for me with the guys."

"Forget about it," Charlie said, looking back over the darkened waters. "We been friends for a while, ain't we? Was nothing."

A comfortable silence settled between them. After a while, Mike said, "You hear anything from Gabe? From Johanna?"

Charlie closed his eyes. "Been a long time."

"You ever call that lawyer? The guy from Fairbanks?"

"Three times."

"And?"

"And there's nothing I can do. No court's gonna make her bring him back to Alaska and I sure as shit ain't gonna get full custody."

"Where are they now? Do you even know?"

He didn't know, not for sure. The last conversation he'd had with Johanna, she and Gabriel were somewhere outside Omaha, holed up in some flea-infested roadside motel, Johanna angry and yelling at him until she finally started crying. In the background, he had heard Gabriel crying, too, and calling for him. *Daddy-Daddy-Daddy* — he could still hear it, echoing out over the ether. In his hand he could still feel the telephone receiver, pushing hard against his ear as Johanna's yelling came through all too clear. All of this: flashes of memory going off like mind-grenades, the images so vivid they singed the filaments of his brain.

But he couldn't say all of that to Mike Fenty. Instead, he kept his eyes focused on the mottled neon hues of the setting sun spilling over the ice floe and trickling down into the black sea. To Mike he said, "She's got no family to stay with, Mike. Nobody I could contact. She and Gabe could be anywhere." The *Borealis* canted to one side as sheets of ice broke apart beneath its bow, the sound like glass being crushed beneath heavy boots. In the distance, covered now in deepening darkness, the seal pups barked at the moon. "This is my last trip out, Mike. Just wanted you to know that."

"Jesus, Charlie, what are you talking about?"

"I can't keep doin' this."

"You're just talkin' foolish."

"Been thinkin' about tryin' to find 'em. Go out lookin' for 'em."

"But you said it yourself, Charlie — they could be anywhere in the country. How you gonna find them? Ain't got a chance in hell."

"Better chance than bein' out here."

"And even if you did find them, it won't change nothing. She still won't let you see him."

"She might. If I took a job nearby, something that kept me grounded without disappearing on the water for weeks or months at a time…"

"Bah," Mike groaned, turning away and looking out over the port side. "That's just happy-talk. You know it."

"Still gotta try."

"And what the hell will you do for a job, anyway? Teach goddamn physics at Harvard? This shit out here—" Mike Fenty opened his arms as if to embrace the world. "This shit is all you know, Charlie. She was wrong to want you to change and you'd be wrong changing."

He sucked hard at the cigar and said, through a mouthful of smoke, "Nothing wrong about goin' after my son, Mike. Nothing wrong with that at all."

Finally, Mike Fenty sighed. He relit his cigar and, after a few moments of silence between the two of them, said, "Yeah, I guess there ain't a damn thing in this world wrong with that."

They remained topside for several minutes more, burning the life from their cigars at equal speed, until Mike

Fenty clapped Charlie on the back and told him he was freezing his ass off and wanted to get some supper before Walper the greenhorn hit the sack.

"Don't stay out here too late, Charlie."

But Charlie hardly heard him. Blindly, without taking his eyes off the passing island of ice, he groped for Mike's coat, catching the captain around the forearm and tugging him back toward the rail.

"Charlie—"

"Jesus Christ," Charlie whispered. The cigar fell from his lips and silently dropped into the sea. "Holy mother of God..."

"Charlie, *what* — "

He jabbed a gloved finger at the icy barge. The trawler had sidled up alongside it in the encroaching night, so close Charlie could see the individual fissures in the ice, the moonlight casting a palette of shadows along the bluish ridge. They'd passed the seal rookeries some time ago, leaving their ghostly barking far off in the distance now. Still, there was movement out on the ice, movement—

"What the hell are you—" Mike began, peering through the darkness. The sun had fully set and there was nothing more to go on than the moonlight refracting off the snow.

"You see it?" Charlie said, his voice not rising above a whisper. "Holy fuck, man, you *see* it?"

"Can't be..."

"Holy—"

"*Can't*—"

A figure, most definitely human, darted along the nearest ridge of the iceberg. Legs pumping, arms like pistons, the black shape ran along the cusp of the snowy ridge until it climbed to the top, briefly silhouetting itself against the three-quarters moon. A second later the figure descended down the opposite side, vanishing from view. The trawler was close enough and the moonlight bright enough for Charlie to identify with little doubt actual *footprints* in the snow.

"Jesus Christ, Charlie, did you *see* that?" Mike's voice

was no louder than a croak. He was leaning over the ship's rail, gaping up at the ridge where the mysterious figure, only seconds ago, had been standing.

"It was a woman," Charlie said. "Did you see?"

"Charlie—"

Snapping from his daze, Charlie grabbed two fistfuls of Mike Fenty's coat and pried him away from the rail. "Get up behind the wheel and spin this barge around. She went down around the other side of the ridge."

Mike's eyes were as wide as hubcaps. "Christ, Charlie…" A crooked half-grin broke across his face. "How do you suppose…?"

"Go!" he barked, shoving Mike across the deck. Mike staggered for a couple of feet until he regained authority of his legs and began running for the pilothouse.

Charlie rushed to the port side of the trawler and nearly became entangled in a coil of line left haphazardly unspooled on the decking. He kicked the line off his boot and peered over the side of the ship, his heart beating heavy in his chest now. In the pilothouse, Mike Fenty had taken the wheel and was already bringing the *Borealis* around the side of the iceberg. As the ship navigated around a tongue of ice and dipped back close to the iceberg, Charlie was immediately overwhelmed by the enormity of the floe. From this side, beneath the bleeding moonlight, he could see the entire length of the iceberg. It nearly glowed with phosphoresce, the sloping ridges frozen into icefalls that bled directly into the sea. The ocean opened up—a blanket of tar whose surface glittered with jewels—and the *Borealis* chugged around the perimeter of the floe.

Charlie looked down. The port side of the trawler was cutting through a crust of ice. Any closer to the ice floe would put the boat at risk. He glanced up at the pilothouse, a triptych of paneled glass illuminated from within by smeary, tallow light. Mike's slender silhouette was clearly visible through the glass. Charlie held up one hand and Mike prodded the air horn—*maaaawh*—in acknowledgement.

The rest of the crew began filing out onto the deck. Joe hurried over to Charlie, still clinging to a half-eaten ham sandwich. "What in the name of holy hell are you two doin' out here?"

The trawler passed beneath the lee of a great cone of ice. The moon was wiped out, dousing the ship into darkness greater than a thousand midnights.

"There's someone out here," Charlie said. For whatever reason, he was still whispering. "There's someone out on the ice."

"What?" Joe cawed, incredulous. He perched himself along the rail and peered through the darkness at the looming iceberg. "Are you insane? And we're too close to this thing." Joe turned around and started waving his arms at the pilothouse. "Asshole's gonna pull a *Titanic!*"

"We're fine, we're fine," Charlie said, his breath coming in excited gasps now. He was staring through the dark, his eyes cutting through the undulating depths of the mountain of ice. The shadows appeared to be alive. If he looked at any particular place for too long, the landscape appeared to shift. He blinked and pressed the heels of his rubber gloves into his eye sockets.

Billy McEwan materialized beside Charlie. One of McEwan's large white hands closed around Charlie's left wrist. "The hell's going on, Charlie?"

"I saw someone on the ice. A woman."

"We can't be cutting this close to the ice, man. You know that." McEwan still had his wrist.

"Mike knows what he's doing." He yanked his wrist free and locked McEwan in a heavy stare. Billy McEwan stared back, his too-white face framed in a black, rubberized hood, the loose threads of his knitted cap spiraling down over his forehead. McEwan had spent a good chunk of his career as a pilot with the U.S. Fish and Wildlife Service out of Alaska until he got caught doing flyovers for poachers in his private Cessna. As a deckhand, McEwan was a strong and silent worker…but Charlie always got the feeling that the man resented his current lot in life and thought of the rest of the crew as no better than a mob of uneducated roughnecks.

McEwan's eyes pulled away, cutting out across the flank of ice. Charlie let his gaze linger just a bit longer, nothing more than a childish exercise in superiority of course, until he watched McEwan's eyes widen and his lips purse. A waft of cloudy vapor rose from between McEwan's lips and vaporized in the freezing air. Charlie swung back around and stared over the ice just as McEwan mumbled something unintelligible under his breath.

The figure reappeared down the opposite side of the ridge—just a black blur among a density of deep shadows.

"There's someone out there," Billy McEwan breathed.

"There!" Charlie yelled, waving again at Mike inside the pilothouse. He began pointing vigorously at the ridge. "There! There!"

The rest of the crew, including "Dynamo" Joe Darling, turned and stared at him as if he'd lost his mind.

Just then the trawler cleared the shadow of the icy spire and the three-quarters moon reappeared in the sky. Moonlight washed down the frozen slopes of the iceberg and spilled down to the frozen shores. The figure was illuminated coming down the ridge—white, glistening skin, athletic build, undeniably female. Smallish breasts capped in dark areolas were quite visible, as was the narrow thatch of dark pubic hair nestled between the V of her thighs.

"She's fucking *naked*," McEwan uttered. The incredulity of his statement would have been a cause for good laughter had the situation not been so absurd.

The young woman—for Charlie already decided she was somewhere in her early twenties—whipped her head around at the sight of the boat just as Mike turned on the floodlights. The entire wall of ice lit up like a dance floor, the mysterious young woman suddenly at center stage. She had long, dark hair, wet and plastered down against her shoulders, her skin glowing in a freezing sheen of icy water. Eyes large and black, she stared directly at the trawler's floodlights without wincing, frozen as if in spectacle without movement, her narrow little breasts quivering, her mouth opened in a partial snarl through which the vague gleam of teeth glowed.

Joe, Bryan Falmouth, and Sammy Walper dashed to the portside in unison, causing the 200-foot trawler to list to one side. All of them speechless, the only sound that could be heard above the chugging of the trawler's diesel engine was a commingling of raspy, exhausted breathing.

The young woman turned away from the floodlights, her hair whipping in a single frozen fantail from one shoulder to the other, and stared down the length of the ice floe. Then she turned back and stared at the men. By inches, the trawler crept closer to the edge of the ice floe. A second later, Mike cut the engine and the ship, following a heavy growl, went silent.

The girl collapsed into the snow, seemingly unconscious.

"Jesus," Joe gasped.

Charlie spun around and grabbed the coil of line that he'd nearly tripped over moments ago. He found the end and slipped it around his waist, tying a halfway decent lasso. Kicking out the length of line to relieve the tension, he was about to make sure the other end was firmly fastened to the hydraulic arm when Joe grabbed his shoulder and spun him around.

"The hell you doing, Charlie?"

"Going out there."

Joe blinked twice, shaking his head. "You've lost your mind or something?"

"Not unless I'm the only guy who sees a naked girl lying facedown in the ice."

"How—"

"Listen up," he said, stepping away from Joe and addressing the rest of the crew. Mike was already hurrying down the pilothouse steps, pulling his coat tighter around his waist. "I'm gonna go down there and grab her. Bryan and Sammy, you guys lower me out over the ice with the hydro arm then pull me back up when I give you the okay."

Bryan and Sammy just stared at him, equally dumbstruck.

"Whoa, whoa," McEwan said, raising both hands. "Calm down, hero. We ain't sending a man overboard tied to a goddamn piece of cable—"

"Is there a better idea?" Charlie returned.

"We've got grappling hooks down below," McEwan said. "Ain't nobody's life on the line. We yank her up and over with the hooks the way they used to yank people off stage in the old vaudeville days."

"Sure," Joe countered, "and we stab her full of holes in the process. Nice thinking."

"Neither one of you assholes is the captain," McEwan said, suddenly leveling his gaze on Mike Fenty. "What say you, Cap?"

Mike glanced over the side and down at the broken white form crumpled in the snow. Her skin had started to crystallize and turn blue. "Much as I don't like it," he said, "we'll send Charlie down. Dynamo's right—those grapping hooks'll turn her into a spaghetti strainer."

Charlie tightened the knot at his waist. "All right, then. Clock's ticking."

FOUR

In hardly no time at all, the hydraulic arm began to whir. Joe and Mike, positioned on either side of Charlie, steadied him as he stepped one foot up onto the narrow railing. As the hydraulic arm positioned itself at the proper angle, it began to raise Charlie up off the railing. Mike's fingers trailed down the length of Charlie's left leg while Joe took a step back, feeding the cable out over the side of the boat.

"Keep steady," Mike called up to him. "Try not to swing."

Thankfully, there was very little wind. Still, Charlie could feel the cold air seeping into every open pocket; he tried to hug himself against the chill, his teeth already beginning to rattle in his skull, as the hydro arm rotated out over the water. He looked down and saw his mirrored self in the glassy surface of the night waters. The hydro arm began to hiss as it extended itself out over the water and toward the floating island of ice. He could smell the gears burning. It seemed to go impossibly slow.

On deck, Mike raced back up to the control booth and manually swiveled the spotlight toward Charlie, catching him suspended in midair like a yoyo having run out of string. Slowly Charlie rotated in the beam of light, shielding his eyes with one gloved hand as he wheeled around to face the spotlight.

The arm jerked to a stop, causing Charlie to swing gently from side to side: a hypnotist's watch on a chain. "What happened?" he yelled. His eyes, which had been trained on the slight, pale form of the young woman sprawled on the ice, turned now to Sammy and Bryan back on deck. "The hell's going on?"

"It's fully extended!" Bryan called back, his hands cupped around his mouth.

Charlie looked down. The ice below was thin and gray, sloping gradually up toward the snowcapped mounds of ice that made up the first ridge of the massive floe. The boat, he knew, would be unable to get any closer.

He called back to Bryan, "Lower the arm!"

Bryan was clearly shaking his head. "No way! Ice is too thin! You'll go right through!"

"It'll hold!" he shouted back. Glancing down a second time, however, he had serious doubts…

"Bullshit!" Bryan returned. "We'll try to get closer!"

"Impossible," he called back. Mike was outside on the deck now, shaking his head as well. "Just lower me down." He added, "Slowly."

Bryan and Sammy exchanged a look. A second later, the gears above Charlie's head once again started to whir. He felt himself slowly descending, keeping his eyes locked on his all-weather boots. He could see water dripping from the boots and striking the ice below, already frozen. In his head he was already doing the math: he was a two hundred twenty-nine pound man with approximately forty pounds of gear on; below, the tongue of ice was maybe four inches thick…if he was lucky. He could have taken one of the grappling hooks, prodded the ice to test its strength, but he didn't want to make his fear a reality as the ice broke apart under the weight of the hook. He would just go ahead and do it the same way he'd done everything else in his thirty-nine years, including his relationship with Johanna all those years ago: he'd simply close his eyes and take a single step toward the abyss.

In fact, he realized his eyes were closed as he felt the world come up to meet the soles of his boots. He opened his eyes just as the hydraulic arm wheezed to a stop. He was standing perilously on the narrow peninsula of ice, conscious of the distribution of his weight equally between both feet. Above his head, the cable slid from the runner and spooled down around his feet. Back on the boat, Joe continued feeding slack.

Holding his breath, he took one step up the incline. Solid. He took another step—and a distant breaking sound echoed back to his ears, hardly perceptible yet as loud as the rumbling of a cement truck at the same time, causing him to freeze. He sucked cold air through his teeth. There was a hairline fissure in the ice running directly beneath his boot.

He looked away, focusing straight ahead. Backlit by the trawler's floodlights, Charlie's shadow, projected onto the iceberg itself, loomed enormous. Arms outstretched for balance, he crossed the finger of ice quickly then mounted the incline, dropping down on all fours to scurry up the slope. Behind him, he heard the cracking ice peel away from the floe. He turned to see chunks of gray ice float away on the inky waters.

"Perfect," he grunted.

Still on all fours, he spied the young woman's frail figure fallen slumped, face-first, in the snow. Maybe ten, twelve feet away. Mesmerized momentarily, he stared at one narrow buttock, the flesh so white it was almost translucent, before Joe's urgent cries sent him scrambling toward her.

Sitting up on his knees, he touched one of her shoulders and rolled her on her back. Her head lolled, filled with ball bearings. Charlie gasped. Her eyes were still open, milky and cataract-blind. Her thin lips had purpled and split in the cold; blood from open sores had frozen in spidery calligraphy down her chin. She wasn't breathing.

"Come on, hon." He managed to hoist the girl up in his arms while standing simultaneously. She was as light as an empty husk, her arms and legs already beginning to stiffen. He shouted out to the *Borealis* and Bryan Falmouth gave him a thumb's-up. A second later, the mechanical hoist reeled the extra cable up into the hydraulic arm, pulled the rope taut. Charlie hugged the girl against him, squeezing his own eyes shut. The rope around his waist tightened and pulled up. The cable was set at an angle, causing him to swing violently the moment his boots lifted off the ground. Keeping his eyes shut, holding tight to the girl's rigid body, he felt his stomach lurch with the swinging of the rope. On deck, a couple of the guys cried out and someone told Bryan to steady the rope, steady the rope, steady the fucking rope.

The arm retracted and swiveled over the deck, dangling Charlie and the girl like two fish caught on a line. Overzealous, Sammy Walper struck the release too early and sent Charlie and the girl crashing to a sopping wet heap on the floor of the deck.

The girl's stiff body sprang from Charlie's arms and rolled like a mannequin away from him. Scrambling backward on his hands and feet, Charlie slammed his back against Joe's legs. Joe reached down and tweaked his ear, clapped him on one cheek.

"She's not breathing," Charlie said, struggling for breath himself. "I don't know CPR."

McEwan dropped to one knee over the girl. He reached

down to roll her over on her back but jerked away the moment his fingers touched her bare flesh, as if shocked by a current of electricity.

"What? What?" Joe yelled.

"She's freezing," said McEwan.

"And not breathing," Charlie said again, struggling to his feet. Joe helped him, slinging one arm around his shoulder. "Does anyone know CP-fucking-R?"

Surprisingly, Sammy Walper came bounding off the crank rig and hurried over to the girl. Without a word, the kid shouldered McEwan out of the way. He peeled off his gloves and placed one hand atop the other, braiding his fingers together, and proceeded to pump stiff-armed down on the girl's chest.

"Go to it, kid," McEwan muttered, standing and sliding out of Sammy's way.

Mike scurried down the pilothouse steps breathing just as heavy as Charlie. Briefly, their eyes locked across the bow. Mike nodded once. Charlie wordlessly returned the gesture.

McEwan pulled back his hood and grabbed his knit cap off his head. Eyes locked on Sammy Walper and the girl, he raked thick fingers through his corkscrew hair.

"Jesus, Sammy, she breathing?"

Sammy didn't answer. When he dropped his face down towards hers, pressing his lips against her lips, Charlie turned away. He was thinking of how her lips had ballooned up and split at the creases...the way the blood had dried on her chin...

Bryan sloughed off the crank platform and staggered over to Charlie and Joe. He seemed unable to look away from the spectacle. In a small voice he said, "How the hell did she get out here?" When no one answered he said, "And what happened to her clothes?"

Mike bent down beside Sammy, who was back to administering chest compressions. "You're doing real good, kid. Real fucking impressive. Come on, Sammy. Come on, Sam—"

Sammy cried out, high-pitched as a schoolgirl. Startled, Mike staggered backward a few steps, his arms splayed, his knees wobbly. With unmatched agility, Sammy Walper popped to his feet and practically moonwalked back across the deck.

The girl's eyes were open. Stiffly she turned her head to one side, appraising the crew one by one. When those cold, black eyes fell on Charlie, he felt something tighten in the center of his gut.

She sat up. Color was already beginning to filter through her veins. Clumps of ice slid down her wet hair and splashed to the deck in muddy pools.

Mike clapped his hands. "Come on, guys! Let's get her downstairs, warm her up!" He grabbed Sammy's sleeve and dragged him back down toward the girl. "Help me get her on her feet, Sammy."

Sammy jerked his sleeve free and pulled his arm up to his chest, as if injured. In a small voice he said, "I ain't touchin' her."

McEwan rolled into place. He slipped two hands beneath the girl's armpits and, after a quick one-two-three count, lifted her off the deck. Upright, her body was as pale as moon-glow, slender yet muscular, fragile as glass. Mike rushed to assist McEwan, each of them grabbing one of the girl's arms. They proceeded to lead her to the hatch. At one point the girl turned and looked over her shoulder. Charlie thought she was looking directly at him.

FIVE

Charlie gathered dry towels from the pantry while Joe boiled water on the petrol stove in the galley. There were only a few towels, which Charlie stacked under one arm. There were warm, clean clothes on his bunk—fresh socks, sweats, a hoodie—so he jogged down the narrow corridor which led to the tiny compartment he shared with Joe and Sammy.

Sammy was in the room, sitting on the edge of his own bunk. His presence startled Charlie, who paused briefly before setting the towels down on Joe's bunk.

"Nice work out there, kiddo."

Sammy nodded.

Charlie grabbed a laundry bag and stuffed it with two pairs of clean socks, a pair of LSU sweatpants, and a sweatshirt with a drawstring hood. He balled the towels up, too, and squeezed them into the bag.

Before leaving he turned back to Sammy. "You okay?"

The kid sat on the edge of his cot, a runnel of snot leaking from one nostril, his legs bouncing up and down like pistons. He had his hands folded together between his knees. At the sound of Charlie's voice, the greenhorn lowered his head and refused to look Charlie in the eye.

"Sammy," he said.

"Who," the kid began. He swallowed what appeared to be a hard lump of spit then continued: "Who do you think she is?"

"I have no idea. What's the matter with you?"

"You picked her up." Sammy turned to him. His eyes were haunted, frightened. "You feel anything funny?"

"Like what?"

Sammy opened his mouth as if to speak but no words came out. Instead, he merely shook his head and turned his face away. His legs, those twin engines, were going a mile a minute now.

Charlie left, hurrying back down the corridor toward the captain's quarters. Mike's cabin door was cracked halfway, allowed Charlie to see movement on the other side. He knocked once then eased the door open.

The girl sat on Mike's cot, the towel around her shoulders already soaking wet and dripping water onto the floor. She looked up at him as he entered. Her face was expressionless. Curls of dark hair hung down over her face.

Mike was digging through an old footlocker, presumably for more towels or warm clothes, while McEwan leaned against one wall, his big arms folded across his chest.

"Here," Charlie said, tossing the laundry sack at McEwan. "Clean clothes and towels."

Mike stood with a groan and intercepted the sack from McEwan. Undoing the drawstring, Mike emptied the contents beside the girl on the cot. Taking one of the towels, he unfolded it and draped it down over the girl's head.

"You speak English, honey?" McEwan said.

The girl was busy watching Mike; she didn't look in McEwan's direction.

"¿Habla ingles?" McEwan grunted. He thumbed his nose then, with a kiss-my-ass grin, looked at Charlie. "You win the prize for best catch of the day, Mears."

He was about to say something when the cabin door swung in and slammed against his back. Joe's head poked through the opening, wincing. "Shit, Charlie, sorry about that." He was holding a steaming mug of tea wrapped in a dishtowel with both hands.

Mike bent down to eye-level with the girl. "What's your name, honey?"

Her dark, oil-spot eyes flitted from Mike to McEwan... then Joe, Charlie, and back to Mike.

"Can you talk?" Mike tried again. "Can you tell us your name?"

She looked away again, only this time at the fresh clothes spread out on the cot.

"She wants to get dressed," Joe said, setting the mug of tea down on Mike's footlocker. "Why don't we step out for a couple seconds, give her some privacy?"

Mike sighed. He clapped both hands on his workpants then stood with his trademark grunt. "You're right, Dynamo." He nodded toward the door. "Everybody out."

They gathered in the galley, where Bryan was already pouring shots of vodka. He passed them out as the others filed into the room and slid around the table. Holding one extra shot, Bryan frowned and said, "Where's the kid?"

"In his room," Charlie said.

Bryan leaned out into the corridor and shouted, "Hey

Walper, get your CPR-pumpin' hands in here!" Claiming his own seat in the booth around the table, Bryan knocked back both his and Sammy's vodka and grimaced. "You see that kid out there? His first time out and he's saving people's lives and shit."

"Let's not jump to conclusions," Joe said.

Pouring himself another shot, Bryan said, "Conclusions about what?"

"About what constitutes being a person."

Everyone looked at Joe. McEwan said, "The hell you talkin' about?"

"Did you see her in there?" Joe was running one finger around the rim of his own shot glass. "It's fucking January and we're how many nautical miles off the coast of fucking Alaska? And she's out runnin' around naked as a jaybird. Fellas, she ain't even *shivering* in there. Not to mention the fact that she's simply fucking *alive* to begin with…"

"So what is she?" McEwan said. "Let's hear your theory, Einstein."

Joe cracked an awkward grin. His eyes looked aloof, delirious. "Fuck should I know? She could be a mermaid, a ghost, a fucking vampire. I don't know. All I know is there's no rational explanation for what she's—"

Mike held up one finger. He turned to Bryan. "Flip on and see if you can get Saint Paul on the radio. Find out if there's been any distress calls from ships within the past twenty-four."

Bryan saluted and jumped out of the booth. His heavy footfalls were heard tromping the steps up to the pilothouse.

They drank their shots and Mike passed around the bottle for refills.

Charlie rubbed two thick fingers across his furrowed brow. "You think she was on a ship that went down?"

Mike shrugged. "It's possible."

"Fuck," McEwan countered. "We would have heard the distress call come over the line, too."

"Hell," Mike said, "for all we know, she could have

fallen off a goddamn cruise ship. I'm just covering all the bases."

"Do you think..." Charlie began then cut himself off. When Mike prompted him to continue he said, "Do you think there could be more people out there?"

There was silence around the table as this notion sank in.

"Nothing we can do about it now," Mike said. He sounded dejected, worn out, beaten. "Unless we hear something specific from Saint Paul dispatch, I ain't risking running this boat into a 'berg searching for people who ain't there." He rubbed his weary face with his big hands. "We'll decide when to head back tomorrow morning when—"

"Whoa," McEwan said, holding up one hand. "Head back? What the hell, Mike?"

"What's wrong?"

McEwan coughed up a strangled little chortle. "You're kidding, right?" He leaned closer toward Mike across the tabletop. Charlie could smell the dried perspiration on his skin, mingling with the odor of the codfish used for baiting the pots. "You were out there today, weren't you? We keep this up for the rest of the week we're liable to pull fifty thousand pounds before the next snowfall." He shook his burly head. "No. No fucking way, Mike. We killed a whole week out here catching nothing but runny noses *at your direction* and we've got the chance to make up for lost time. We hit the mother-load today, man. Think about it."

"But what about the girl?" Charlie offered before Mike could come to his own defense.

McEwan rolled one massive shoulder. "What about her? Keep her nice and warm, give her a few paperback westerns to read, and we drop her off on Sheriff Lapatu's doorstep the second we get back."

"And what if she freaks out?" Mike said. "What if she has a goddamn seizure or a heart attack or fucking *dies* out here, Billy?"

"If she didn't die up there on the fucking deck twenty minutes ago then I think she's out of the woods. I get your concern, Mike. This is your boat and everything on it—every person—is your responsibility. I get that. But I ain't gonna let you cash in for no goddamn reason."

Charlie opened his mouth to speak but Joe cut him off, quick to the punch.

"He's got a point," Joe said, though unable to meet Charlie's eyes. As if he owed some explanation, he added, "Got mouths to feed, Charlie. Sorry, Mike."

Bryan came bounding back down the pilothouse stairs and into the galley, a grim look on his face.

Mike turned to him. "Well?"

"Well you're not gonna believe it but the fucking radio's down." He tossed both hands up in mock surrender. "So's the GPS."

Mike sat forward. *"What?"*

"It's juiced," said Bryan. "I mean, it's getting power. It's just not turning on. I rebooted the whole console but it ain't working."

"Christ." Mike sank back in his seat. "I'd say we check the generators but if the board's getting power…I mean, the fucking lights come on and everything?"

"Lights, meters, gauges, you name it. No GPS screen and no radio signal. Power light comes on but I can't locate a channel."

Mike rubbed at his face and stared at the shot of vodka that stood before him on the table. Disgusted, he slid the shot over to McEwan. Through his fingers, Mike said, "Let's drop console power for the night. We'll reboot in the morning and deal with it then. It's been a long day. Any other suggestions?"

There was a resounding grunt of approval from the others.

"All right," Mike said, standing up. "I'll go down and double-check the generators. Last thing I want is all the power to cut out. Lose heat. I think—"

The girl appeared in the doorway. She was swimming in an oversized sweatshirt and baggy sweatpants, her tiny feet bound in two pairs of socks. Though still damp, her long dark hair had begun to dry in silken, raven-colored waves around her face.

The men stared at her, speechless.

"Do you have any food?" she said, startling them all.

No one moved.

"I'm hungry," she said, and this time Bryan snapped into action, climbing over the booth and pulling open cupboards.

The girl eased herself down into Bryan's seat while everyone else slid over to make room for her in the booth. Mike put his hands on his hips and looked like he wanted to laugh.

"You can talk, huh?" Mike said. "How come you wouldn't talk to us before?"

"I didn't know what to say," said the girl.

"What's your name?" Mike asked.

"I don't have one."

"Did you fall off a ship?" Charlie said from across the table. "Did a ship go down out here or something?"

"I don't think so," she said. She seemed unconcerned. Bryan placed a bowl of cornflakes in front of her, which she proceeded to eat with her fingers. "This is good," she told him, holding up individual flakes to examine them up close before eating them. "These taste good."

"Honey," Mike went on, "how the hell did you get out here?"

"Wait." She set both palms down on the tabletop, on either side of the cereal bowl. Across the table from her, the guys recoiled without thinking about it. "There was one more of you."

"The kid's in his room," McEwan said before anyone else could answer. "Sweetheart, what the fuck you doin' running around naked out here in the middle of the devil's icebox? How long you been out here before we came along?"

"I don't remember," she said. "I don't know how long."

"And you don't remember how you got out here?"

She seemed to consider this. Finally, as a coy little smile

spread across her face, she said, "I don't. I don't remember."

They watched her devour several bowls of cereal and even warmed her with a shot of vodka before the totality of the day's exhaustion began to weigh heavily on them all. They slipped out of the galley one at a time, until only Charlie, Mike Fenty, and the mysterious girl remained. The trawler bobbing like a cork on the troubled, icy waters of the Imarpik, the cupboard doors creaked open and banged shut while the remaining few inches of Popov seesawed in the bottle. Between Charlie and Mike the silence was pregnant with speculation. Frequently, sitting across from each other at the Formica table, the two men would exchange similar glances, each attempting to prompt the other into speaking.

Whether he crumbled under the weight of Charlie's unflinching glare or merely surrendered to his rank as captain, Mike sighed and finally said, "Look, darling, it's late. You're eating like a truck driver just drove in from the moon but it's late. Charlie Mears and I, we're hitting the sack. You're welcome to my bunk for the night. There's an extra cot next to Falmouth. Won't be an issue long as he cranks down the snore machine for the—"

The girl stood abruptly. "Goodnight," she said, and marched out of the galley.

Mike turned and stared at Charlie. They broke into laughter together, the girlish giggling subsiding only after Mike stood, yawning. "Fuck it," the captain growled. "Maybe Billy's right. No sense cutting this thing short."

Charlie shook his head. "It's late, Mike. Go to bed."

Later, in his own room, Charlie couldn't find sleep. He stared at the darkened ceiling while on his back, his big hands laced behind his head and one ankle crossed over the other. Joe was snoring soundly. Outside, he could hear the waves lapping against the sides of the trawler.

"You awake, Charlie?" It was Sammy Walper's voice, disembodied in the dark.

"I guess. What is it?"

"She make you feel…" Sammy paused, possibly choosing his words with heed. "Make you feel funny, Charlie?"

"Nearly gave me a heart attack earlier when I saw her running along that 'berg. That's about it."

"She doesn't exist." His voice was small and growing smaller. "Like...I mean, she's not supposed to exist. And maybe she doesn't. Not like you or me, I mean."

"Sammy, what are you yappin' about?"

"She doesn't know who she is," Sammy said.

"Probably amnesia. She'll remember in the morning," Charlie assured him.

"No." Sammy Walper sounded adamant. "No, that's not it..."

It was only when Joe spoke up that Charlie realized his snoring had stopped. "Truth is," Joe muttered, his voice still groggy with sleep, "she didn't say she couldn't *remember* her name. She said she ain't *got* one."

"Well shit," whispered Sammy Walper. The greenhorn's heartbeat was nearly audible in the claustrophobic little room.

"Guys," Charlie said, rolling over. "Let me get some sleep. I need to dream about my kid for a few hours before sunup, okay? Everything," he promised them, "will be fine in the morning."

SIX

In the morning, Sammy Walper was gone. It was impossible, of course—there was no place to go—but the truth of the matter could not be refuted. The kid was gone, vanished, disappeared. After thirty minutes of scrambling about the *Borealis* like frantic rats through a gasoline-smelling maze, the crew regrouped in the galley, confusions rising, to formulate a more ceremonial approach to the search.

"We'll split into teams," Mike said. "Charlie and Joe, you guys check the engine room, the generators, every single poorly lit crevice on this ship." Mike handed Charlie a flashlight then instructed Bryan and McEwan to systematically check every room as well as all the compartments and hatches above deck. "We'll tear the boat apart if we have to."

"What're you gonna do?" McEwan said.

"I'll be in the pilothouse, trying to restore power to our radio and GPS," Mike said. "We good on this?"

"We're good," Charlie advised.

"Good as ever," said Bryan.

As they began filing out of the room—

"Hey." Mike pulled Charlie to one side, leaning close to his ear. "Do me a favor and peek in on our guest before you head down, will you?"

"Sure."

She was still in Mike's room where she'd spent the night. Charlie knocked on the door but when she didn't respond he opened the door slightly. Poked his head inside. The lights were off in the windowless room. The girl sat stock-still on the edge of the cot, her bare feet on the floor, her hands folded in her lap, illuminated by the vertical sliver of electric hallway light coming in through the half-open cabin door.

"Jesus, I'm sorry," Charlie blurted, quickly looking away.

She was completely naked, the curls of her raven-colored hair just long enough to cover the swells of her smallish breasts.

"Oh. Hello, Charlie." Her voice was childlike, simplistic somehow. "You're awake early. It's still dark."

"We're always awake early."

"How are you?

"I'm...I'm okay." He grinned in spite of his embarrassment—or, more likely, because of it—and held up two casual fingers over his eyes. Still, he could see her peripherally. "You didn't happen to see Sammy this morning, did you?"

"The young boy who saved me last night?"

"Yeah, that's the one."

"No, sir." She actually shook her head from side to side, like a stage actor being overly dramatic. "No."

"Sit tight," he told her and quickly departed, a flush of red having blossomed at each cheek.

Down below deck, they wandered through an ink-black labyrinth of industrial pipes and steam valves, of rattling compressors and twitching radium needles arcing across grime-caked dials. Charlie played the flashlight's beam along the ductwork, breaking light into cobwebbed corners and back behind narrow crevices. Behind him, Joe's boots shushed along the planking. The constant hum of the generators resonated in Charlie's back teeth and, at the end of the tapered black walkway, bending down where the pipes came in too close to his head, the vibrations caused an enormous spider's web to quiver like the plucked string of an upright bass. In these temperatures the web's occupant was no longer in attendance, having either vacated by virtue of arachnid intuition just prior to the trawler's departure from Saint Paul Island or simply disintegrated in the subzero temperatures into filaments of frozen bug-dust.

"Sammy ain't down here." Joe's voice, punctuated by the chattering of molars, echoed off the pipes. "Ain't nothing down here, Charlie."

"Sammy?" Charlie called, his own voice booming in the cramped space. "Kid, you down here?"

"Why's it so cold?"

"Dunno."

"Charlie, man, you don't find this strange? First it's this chick running naked on a 'berg, next thing we know the kid's gone missing."

"You sayin' there's some connection?"

"I'm sayin' it's pretty fucked up, amigo. That's what I'm saying."

Something cold and wet fell in Charlie's face. He directed the flashlight toward the ceiling, which was only about a foot from his face, and saw icicles forming along the ductwork.

Joe saw it, too. Muttered, "That ain't good."

The flashlight flickered then winked off. Charlie groaned. He cracked it several times against the heel of one hand but the light did not come back on.

"Let's beat it topside," Joe said, already retreating into the darkness through the maze of pipes.

Topside, the rest of the crew was in a panic. Bryan and McEwan were unsuccessful locating any sign of Sammy Walper and Mike was still fiddling with the power-grid in the control room with no success. The sun had just started to peek up over the horizon, the sea like liquid mercury, and the pots would soon need to be collected.

Charlie rapped knuckles on the control room door three times before Mike, looking haggard and frustrated, opened it.

"No dice," Charlie informed him. "I've got a sick feeling in the pit of my stomach, Mike, that the kid might've gone overboard."

"Don't say that. Anyway, how in the world...?"

"Beats me. He was pretty shaken up last night. Maybe...I don't know...maybe he went topside for a smoke and fell the fuck over the side."

"That's pretty goddamn queer."

"Whole thing's queer," said Charlie. "What're we gonna do about the pots?"

Mike rubbed the back of one hand across his forehead and looked instantly exhausted. "Guess we pull 'em. We're here, ain't we? Fuck."

"Then what?"

"You mean do we head back to Saint Paul? I don't see no other alternatives, do you? Kid's gone, for Christ sake. We gotta report it or something. Tell the police."

"You been in to check on our guest this morning?" Charlie asked.

"Briefly. Talk about queer, she was just sittin' on the cot buck-ass-naked."

"You get a name from her yet?"

"No. And talkin' to her's kinda funny. Leaves me feeling...strange, I guess. Like talking into a tornado—words get all jumbled and lost."

He didn't have to ask what Mike meant. "How's the power situation coming?"

"No soap. Still futzing with it."

"We got ice on the pipes down by the generators."

"Fuck me blue."

"Just thought you should know."

"Yeah, right." Mike Fenty looked shaken. "Goddamn fuckaroo this is turning out to be."

Just then, Charlie happened to glimpse arms waving down on the foredeck from the corner of his eye. He turned to see Bryan Falmouth semaphoring to them from the bow, McEwan crouched on one knee before the hatch that led down into the crab tanks. The hatch was open and McEwan was peering in while dragging a hand across his scalp. Joe was bounding up the stairs of the control room, his eyes blazing like high-beams in his head.

"Oh, shit," Charlie uttered. That sinking sensation in his gut suddenly amplified ten times over. He and Mike burst through the control room door and nearly collided with Joe, who was spouting gibberish, talking too fast.

"Jesus Christ, fellas—I mean, it's—Jesus—"

Charlie brushed past him and took the iron steps two at a time, Mike right behind him on his heels. Looking far from the "Dynamo" Joe who'd stepped onboard the *Borealis* just over a week ago, Joe Darling did not follow Charlie and Mike down the steps; he merely propped himself up against the iron railing and clung to it with both hands, all the color drained from his face.

McEwan held up a single hand, palm out, as Charlie and Mike approached the open hatch. "It's bad," McEwan warned, his voice hollow.

Charlie stopped at the edge of the hatch and peered down into the tank.

Yesterday's catch of crabs populated the water—enough of them to compound the confusion of the scene itself which required Charlie to do a double-take. Then he realized what he was seeing, recognizing the whitish skin and the specifications of the protrusion of a human leg…finally, the undeniable fan of dark hair, undulating in the icy tank water like some undersea vegetation. The reddish, spidery crustaceans heaped on top of what remained of the body, moving with a mechanical, calculated slowness.

He felt his stomach lurch and he turned quickly to the side of the trawler to address the sea below. The vomit came up in a messy, pasty string that burned his esophagus and stank like the bait locker. Eyes squeezed closed, he waited for the nausea to pass before turning back around. Moisture from his eyes froze to his face. He saw Mike Fenty, poised precipitously at the lip of the hatch, not so much staring down as he was staring into a blind abyss. *Like talking into a tornado,* Charlie thought. The captain's mind, it seemed, had temporarily shut down.

McEwan stood, albeit shakily. His small eyes appeared even smaller, almost disappearing altogether in the creases and folds of his weathered face. A sick tone to his voice, he mumbled, "How the hell could this have happened?"

"Shut it," Mike ordered him. He took a step backward and tore his eyes from the opening in the deck. "Shut the fucking thing already."

Together, Bryan and McEwan eased the hatch down and bolted it into the planking. They looked mutually disgusted and equally drained.

"It takes two men to open that hatch," Mike said. He could have been addressing them all or just talking to himself.

"Doesn't make sense." It was Bryan, hugging himself through his bright orange slicker. Bits of frost had collected about his eyelashes. "It's impossible…"

Charlie looked down at his hands. The tips of his fingers were blue. They were shaking something fierce.

SEVEN

Bryan put on a pot of coffee while Mike retreated to the control room once again. In his mounting agitation, McEwan grabbed a pack of Camels from his footlocker and tucked himself away at the rear of the boat where the diesel sauna fought to keep the cold at bay. With the sun full in the sky and the waters stretching around the world looking alluringly calm, they would soon have to reclaim the pots and, in the wake of a unanimous decision, head back to Saint Paul Island.

Charlie crept down the corridor and, without knocking, pushed open Mike's cabin door.

Fully dressed in the clothes Charlie had given her the night before, the girl stood staring directly at him as if in anticipation of his arrival. A cold finger touched the base of Charlie's spine. He cleared his throat and was about to speak when she beat him to it—

"Did you find your friend?"

"Sammy's dead." He cleared his throat a second time, fearful he might choke on his own words. "I want to ask you something."

She eased herself down on the cot, folding her small hands in her lap. "Okay." Again: that helpless, childish voice...

With a grief so powerful it nearly shook him to his knees her voice caused him to think of Gabriel, his son. Before he knew what was happening his eyes began welling with tears, blurring his vision.

Like a puppy plagued with unending curiosity, the girl cocked her head to one side and examined him with coal-black eyes.

The feeling passed and Charlie regained his composure, quickly swiping his thumb over both eyelids. "Have you left this room since last night?"

She shook her head. Said, "No."

"Not even to take a—not even to use the head?"

"The 'head'?"

"The toilet."

"No."

He said, "Then how did you know it was dark out this morning?"

She only stared at him, as motionless as a stone figure.

"When I came in here this morning," he went on, "you commented that it was still dark outside. You said it was early and still dark. How did you know that if you hadn't been outside?"

"I'm hungry," she said.

"Answer my question first."

"But I want to eat."

"You won't get any food until you answer my question." Lowering his voice, he heard himself say, as if from the mouth of someone else speaking from a far distance, "What happened to Sammy?"

Almost imperceptibly, the girl's eyes narrowed.

There's knowledge there, Charlie realized. *There's knowledge behind those eyes.*

"Don't be angry with me," she said, and he could not tell if she was feigning innocence or if it was genuine. "I don't like it when people get angry with me."

Steeling himself, he said, "I want to know what happened to Sammy. I want you to tell me."

"Why do you think I know?"

"Because I do. And I'm not angry. I won't be. But you have to tell me."

"Maybe your friend Sammy couldn't help himself." A pause. "Sometimes people just can't help themselves…"

"If—"

There came a sudden jarring, books and framed photographs flipping off the nightstand, a ceramic coffee mug, and the lights blinked but stayed on. Charlie, his fingers digging into the doorframe, glanced around. "Jesus, I think we hit something."

He rushed down the corridor and out onto the foredeck. An elongated slip of ice, roughly the size of the trawler itself, had rushed up alongside them in some semblance of an attack. The hull of the boat was dented and streaming with heavy scrapes but it hadn't been punctured. At least, as far as Charlie could tell from peering over the side…

A cigarette dangling from his chapped, bloodless lips, McEwan appeared beside him. "The fuck's Mike doing?" he shouted over the sudden grinding of gears sounding up from the engine room. He waved a hand in the direction of the pilothouse but the lights behind the glass had gone dim; Mike Fenty was nothing more than a ghost among shadows.

"Something's funny," Charlie whispered.

"Yeah," McEwan agreed, his voice scratchy. "A regular fucking riot."

Bryan was cursing at the petrol stove when, five minutes later, Charlie and McEwan came down the galley steps.

"Damn thing won't work," Bryan growled, dropping a fist on top of the unit. "Useless."

"Maybe needs more fuel?" Charlie suggested.

"It's full. I just checked. And look." He reached up and slammed one of the cupboard doors, cracking it against its frame. It rebounded, easing itself back open. "See that?" said Bryan. The early stirrings of insanity glittered behind his eyes. Laughed humorlessly. "None of them close." He ran one finger along the inside of the door, prodding the magnetic panel screwed into the wood. "The magnets don't work anymore. None of 'em do."

For the first time, Charlie noticed all the cupboard doors were standing open.

Grumbling, McEwan retrieved a bottle of vodka from one of the open cupboards then dropped his considerable bulk, in tandem with a piggish grunt, into the booth. "Go complain to Fenty," he said, unscrewing the cap off the bottle. "It's his piece of shit rig."

Still glaring down at the petrol stove, Bryan said, "I don't get it. Everything worked fine until now."

"To the kid," McEwan toasted, bringing the bottle of

vodka to his lips.

"How the hell did he get *down* there?" Bryan said, sliding into the booth beside McEwan. He grabbed the bottle from McEwan's lips and took a swig himself. "What was he *thinking*?"

"Mike's right," Charlie said, folding his arms. "Hatch is too heavy for one man to lift. And Sammy, he weren't no superman."

"Sounds to me," McEwan said, "you're accusing one of us of bein' there when it happened." Without expression, he snatched the bottle back from Bryan. "Maybe even insinuatin' we had somethin' to do with him dying."

"I don't know what I'm insinuating," said Charlie.

"Why don't you go ahead and say what's on your mind, then?"

"I'd just like someone to explain to me how that kid got himself killed in the holding tank, that's all. Kid's dead. I'd like to know how it happened."

In the ceiling the lights blinked in their fixtures. All three of them cast wary glances. The ship was keeling to one side, items slid out of the open cupboards and onto the floor. A bag of sugar spilled like beach sand across the counter.

"We're turning around," Bryan observed. "Mike's taking us back."

"What about the pots?" McEwan said.

"Pots ain't goin' nowhere," Charlie said. He turned and rolled out of the galley, both hands planted on either wall for support as he made his way down the canting corridor. The bluish light from the head shone in the darkness. Joe was staring into the commode, his legs folded up under him, a dazed expression on his face. As Charlie approached, Joe turned his head slowly to address him, a silvery tightrope of spittle bowing from his lower lip to the rim of the toilet.

"Hey, Charlie."

"What's wrong, Joe?"

"Sick." And indeed he looked like death. In the bluish

light of the tiny latrine, his skin had adopted a translucence that was almost corpselike. Dark rings encircled his eyes and his lips quivered, vibrating the trail of saliva that held him to the toilet. "Never been seasick b'fore. All my time on boats, ain't never been seasick. Funny, huh?"

Charlie leaned in and pulled the flush-chain. The commode growled and, with a whoosh, devoured the whole mess.

"Mike taking us home?"

"Think so, yeah."

"I'm still seein' him, Charlie. Every time I close my eyes, man, I see him—or what was left of him—in that holding tank. The water all pink, the space-spiders creepin' and crawlin' all over him. His flesh all white and hanging off in chunks like bits of uncooked chuh-chuh-chicken—" He leaned over the commode and retched.

"Go lay down, Joe."

"Those crabs," Joe said, wiping a sleeve across his mouth. "I mean, we can't use 'em, right? We gotta let 'em back out into the sea. Christ, Charlie, they fucking *ate* him."

Uneasy, Charlie turned away and climbed the galley steps that led out into the milky haze of an overcast day. It felt like forty below, the wind practically searing the skin from his face. He chased the tip of a cigarette around with a lighter until he caught it. Sucked vehemently. It was all he could do not to stare at the hatch. How in the world had Sammy managed to open it on his own, let alone fall in there?

He glanced up at the pilothouse. Just barely did he make out the seemingly disembodied face of Mike Fenty, floating like a white moon behind the salt-streaked windows. Lungs tugging on the smoke, Charlie ascended the steps toward the control room, his muscles almost audibly creaking in the cold, running one numbing hand along the iron rail. Around them the sea was growing rough. Behind a veil of cumuli the sun had repositioned itself in the sky, burning silver threads through the clouds.

The control room door was locked.

"Hey, Mike." Charlie knocked against the pane of glass. "Door's locked."

Mike did not turn to look at him; he merely stood behind the wheel facing straight out the windows.

Charlie knocked again, this time with more urgency. Through the pane he could see that the control panel was unlit: still no power.

"Mike?"

Snapped from his daze, Mike craned his neck to stare at Charlie. With the dedication of a death-row inmate, Mike leaned over and flipped the latch on the door. Charlie stepped inside, expecting the usual blast of heat from the floor vents, but it was almost as cold in the pilothouse as it was out on the foredeck.

"You takin' us back to Saint Paul?"

"Sure," Mike said.

"Guess we'll come back for the pots another time."

"Sure will."

"Figure we might not want to touch the reds in the holding tank," he suggested. "In case, you know, Sheriff Lapatu wants to have first look. Scene of the crime and all that, I'm guessing."

"What crime is that?" Mike said. He continued to stare out the grime-streaked, salted windows.

"I guess not a *crime,* per se, but…well, you know, we prob'ly shouldn't go messin' in that tank, is all." He put a hand on Mike's shoulder. Still, the captain would not look at him. "You all right?"

"Sure am."

"Couldn't get the power up?"

"Don't need it. Been navigating these waters since I was a teenager."

"Lights are blinking and the petrol stove is cold." Charlie tapped one of the floor vents with his boot. "Feels like the heat ain't makin' it up through the vents anymore, either. Like she's givin' up on us."

Mike swung his head around to face him, his eyes haunted and nearly fearful. "What do you mean 'she'?"

"The boat. She. Listen, Mike, why don't you head down, get something in your stomach. You're burning yourself out, man."

He returned his gaze to the sea. "Not hungry."

"Then take a nap."

"Not tired."

Defeated, Charlie bent and rummaged through the underside of the console for the first aid kit. Once he located it he stood, his spine cracking, and cast one final glance at Mike Fenty before taking the first aide back below the deck.

Joe was curled in a fetal position on his cot when Charlie entered the cabin. His eyes were closed but he spoke Charlie's name when he entered. Charlie sat on his own cot and opened the kit in his lap. Bandages, adhesive strips, a needle and thread, a syringe, even a flare gun and two flare cartridges. Eventually he located some Dramamine. Joe dry-swallowed two tablets without opening his eyes.

Charlie slid the first aid kit beneath his cot and stood, unsure if the creaking sound he heard was from the cot's struts or his own tired bones. He suddenly felt a million years old. For whatever reason he thought once again of Gabriel. The last time he'd seen the kid had been six months ago, back at the trailer in Saint Paul Village. He'd been sitting on a telephone book at the kitchen table, shoveling spoonfuls of some sugary cereal into his mouth. Through the kitchen windows, the tawny lights of an Alaskan predawn bled up into the sky behind the black serration of distant firs. The boy was up early for school, dressed in oversized corduroys and a Batman sweatshirt. Though seated at the table he already had his matching Batman backpack strapped to his back.

Charlie tousled the boy's hair and kissed the top of his head. He, too, was up early, it being the first day of a new season. Down at the shore, the trawlers would be lined like soldiers along the seal rookeries, dressed and ready for a trek across the Imarpik. He grabbed a bowl for himself and, in sleepy silence, sat opposite his son at the small table, pouring his own bowl of cereal and milk. They ate without talking, content merely with their proximity, for the boy loved his father and the father loved his boy, and in the pauses between their crunching Charlie could hear Johanna's light snoring emanating from the back bedroom.

When he'd finished eating, Charlie stood, raking the legs of the chair across the linoleum, and paused to grip the boy's chin. Pinched him gently.

"You do good in school," he told the boy.

"I know, I know."

"I'll see you in a couple weeks."

"You do good, too," the boy said.

"I know, I know," he said, mimicking his son's tone.

Yet two weeks later, Charlie Mears returned from the great salt seas to an empty home—empty, it seemed, for so long that the smells representative of his wife and child no longer haunted the empty rooms…

"Where you goin'?" Joe practically croaked from the cot. The sound of his voice dragged Charlie back from his reverie.

"Finish talkin' with our no-name little guest in the next room," he said, and left.

EIGHT

Unable to prepare any warm food without the use of the petrol stove, he entered Mike's cabin carrying a bowl of cereal and a glass of milk. The girl stood beside the dresser, holding one of Mike's framed photographs in her hands. It was a glamour shot of Mike's wife, one of those airbrushed, angelic portraits you can get at Kmart or some such place, her hair a nest of springy platinum curls, too much makeup on her face.

"She's pretty," the girl said, setting the picture back atop the dresser as Charlie came in.

"Brought you some food." He set the bowl of cereal and glass of milk on the dresser. "I wanted to pick up where we left off before."

"About your friend who died?"

"About who you are," said Charlie. He sat on Mike's footlocker, folding his hands between his knees, and motioned with his chin for the girl to sit on the cot. She sat without protest, her eyes never leaving his. "Who are you?" he said after a few moments of uninterrupted silence fell between them.

"I'm your catch," she said. "I'm your find."

"That makes no sense."

"You found me, didn't you?"

"What's your name?"

"I don't have one." Again—that timid head-cocking. "You can give me a name, if you like."

"Forget names," he said. "Tell me how you got out here."

"You picked me up," she told him. "You brought me on the boat."

"No. Not how you got on the boat," he clarified, growing increasingly irritated at her evasiveness. "How did you wind up out here in the sea? On the iceberg?"

She held him in her gaze for several seconds, unspeaking. A cold, marrow-freezing chill overtook him and settled deep within his soul. He had to break her stare, to look away from her.

"You're one of the hard ones," she commented after a while.

"What does that mean?"

"It means some people are easy to reach. Most people, actually. But not all. You're one of the hard ones to reach. I think…I think it's because you're overtaken by something else." Wrinkling her nose and creasing her brow, she was trying to read something in him, something deep below the surface. "There is something keeping you shielded." She added, suddenly brightening, "It is a little boy."

This statement, for whatever reason, did not jar him. "My son, yes. Gabriel. He's been on my mind a lot lately. You can tell that?"

"You're a hard one," she said again, "but you're not difficult to read."

He sighed and leaned away from her, sitting straighter on the footlocker. "You did that to Sammy, didn't you?"

"Sammy did what he did to himself."

"He couldn't have opened that hatch by himself. Someone had to have helped him."

"There are a lot of big strong men on this boat," she offered.

"None of them would have done anything to him. Let's stop playing games. Tell me how you got out here."

At first, he did not think she was going to answer. The only sound was their intermingled breathing and the ticking of Mike's wristwatch on the nightstand. Then, surprisingly, and with evident surrender, the girl said, "I was brought out here by a man. His name was Calvert Tackler. We came out on a boat, much like this boat, and he left me out here, presumably to die."

"Why did he do that?"

"Because," she said, "he was thinking the same thoughts about me that you're thinking right now."

This startled him. He began bouncing one leg up and down, up and down, up and down. "How long ago did he leave you here?"

"A very long time ago," she said. "I don't know exactly."

"Who was he? This Calvert Tackler?"

"Just a man."

"How did you know him?"

"We came to meet. He thought he loved me, or was in the process of falling in love with me, but that was not why he brought me out here. He brought me out here because he couldn't bring himself to kill me. Maybe it was because he loved me or maybe it was because he simply did not have it in him to kill a person—"

"But why would he want to kill you?"

"Not just him."

"What do you mean?"

"There have been others," she said. "My whole life, there have been people who've tried to kill me. I can remember their names, all these people, and what each one looked like. I can remember the first one, a man named Frank Bodine, who nearly managed to kill me in a motel room outside Las Vegas. But in the end I eventually got to him. I eventually got to them all, even the strongest ones. Strong ones like you, Charlie Mears. Ones that put up a mental wall, put up a fight. Strong ones like you."

Charlie stood. "I get it. You're out of your mind. Either that or you just like to play games. Well I don't like games. I don't have time for them. You've got three seconds to start talking sense—"

"Don't yell, Charlie."

"—or you're gonna spend the rest of the trip back to Alaska locked in this room. Do you understand?"

"Don't be angry with me." She smiled.

"One," he said.

"Poor, poor Charlie. Misses his boy."

"Two." Grinding his teeth.

"You'll never see him again. You know it's true."

"Three—" simultaneously swiping the bowl of cereal and glass of milk from the top of the dresser and onto the floor.

"Look at the mess you've made." She cast her eyes to the cornflakes and broken shards of bowl in the puddle of milk. "Very messy, Charlie."

"You can talk to the cops when we reach land." He stormed out into the corridor, slamming the cabin door. In the darkness of the corridor, he nearly ran right into Joe, who was leaning against one wall, shrouded in darkness.

"She tell you anything?" Joe said. Charlie couldn't see his face in the dark but it sounded like he had something in his mouth.

"She'll tell Lapatu when we get back to Saint Paul," he promised Joe. "You should be in bed."

"You need to push her more, Charlie. You need to get her to stop."

"Stop what?"

"What she's doing to me."

"You're just seasick."

"Ain't never been seasick in my life, Charlie."

He pressed a hand to Joe's forehead then quickly withdrew it, disgusted by the moist clamminess of "Dynamo" Joe's flesh. A skein of mucous came away with his hand, cool like menthol.

"Fuck, Joe. You're burning up, man."

Joe took a lumbering step forward, his face suddenly illuminated by the red emergency lights recessed in the ceiling. A living skeleton, his skin looked like latex stretched taut over a large stone. Charlie could smell him, too, and it was a sick-sweet, organic smell that reminded him of the breweries down in Anchorage. Though he didn't want to touch Joe again, he placed a hand on one of the man's shoulders and directed him back toward their cabin. Inside the room, Joe winced and recoiled from the lamplight. Joe growled for him to turn it off. Charlie flipped the switch and assisted Joe as he climbed back onto his cot.

"Fucking fuh-freezing," Joe stuttered.

"I know." Charlie grabbed the blanket off his own cot and draped it over Joe's quaking body. Even as he left the room he could hear Joe's teeth chattering in his skull—could hear them as he walked all the way down the corridor.

In the galley, Bryan was looking down forlornly at the petrol stove. Billy McEwan was at the table getting drunk. Charlie paused in the doorway and McEwan's eyelids fluttered. He waved a hand at Charlie. "C'mon, Mears. Drink with me."

"Damn thing," Bryan muttered, seemingly oblivious to Charlie's arrival.

"Is Mike still topside?" Charlie said. When no one responded he reached out and touched Bryan's elbow. As if shocked, Bryan jerked his arm away and practically threw himself back against the far wall. He stared at Charlie with wide eyes.

"Mike," expounded McEwan, drawing Charlie's attention to him, "is a damn fool. He got lucky yesterday with the catch, Mears, but there ain't no luck left out here. Not for us." Again—that sloppy wave of the hand. "So come on over and let's you and me kill this bottle, eh?"

Charlie stepped down into the galley and, with two hands, ripped one of the cupboard doors off its hinges. Bryan's jaw dropped, still pressed against the wall as far away from Charlie as the cramped little room would permit. McEwan, even in his stupor, watched with speechless detachment.

Tucking the cupboard door under one arm, Charlie plucked the flashlight off the countertop. "I'm going down to the engine room for some tools. You two keep an eye on Mike's cabin, make sure that girl doesn't come out."

"What're you doing?" boomed McEwan, but Charlie was already gone.

NINE

Despite the pump of the generators and the grind of the diesel engine, it was freezing in the bowels of the trawler. Wagging his flashlight around the network of pipes, it didn't take Charlie long to locate a suitcase-sized metal toolbox, already open on the floor. Charlie crouched over it and fished around for a handful of carpenter nails and a recoilless hammer.

He heard it—the steady *plick-plick-plick* of dripping water. Charlie cast the beam of light onto the floor and found he was crouching in a puddle of filthy gray water. Rings expanded in the puddle as drops of water fell from above. He followed the droplets up to the ceiling to discover that the drops were actually sloughing off the tips of icicles clinging to the underside of the entire system of pipes.

It was ridiculous, he knew, but he stood and touched the pipes nonetheless. Cold as bone, powdered in frost. He traced the pipes with the flashlight back to the wall of generators. The pipes, he learned, led to the heating unit.

"Goddamn it…"

He approached the unit only to discover, with increasing horror, that it was dead. The dials all ran to zero; the archipelago of bulbs stood unlit. He pressed one hand against the heating unit to find it was still slightly warm but was quickly losing heat.

Frustrated, he administered a swift kick to the side of the unit. The clang played off the metal pipes for an eternity. He didn't want to think about what it would mean to be caught out here for an extended period without heat. Silently he prayed that Mike Fenty knew what the hell he was doing—that, in fact, he would find their way back to Saint Paul Island without the use of the GPS and the navigational system.

Back on the quarterdeck Charlie cracked open the door to Mike's stateroom. The lamp on the nightstand was blinking sporadically. The girl was sitting up on the cot, staring at him through the crack in the door.

"You ready to start talkin' sense?" he said to her.

That coy little smile…

Without another word, he shut the door and proceeded to nail the section of cupboard across the stateroom door and the frame. The sound of the hammering was nearly deafening in these close quarters; still, he drove every nail home until he was left, exhausted and breathless, panting like a lion outside the door. When the hammer slipped from his hand and dropped on his foot, he was brought back to reality. Shaken, tired, he crept down the corridor to his own room. Careful not to wake Joe who was snoring wetly beneath a heap of blankets, Charlie peeled off his sweat-smelling clothes and, in nothing but long johns and wool socks, settled down on his own cot. The trawler rocking, the struts creaking and sighing and moaning all around him, he knew right away, despite his fatigue, he would not find sleep.

Eventually Gabriel worked his way into his head—out

in the yard, overburdened by a heavy winter coat and snow pants, scooping up handfuls of graying snow and throwing them over the fence at Dale Carver's German shepherd. Johanna was there, too, a wool cap on her head and a knit scarf around her neck. She looked fresh-faced and pure in the snow, her face barren of makeup. Calling to Gabriel as a gentle snow began falling in the yard. Dale Carver's German shepherd yelped and bounded after the fistfuls of snow tossed over the fence, confounded by the fact that the mysterious white balls disappeared the second they touched the snowy ground.

Charlie was there, too, of course. In his bright red ski parka, his reddish beard neatly trimmed, he came out of the trailer and proceeded to chase Gabe around the yard. Giggling and wailing, his small legs pushing hard through the deep snow, Gabriel tore around the yard as Charlie pursued him, the German shepherd bounding after them from behind its fence. Barking.

Charlie's eyes flipped open. Not barking. Something struck the hull of the trawler. Maybe another iceberg.

"Joe?" His voice was empty, void of substance. "You awake?"

No answer. He could no longer hear Joe's snoring, he realized.

Sitting up on one elbow he peered through the absolute darkness but could not see a thing. Fumbling on the floor for the flashlight, he located it and clicked it on. The dim, cataract light opened up on Joe's empty cot. The mound of blankets were strewn on the floor.

It wasn't until he sat up and squeezed his feet into his boots that he realized he was still mumbling Joe's name over and over.

Yeah, he thought. *Losing my mind like a regular champ.*

He dressed, the room bitter cold, and he could feel every muscle in his body wanting to cramp up. In the vague gloominess of the quarterdeck he could see his breath, billowing out like tufts of cotton, nearly freezing to the walls.

He all but collapsed in the doorway of the galley. Breathing hard, sweat freezing to his temples, he struggled to catch his breath. McEwan, seated alone at the table, glared up at him. Both his big hands were hugging the bottle of vodka, which was now mostly empty. Dead eyes lifted to examine Charlie, partially slumped in the galley doorway.

"Joe's very sick," he managed, realizing as he said it that it was probably the understatement of the year. "He's not in his room. Have you seen him?"

"This," McEwan grumbled, his rheumy eyes moving wetly in their sockets, "is all your fault, Mears."

"What are you talking about?"

"You're always trying to be the hero," McEwan said. "Always trying to save the world. Funny thing is, you can't even take care of your own domestic problems."

"Man—"

"We're no different than the crabs," McEwan went on. "You know it? We're no goddamn different than the moonbugs in the tank. Each of us, we're all in our own tanks, all scuttlin' and clackin' and spittin' bubbles. Sure." He grunted in approval of himself. "Sure as shit." Those sloppy eyes worked their way up to meet Charlie again. "You know what happens to the spiders they stay in that tank too long, don't you, Charlie?"

Charlie exhaled slowly. Said, "What's that?"

"One of two things happen. Neither's very good." A grimace. "One—they freeze in that tank. Ain't enough to circulate the water so it gets icy, even colder'n where they come from on the sea floor. They freeze and then they start exploding, bits o' shell and claws—pincers, clusters of spidery red legs—all of that, just *poof!* Like puttin' an M-80 in a mailbox, way we all did when we was kids.

"Then there's the other way," McEwan continued, not missing a beat, "an' maybe you'd think this way is worse, mostly 'cause it ain't as quick as explodin' into pieces of spider-shell, but also 'cause what it means—what, see, it *means—*"

"You're drunk," Charlie said flatly.

"They eat each other." Billy McEwan's voice was equally as flat. "Cannibalism. They get to starvin' in that tank, get to fightin' and gettin' on each other's last nerve. Close quarters, scrabbling over each other, probably learn to hate every other space-spider in there with you. You start pulling off a leg here, a claw there. Pretty soon you can't pull no more 'cause your *own* claws are filled with the claws and legs of others, and anyway it's only a matter of time b'fore they start pulling you apart and eating out your guts while you're still alive."

Grabbing the bottle by the neck, McEwan smashed it against the edge of the table. It broke into a crystal spray, pellets of broken glass scattering across the table and onto the floor. The liquor sprayed everywhere, darkening his chambray work shirt.

"We have to do something about our situation here b'fore we resort to eatin' one another, Charlie," said McEwan. A silvery thread of saliva drooled from his mouth. "Or before we start explodin' like mailboxes full of firecrackers." He was breathing heavy, practically panting. "You an' me, Charlie. We have to do something." He brought up his free hand and pressed an index finger to his left temple. "Before we start losin' it in here."

"You're drunk, man," Charlie said.

Those soul-piercing eyes—Charlie couldn't shake them off him. Then, to his amazement, Billy McEwan's ruinous lips splintered into a mock-smile. His teeth were narrow, gray pickets protruding from purpling gums. "Oh, yeah," he said, still smiling. "I'm drunk, all right. To hell and back. Right, Charlie?" The lip-splitting grin widened. "Right, homeboy?"

"Joe's—"

"Haven't fucking seen Joe."

"Where's Bryan?"

Angrily, he tossed the broken bottleneck into the stainless steel sink. "Topside."

TEN

Out on the deck, the air tore into his face, neck, and hands. His cheeks tightened and the moisture around his eyes seemed to freeze instantly. Still, with Billy McEwan's words still fresh in his ears, he was glad to be out here in the open and away from the increasing claustrophobia of the quarterdeck.

Pulling his slicker tighter around his body, he spotted Bryan Falmouth standing at the end of the bow. Beyond, the sea was growing rough, a gray-black patchwork of ice fields miles in length drifting along the shimmering surface. Too much ice. The sun was still struggling to break free of the clouds.

Suddenly, the boat rocked. A sound like tree limbs breaking sounded out over the bow. Steadying himself against the railing in case a second blow should accost the boat, he diligently maneuvered his way to the front of the trawler.

"Hey," he said, coming up behind Bryan. "The hell's Mike doing? There's too much ice out here."

Bryan spun around, instantly shocking Charlie with the emptiness that was so evident on his face. He brought his cigarette to his lips, his hand vibrating like a tuning fork, and displayed some difficulty actually getting it into his mouth. He sucked hard, his cheeks nearly touching, and blew a shaky pillar of smoke into the wind.

"You fucking leave Mike alone," Bryan uttered through chattering teeth.

"What?"

"Don't think I'm not on to you, Charlie. Tryin' to stir the fucking pot."

"Bryan, man, I don't know what you're talking about." He took a step forward, one hand outstretched—

"Don't come near me," Bryan said.

As if stung, Charlie quickly retracted his hand. "Bryan—what's going on, man? What the hell's happening?"

"Don't fucking play with me, Charlie. You just stay right where you are."

"Bry—"

"I'm not fucking playing with you, Charlie, so don't try to play with me!" Bryan screamed, spittle firing from his lips.

Speechless, Charlie backpedaled with his hands up in surrender. Bryan watched his retreat, not trusting himself to look away, the cigarette stuttering between two mercurochrome-colored fingers. As Charlie watched, something poked briefly from Bryan's right nostril. A second later it appeared again, more prominent this time, and Charlie realized, with a sinking sense of dread, that it was a bubble of dark blood.

"Bryan, please—"

"She's drilling holes," Bryan said. His teeth rattled in the cold. Charlie watched as the cigarette dropped to the foredeck and smoldered on the planking. "Holes everywhere." In a terrifying mimicry of McEwan, he brought up a set of fingers and jabbed at his temple. "In here," he said. "In the boat, too." Looking briefly out over the roiling sea: "The goddamn *world*, Charlie." A half-curled, lopsided grin—again, just like McEwan's. "You get it, man? The whole goddamn *world*."

In a whisper, Charlie said, "What about the world, Bryan? What is it? Tell me."

Eyes wide and rimmed red with terror, Bryan Falmouth whispered back: *"Infected."*

"Infected by what?" When Bryan didn't answer—he just stood there, his eyes afire, his entire frame quaking in his slicker—he said it again: "Infected by what, Bryan?"

There came a sound similar to metal sheeting being crushed under a great weight, followed by a rumbling from beneath the boat. The whole trawler shook. Bryan lost his footing and slipped on the wet deck, his arms pinwheeling. Charlie ditched to the side and grabbed hold of the railing. Looking down over the side he watched as a small drift of ice was sucked underneath the boat. He heard a snapping, recoiling sound and looked up in time to see the trawler mow through a second sheet of ice closer to the bow. The sheet literally split down the middle and parted in half by the cutting trawler.

At the bow, Bryan had righted himself against the railing and was also leering over the side of the boat, although he seemed unimpressed by the fact that the *Borealis* was currently cutting through an ice field. As he looked a length of salt-encrusted fiberglass siding, perhaps two feet long, snapped off the ship's hull and flipped end over end in the air until it crashed onto—and slid along—a shelf of frazil ice.

Charlie looked toward the darkened pilothouse. Sea-salt had calcified on the paneled glass, making it impossible to see inside…and, he thought, impossible to see out. Nonetheless he began waving his arms high above his head, suddenly shouting Mike's name.

"No use, Charlie," Bryan called to him. He was fumbling another cigarette from out of his slicker. "He's locked on course now. You guys will be home soon."

He *almost* didn't pick up on it. "What do you mean 'you guys,' Bryan?" he said. "What about you? You'll be home, too, Bryan. We'll all be home."

Unable to light his fresh cigarette in the strong wind, Bryan flicked it over the bow. "No," he said. "Not me. Ain't supposed to be me."

"Bryan, please, what—"

Bryan appeared to crouch, lowering his center of gravity. For one bone-chilling moment Charlie thought the man was preparing to rush him. And in fact Bryan *did* lower his head, ready to charge. Had it been his intention to execute a full-on rush into Charlie's solar plexus, he would have accomplished just that, as Charlie Mears was too slow getting out of the way. But as it turned out, such was not Bryan's intention. Head lowered, eyes ablaze, Bryan charged like a locomotive straight *past* Charlie, his all-weather boots slamming on the foredeck, his arms and legs pumping like machinery. He ran straight across the planking toward the stern where, in a bluish cloud of exhaust, Bryan Falmouth spread wide his arms and, without pause, launched himself over the side of the trawler.

Charlie shrieked his name, already running in Bryan's direction. But by the time he reached the stern there was no sign of Bryan—not even the ripples in the ice-black water. Still, he kept screaming his name, as if mere recital would affect the man's return, his own hands biting into the framework of the stern. As the trawler peeled away, carving a white-capped tract through the frozen sea, Charlie saw— or imagined he saw—one of Bryan's boots briefly bob to the surface.

Holes everywhere, Bryan's voice echoed in his head. *You get it, man? The whole goddamn world...*

He spun around and ran for the pilothouse, mounting the steps in just three giant strides. He slammed his considerable weight against the pilothouse door which, once again, was bolted from the inside. Shouting Mike's name, his breath blossoming on the filthy pane, he rattled the doorframe with his fists.

Mike, stock-still behind the control panel, did not turn and look at him.

"Goddamn it, Mike, open the fucking door!"

"Mears!" The voice boomed over the snarling engine, just barely audible despite the urgency of tone. It was McEwan, his features muddied by the low-hanging thunderheads trembling with snow. He was wearing only an open chambray shirt and, beneath, an unwashed wifebeater—no coat. The bristling tufts of his hair, unraveling in every direction, rustled like oak leaves in the strong wind. In his hands he held an ice-axe.

Charlie took a step back, his blood freezing in his veins. "Bryan's dead," he heard himself say, his voice flimsy and paper-thin. "Jumped off the stern."

"Come on down from there," McEwan said. There was a calculated levelness to his voice, Charlie noticed—a noticeable restraint. Something was trembling just below the surface. "Leave Mike alone."

Another grinding, peeling sound as jagged fingers of ice cut into the hull—

"He's gonna sink us," Charlie warned.

McEwan placed one heavy boot on the first iron step. His eyes settled hard on Charlie, dull like the heads of iron spikes driven into his skull. "He's a good, strong captain," said McEwan. "Said it yourself. He knows what he's doing."

Charlie shook his head. "No. She got to him." He cleared his throat as McEwan mounted another step. "She got to you, too, Mac."

"Ain't nobody gettin' to me, Mears. Why don't you come on down? We'll talk it out."

Mike Fenty's face suddenly appeared at the pane of glass in the pilothouse door—just inches, despite the shield of glass, from Charlie's own. Charlie's heart leapt in his chest. Mike's eyes had soured, the sclera textured like curdled milk, and a network of whitish blisters had cropped up along the right corner of his mouth. As Charlie looked upon him, Mike Fenty grinned. His gums receded, his teeth looked wolfish.

"Can't have you messin' with the captain," McEwan said. He hefted the ice-axe in his hands as he climbed yet another step. "We're almost home, Charlie. Then we can go about our shit. Like you." Just as the girl had done before him, McEwan cocked his head to one side like an inquisitive mutt. "Ain't you got a kid out there you're anxious to start lookin' for, Mears? A little boy? Hell, man, once we get back to Saint Paul you can do all the lookin' you want. Hell, man, you can use my goddamn car. Got a brand new F-450, chains on the tires, the whole nine. All yours, amigo. Whatever you want." McEwan paused, halfway up the stairs. "Just come on down with me, huh? What'd ya say?"

Behind the glass Mike Fenty's face appeared to blur like someone moving too quickly just as a photo was being snapped.

"Listen to me," Charlie said, trying to watch both Mike

and McEwan at the same time. "You guys ain't thinkin' right. Did you hear what I said about Bryan? He jumped over the *side*, Mac. He's dead."

"Parasites," McEwan said matter-of-factly. "In the head."

"I can't let this boat reach Alaska. I think that's what she wants."

"Talkin' crazy now, Mears."

"Someone dumped her out here for a reason. We can't let her get back."

"Hey Mears—" taking another step, "you remember what I said 'bout them crabs? How we ain't really no different so's we gotta be careful, keep an eye out, make sure we don't do what they do?"

"Don't come up any farther," he warned.

"Well," McEwan continued, ignoring him, "you ain't kept such a close eye. Seems to me you started coming apart, gettin' ready to explode on y'self."

"Billy—"

Scraping: nails on a chalkboard. Wincing, Charlie looked to find Mike dragging the blade of a ten-inch boning knife down the length of the windowpane. His menacing, grin widened, skeletal in its appearance.

With a grunt, McEwan lunged forward, swinging the ice-axe in a wide arc. Overcompensating for the distance between them, the swing was undisciplined; the tapered point of the ice-axe missed Charlie's thigh by a good foot and a half—though it seemed much closer to him—and wedged itself into the pilothouse door. Before McEwan could yank it free, Charlie administered a swift kick that connected squarely with McEwan's chin. McEwan's head rocketed back on his neck, his bulky torso bowing backward until the distribution of his weight sent him spilling down the iron steps. The foredeck sustained the full brunt of his weight, the planks buckling but not breaking, while the back of McEwan's head rebounded off a slatted wooden crate.

Charlie vaulted down the steps and bounded over

McEwan's prone form. As he rounded the foredeck he happened to catch sight of an immense pillar of ice, its summit carving a notch in the silvery sun, rushing up to greet the starboard. Too late to brace himself against the collision, the flooring was ripped from beneath his feet, launching him into a succession of cartwheels from starboard to portside in the blink of an eye. A moment later he was knocked stupid by a blood-freezing pummel of water that reached over the starboard side and, like the smiting Hand of God, smacked down on the foredeck. The icy wave burned through him. It seemed an eternity for it to spill away and for the trawler, now bobbing like a Coke bottle at sea, to right itself.

Gasping for air, his entire body flash-numbed, Charlie scrambled to his feet just as McEwan, dazed in his own right, was trying to prop himself up against the pilothouse stairs. As their eyes locked—

"*Mears!*" It was a roar, no more human than the guttural articulation of some mythical Himalayan beastie. "*Get the fuck back here, goddamn you!*"

The trawler shook again then tipped gradually to portside. All the crates, deck furniture, lines and hooks, loose tools and tool-chests slid in that direction. Hands up in a defensive posture, Charlie felt the equipment slam into him, biting his flesh and snagging his clothes. Something solid ricocheted off his forehead causing a fireworks display to erupt beneath his eyelids. Dizzy, he managed to climb to his feet and, staggering like a drunkard, propelled himself across the foredeck toward the narrow cutout of steps descending beneath the pilothouse station.

McEwan, having successfully retrieved the ice-axe from the pilothouse door, lurched across the foredeck in pursuit. Chunks of graying ice adrift on silt-blackened water pooled around McEwan's ankles. The trawler was foundering, the rising water breaching the sides quicker than it was able to dispatch it back into the sea.

Charlie slammed down the stairs and hurried down the corridor toward his cabin. The walls were frozen, the pipes dripping icy condensation from above. He burst into his room and slammed the door behind him, engaging the meager, useless slide-bolt. A swift kick and the door would splinter down the middle.

He tipped over his cot, the four metal legs jutting up like the stiffening legs of a dead gazelle, and quickly scrambled for the first aid kit. He located the white aluminum box but his big fingers, in their panic, fumbled at the latches. Out in the corridor, McEwan's bullish laughter erupted. Charlie froze. A second later, the cabin door buckled down the center in a perfect vertical stress-line through the center of which projected the tapered iron tip of the ice-axe. There was the sound of splintering balsa as the ice-axe was withdrawn. A second strike punched a fist-sized hole in the flimsy door.

"Mears!" McEwan shouted from the other side. "Goddamn you, Mears, you're fucking it all up!"

Finally, after what seemed like an eternity, the first aid kit popped open. Charlie fumbled the flare gun out, shaking the flare cartridges into his lap.

"Mears!"

McEwan rammed the door with his shoulder, the weightless balsa disintegrating nearly to sawdust. The big man stumbled a few steps, the ice-axe now poised over one shoulder like a baseball bat. When his eyes lit on Charlie, who was crouched in the farther corner of the room, they seemed to briefly emanate a fiery luminosity. Like the eyes of a lion.

"Goddamn you, Mears, you stupid son of—"

Flare gun raised, Charlie slammed the trigger. All in a single second there issued the faint hiss, the acrid burning smell, and—finally!—the belch of dazzling pink radiance from the muzzle of the flare gun. Almost in slow motion Charlie watched the sparkling pink ball of fire propel across the room, flagging behind it a blackish contrail of sulfur-smelling smoke.

McEwan shrieked and attempted to sidestep the assault, but his great bulk moved too slowly; the sparkling magnesium flame, pink as a neon strip-club sign, drove itself into Billy McEwan's face where it seemed to grow brighter and larger, expanding, breathing like new lungs, and the ice-axe clattered heavily to the cabin floor. McEwan's screams reached a girlish timbre, enough to fuzz-out Charlie's eardrums, while his large, club-like hands began pawing at his face. The pink, starlight brilliance of the flare quickly diminished, and between the swiping of McEwan's hands Charlie could see the charred, smoking crater that had replaced the man's left eye—

"*Muh—!*"

The half-word was actually punctuated by the expulsion of thick, charcoal-colored smoke from McEwan's mouth. As Charlie watched, McEwan accomplished a single uncertain step forward before his bones surrendered, sending him face-first—not to the floor but toward one of the jutting metal legs of the overturned cot. There was a wet crunch as the metal pole impaled itself through the center of Billy McEwan's chest, followed by the softer susurration of McEwan's heavy bulk sliding lower and lower on the implement until, eventually, and like the conclusion of some dramatic stage play, Billy McEwan came to rest against the underside of the cot, the cot-leg itself, glistening with blackish-red gore, projecting from between his shoulders. In seemingly no time at all, a dark oil slick of blood expanded from beneath McEwan, filling in the grains of the cabin floor.

Charlie sat wide-eyed, staring, hugging both his knees with one large arm. The flare gun was still in his right hand, still pointing in the direction where, less than five seconds ago, McEwan had been standing. Smoke still trailed up from the muzzle and the entire cabin was suffocating with burnt sulfur.

How much time passed while he sat there, the gun still aimed at the empty space across the cabin, Charlie could not be certain. But when he finally lowered his arm, the muscles had tightened and grown sore and the flare gun itself felt like it weighed two hundred pounds.

Eventually, he pulled himself up off the floor, his entire body trembling like an electric cable. The entire cabin floor was now soaked in McEwan's blood. He refused to look at McEwan's face—at the blackened, roasted divot where his left eye had been...and where wisps of ghost-smoke still spiraled from the gaping socket.

He toed the ice-axe across the floor, leaving an arc of blood in its path. The ice-axe itself was wet with blood; it took great control over his tensing stomach muscles for Charlie to reach down and pluck it from the floor. The blood around its hilt had already begun to congeal—how the hell long had he been sitting here?—and it made his arms weak to carrying it through the doorway.

The corridor was pitch black, the lights having burned out in their fixtures, with only the faintest suggestion of light issuing from beneath the closed door of the latrine. His heartbeat suddenly in his ears, he proceeded down the corridor toward the latrine, one hand trailing along the wall. The whole corridor was canting to one side, taunting his equilibrium. He passed Mike's stateroom, his fingers running over the cupboard door still nailed across the frame...

As he approached the latrine, the ghostly bluish light outlining the door, the sound of gravelly respiration could be heard coming from the other side. The sound of it caused Charlie to freeze just on the other side of the door, his skin suddenly clammy with sweat. Shaky-handed, his fingers tacky with McEwan's blood, he reached out for the door and gripped its anchor-shaped handle. Tugged on it. Heard the bolt retreat from the frame. Opened the door—opened—

"Oh, Joe—"

He laid crumpled, nude, curled like a prawn on the floor of the claustrophobic little bathroom. Lids fluttering, only the milky whites of his eyes shown while a greenish, sudsy foam bubbled out of his mouth. The muscles in his thighs were so tense Charlie could make out, beneath the taut, bluish skin, the individual filaments of musculature like piano cables strapped over the leg bones. Vomit pooled beneath Joe's head while a fouler, darker viscous fluid seeped from Joe's rear.

Charlie bent and clamped one hand around Joe's knobby, bluing shoulder. Touching his flesh was like petting damp, featherless gooseflesh and Charlie instinctively recoiled, leaving bloody fingerprints on his pale flesh. Joe rocked on the hump of his spine; membranous webbing veined with black, pubic-like filaments revealed itself as his legs parted. The membrane pulled taut then retracted like a mesh of elastic, clapping both of Joe's knees together with a hollow pop.

Charlie shuddered and threw himself backward, spilling back out into the corridor and down hard on his ass. The head of the ice-axe clanged hollowly against the wall. A pathetic cry escaped him. As he watched, an inky jet of bile squirted from Joe's mouth and dribbled from both nostrils.

Managing to stand, righting himself against one wall, he began staggering backward down the corridor. Framed in the fading blue light of the latrine, Joe continued to convulse on the latrine floor, the chalky, foul-smelling liquid maintaining steady evacuation from his body. One of Joe's hands slid blindly through the pool of thickening black fluid. There was the sound, *sssssllllit*, of the sliding, the fingers—

A moan escaped from Joe's mouth, bubbles of dark green foam snapping and popping, but was instantly amputated by a wet, muddy cough, which sprayed thick crimson clumps of fibrous tissue onto the floor.

Charlie turned and ran, slamming one shoulder against something solid and immobile in the darkness. Stars exploded before his eyes. He reached out, sightless, grasping a pipe. Cold as ice. Above, the vents pumped frigid air into the corridor—*uhhhhhhh*, moaning like the damned. In his frustration he swung the ice-axe into the pipe, piercing its shell without difficulty. A sludgy black stream of frozen water spouted from the rent.

Heating ducts filled with water...
They were floating on a frozen coffin.
Who's "they"?
Sammy Walper—dead. Bryan Falmouth—abandoned ship. Billy McEwan—impaled on an overturned cot-leg. And Joe...*Jesus fucking Christ, Joe, what the hell?*

There would be no reasoning with Mike. The man was already too far gone. And he was determined to navigate the *Borealis* back to Saint Paul Island. As keenly as he had ever understood anything in all his life, Charlie Mears knew he could not let that happen.

"You're not getting back," he bellowed, his voice like thunder in the lightless corridor. "You're going to stay out here."

He was speaking to the barricaded cabin door—Mike's old stateroom—behind which the trawler's mysterious guest was held prisoner. If he could—

But a fresh thought stopped him cold.

He was alone with his breathing again, his heartbeat. Reaching out, he tugged at the panel of wood—the cupboard door—he'd nailed across the cabin's doorframe. It was still securely in place...

Kill her, a voice spoke up at the back of his head. Strangely, a woman's voice: eerily similar to Johanna's. *You have to kill her, Charlie. If she reaches land...if she reaches Alaska...*

He knew what would happen. All that had transpired aboard the *Borealis* was a microcosm, was the world in miniature.

With the curved head of the ice-axe, Charlie pried the cupboard door off the doorframe, the nails groaning as they were extracted from the wood. He kicked the door open with one boot; it swung inward, hinges squealing, upon a murky darkness. A smell not unlike something fetid and rotting struck Charlie and he shrunk back from the doorway, the ice-axe, as if in protection against olfactory aggression, held up before his face.

The room was empty.

Charlie slumped against the wall. He clutched the ice-axe tighter. Someone had let her out, of course. *Someone*— McEwan before going fucking screwball? Bryan, just prior to flinging himself into the frozen sea? Or was it possible, he wondered, that she let *herself* out? Anything, it seemed, was possible.

The *Borealis* jerked and seemed to come nearly to a stop. Charlie stumbled forward, spilling into Mike's empty, reeking stateroom, the ice-axe clattering to the floor somewhere ahead of him in the darkness. A moaning, clangorous sound shrilled up through the flooring: banshee cries. Charlie actually felt the trawler's hull cutting through clutching mires, an unseen net of impenetrable ice, and the grinding of metal being sheared away grew to an intensity so great he had to clamp both hands over his ears. Something somewhere in the distant bowels of the ship popped—*thwanggg!*—and the *Borealis* shuddered forward again, clear of whatever it'd run over.

The fuel lines. The thought blossomed in his head like a dazzle of Broadway lights. *The fuel lines are down in the engine room.*

Fumbling around in the darkness of Mike's stateroom—

(*not Mike's stateroom*)

—his hands eventually fell on the ice-axe. He gripped it and slammed back out into the corridor, the red emergency lights wholly useless save for drenching everything in a foreboding vermillion, and hurried toward the rung-ladder leading down into the engine room. He moved quickly by the galley, food articles and utensils tossed in tangled nests, broken coffee mugs, the oily pool of running petrol seesawing across the granulated sole, operative notebooks and *Penthouse* calendars, Scotch-Brite scouring pads, flecks of cornflakes sprayed in Big Dipper fashion along the sticky countertop, a sepia-toned map of the Aleutians, unfolded like an accordion—

Below deck, it was intestinally dark. The cold was instantly unbearable. The last rung of the ladder had been swallowed by dark, standing water, atop of which a film of filthy slush had already begun forming. Unfortunately, Charlie didn't see this until he'd already driven his boot straight down to the floor—hearing the *plosh;* feeling, a second later, the ice water seeping through the worn creases of his boots. His foot bristled with needles then went immediately numb.

Steeling himself, he dropped his other foot down—hissed like a cat—and, poising the ice-axe over his shoulder, pushing through the freezing water toward the rear of the engine room. Gears growled and chugged. The furnace was a dead cylinder, hardly visible without its flickering yellow faceplate. Yet despite the loss of power throughout the rest of the boat, the turbines continued to hum from within an ancient steel enclosure.

He knew the fuel lines ran against the far wall, though he couldn't see them in the dark. On deadened feet, his lower jaw shaking like a maraca, he stepped around the turbine enclosure, feeling with hands pained by the sharp, cutting temperature, for the line-spout. He could feel his breath freezing in front of his face—could imagine the vaporous cloud crystallizing in midair and raining in a shower of ice pellets to the sloshing water around his ankles. Touched something—the goddamn blessed motherfucking *line-spout,* thank you Jesus.

And the water level was rising; he could feel it creeping up the legs of his cargo pants. Mike's carelessness in traversing an ice field...

And there was *someone else down here with him—*

His breath caught in his throat. Froze. Dripping water sounds among the steady snarl of the turbines...and, somewhere *behind* him, the sound of someone wading through the water.

"Who's there?" It was hardly a whisper—weak, ineffectual.

No answer.

He was shaking uncontrollably now, his entire body, the ice-axe growing increasingly heavy. Gripping it tighter, he gathered what strength was left in him to mutter, "Who the *fuck* is there?" This time the sounds of the wading stopped but, again, there came no answer.

Fuck it, he thought. *I'll drag this whole fucking boat — and everyone on it — straight to hell.*

Hoisting the ice-axe back over his shoulder, he expelled an exhausted grunt and swung the tool straight into the hub of the line-spout. It was a solid strike, ringing through the heart of the *Borealis.* There came a teakettle hissing followed by a burning stream of hot fuel sprayed into the dark, scorching his flesh. Burned, he foolishly dropped the ice-axe where it plunked through the frozen sludge. He dropped to his knees without thinking, though he immediately regretted his actions as his testicles retreated into the cavity of his abdomen and his muscles seemed to stiffen to broom handles.

Cold fingers clutched the nape of his neck. Charlie cried out and launched himself forward, sprinting in his sightlessness for the rung-ladder. He heard the thing —

(the girl)

—slam through the water in quick pursuit. Hand over fist he scrambled up the ladder, heavy boots tolling on the iron rungs, shrieking like someone in furious pain until he broke through the hatch and crawled across the floor toward the galley. But the corridor was midnight-black, cramped like a coffin; there was no place to go.

Sour breath sawing from his lips, his chest hitching, Charlie Mears pulled himself into a ball and waited. Despite his blindness, he nonetheless trained his eyes in the direction of where he knew the engine room hatch to be.

Listening…listening…listening…

But she never appeared. There were no more sounds from below, save for the occasional thumping of ice against the bottom of the *Borealis.* He would have thought such a feat impossible but in his exhaustion and before he knew it was happening, Charlie Mears fell asleep.

ELEVEN

And awoke with a scream caught in his throat.

Couldn't feel his fingertips; couldn't feel his toes. Could he move them? He couldn't tell. How long had he slept? There was no way to tell. Was he dead? He didn't know.

But if he was dead, this was Hell.

He found matches in the galley. Igniting the corner of one of McEwan's paperback westerns, he carried it like a torch while traversing the inner-deck of the *Borealis*. The corridor closed in around him, the darkness diluted to a chalky grayness. The walls themselves were overgrown with frost, the corridor a frozen white throat which, upon bringing the makeshift torch too close, would weep runnels of melting ice like tears onto steel-colored frozen pools on the floor.

"Dynamo" Joe Darling was now a mummified, dehydrated husk webbed in a gelatinous black tar on the floor of the latrine.

Charlie walked through the cabins, smelling the disuse and, beneath that, the stronger vein of putrefaction. Had he anything in his stomach he would have vomited.

He noticed that the ship was no longer rocking. In fact, it seemed unusually calm.

Lastly, he poked back inside Mike Fenty's old stateroom, still vacant. However, there was a moist, almost breath-smelling condensation to the air in the room. The flames danced off the paperback, already having consumed half the book while managing to fill the ceiling with black columns of smoke, and Charlie had to creep farther into the room to make sure he was actually seeing what he thought he was.

The place on the cot where the girl had sat was *darker* than the rest of the fabric. It was a stellated, tentacled shape, like a cannonball-sized asterisk, that Charlie at first thought was due to water dripping down onto the cot's fabric from somewhere up above. Dampened, darkened fabric. But when he touched the spot his fingers came away dry as bone.

Taking a step back he noticed two similar spots moldering on the floor—where, naturally, the girl's feet would have been while she sat on the edge of Mike's cot. It was a darkening of the wood, each one practically foot-shaped. As if her flesh, not belonging to this world, was rotting whatever it touched, soiling it, marking it the way a wolf may mark its den.

He crept up to the foredeck and pushed open the double-hatch. Shafts of hoary light stung his eyes though he couldn't tell what time of the day it was. Or *what* day it was.

Topside, he crossed over to the bow and looked out upon a vast ice field, its size indeterminable, upon which, at some point during his unconsciousness, the *Borealis* had run aground. The hull was destroyed, stabbed by countless knives of ice, an explosion of boat pieces sprayed across the snow.

He turned and proceeded toward the pilothouse. Walking was less about moving his legs independently of each other but merely pivoting each foot and twisting at the hips, for this seemed the best way to conserve what warmth hadn't evacuated his body. At the control room door, he wiped away thick grime from the window and, cupping his hands at either side of his face, peered inside.

Mike was on the floor, his hand still clutching the hilt of the boning knife that he'd used to open his throat. His skin was gray as bird down, his eyes milky pustules overloaded in their sockets.

Shaking, shaking—

Breathing into his hands, he retreated down the steps and noticed something in the snow he hadn't seen when he'd first looked over the bow.

Footsteps.

She.

And *she*—

TWELVE

Down in the galley he scooped handfuls of cereal off the countertop, which he ate without expression, then ate two slices of wheat bread which were covered in frost. Afterward, he urinated in the galley's steel sink—a stream so pungent and yellow it was nearly solid. From his cabin he retrieved the flare gun then, on second thought, packed the entire first aid kit in his laundry bag. He pulled tight the laces on the bag and slung it over one shoulder.

There was a flashlight in Mike's room. It didn't work but, for some reason, Charlie was confident the farther he got from the trawler the greater the chance the flashlight might start to work. Again he thought of those blackened footprints on the sole of Mike's stateroom, the tentacled star on the seat of the cot. The girl, he knew, had poisoned the *Borealis,* and everything on it. Well, almost everything.

While he prepared his gear and changed into warm clothes, he thought of Gabriel. When he was born, on the day Johanna and he had taken him home from the hospital, the infant had been silent as a dormouse. This reddened, squinty-eyed little garden gnome with a tiny, upturned nose and square little pink fists. And the hair on his head! Dark as the pelt of a black bear. They'd been living in Oregon then, in a small cabin backed by redwood trees as formidable as minarets while the front yard opened up on a pebbly gray beach where the cold Pacific waters rushed up to lap against the bulkhead. He'd been piloting charters back then while sustaining a hunger to get his hands back into the gullets of cod instead of just coolers of Bud. It was what he hoped for that pink, squirming little baby, too—a lifetime of *doing* as opposed to the *pursuit* of doing. Anyway, he'd get back to the sea, the real sea, in due time. There was the baby. Gabe. Gabriel. The way Johanna, slight in frame and just as beautiful as she'd ever been, nursing the baby in the half-gloom of midday coming in through the cabin's windows, framing her in some angelic penumbra while she rocked gently in the old rocking chair that had once been her — or his? — grandfather's...

Back above deck, the world was colorless. Snow snowed. The boat's prow had shriveled and turned black as rotting fruit. There came the steady *glug-glug* from the hull as the trawler slowly took on more and more water. With a pair of field glasses, Charlie surveyed the expansive strip of ice, miles long, practically its own continent. He could see the girl's footprints in the snow, soon to be covered over by the fresh fall.

Shouldering his gear, he climbed down the side of the trawler via an overhang of cable. The ice-nails in the soles of his boots left pockmarks in the fiberglass hull. Touching down on the ice field, he found the frozen terra firma solid as pavement. Charlie hefted his gear and, without a second thought, pushed forward through the twirling snow. He followed the girl's footprints until the storm covered them up. Then he continued in their estimated direction, up over frozen buttes, across jagged crevasses, and down the throat of winding, bluish canyons through which dense, crystalline fog called "pogonip" hung like spectral gauze. He walked until hunger cramped his stomach and the silver aurora of sun bled away behind the sea, leaving a velvety, star-encrusted firmament in its place.

In the dark and miles from the *Borealis*, the flashlight came on.

Trudging through the snow, his head down and his stiff-bristled beard glistening with ice crystals, he pursued the ghostly mirage. When he caught a glimpse of her, glistening in the pale cast of moonlight, white against a whiter background, he had to question what he was seeing — was it real or only in his mind, a trick of his eyes? Had she *ever* existed? Had any of them?

Holes everywhere, Bryan's voice came back to him. *You get it, man? The whole goddamn world...*

At one point he collapsed in the snow. Thinking, *Mailboxes full of firecrackers.* Thinking, *Moon-bugs.* He managed to roll onto his back and, with some semblance of consciousness, propped himself up against a pillar of ice. Shivering, he pulled his gear into his lap for warmth against the biting, unforgiving wind. However, the seat of his pants soon grew wet and cold, the snow soaking through both pairs of underwear, long johns, his BDUs. His buttocks went numb. Thinking of Gabriel, zigzagging around the yard in Saint Paul, lobbing fistfuls of snow over Dale Carver's fence. Dale's German shepherd barked wildly, poking its snout through the quadrangular rings in the fence. He chased the boy around the yard, feinting for him just as the boy pivoted in the snow and darted in the opposite direction. From the trailer's stoop Johanna looked on, dressed in a heavy pink bathrobe and rabbit-fur slippers, her arms folded in mock-disapproval across her chest.

Just as his fingers looped into the collar of Gabriel's parka, he happened to look up and meet Johanna's eyes. Laughing, shrieking, Gabriel eventually pulled free and sprinted across the yard. Dale's hound loped wildly in the snow.

"Why you gonna leave?" he said suddenly to Johanna.

"What are you talking about, Charlie?"

"I know you're gonna leave."

"I don't know what you mean, Charlie."

"Yes you do." Gabriel's laughter faded into blackening ether. "You're gonna wait for me to go out so I won't know until I come back home. It'll give you a good head start."

"Charlie, please. You don't know that. You're dreaming this now and it's not real. It already happened. That's how you know. This isn't real."

"Don't go," he begged her, tears suddenly spilling down his face. He crossed the yard and, before the trailer's steps, dropped to his knees in the snow. "Please, Jo. Don't leave. Don't take him away from me. If you're unhappy—"

"It's not about me being unhappy. The boy shouldn't live like this, Charlie. Look around. This isn't normal for him. And with you gone half the year—"

"Please, Jo," he begged. "Please…"

THIRTEEN

And opened his eyes—

He was covered in frost, the back of his coat frozen to the pillar of ice. Likewise, his gear lay frozen to his legs. He had no feeling from the waist down. The snow had let up to a lazy flutter, the large flakes twisting and spiraling in the clear, crisp night air. Overhead, he saw—or imagined he saw—the great bruise-colored northern lights, the aurora borealis, the spirit of the great north. It gleamed like heat lightening.

Over the nearest bluff a figure appeared. Small, inconsequential. Almost nonexistent. Charlie blinked his eyes and, with much difficulty, managed to bring his gloved hands, hooked now into inflexible talons, up to his face. He scrubbed the ice from his lashes and peered out along the moonlit pass. The figure was descending the bluff, coming toward him.

Charlie's breathing quickened. He tried to move his legs but couldn't. Moving anything but his arms—which were weak and practically useless anyway—was impossible.

"Huh...huh...*huuuuhhh*..." Clouds of vapor wafted before his face before being carried off in the wind.

The figure stood before him now, peering down at his broken, immobile form.

"G-G-*Gabriel*," Charlie managed.

The boy was wearing his ski parka and Ninja Turtle earmuffs. Red mittens, yellow boots with the bright red buckles.

"Daddy," said the boy.

"G-G-*Guh-Guhhh*—"

The boy crossed over to him. Bending down, he peeled Charlie's pack from his legs, the frost popping and tearing, until he was able to roll the pack down a nearby embankment. Then the boy climbed up into Charlie's lap, his weight and warmth so real Charlie could not deny the boy's existence.

"How d-d-d-did you guh-*get* – huh-how…how…"

"Daddy," the boy said, pressing his face to Charlie's chest. His small arms found Charlie's neck, looped around it. "I missed you, Daddy."

"Oh, pal," said Charlie, his eyes welling with tears that froze the second they spilled from his eyes. He managed to bring one arm up and encircle the boy with it. Hugged him gently. "I was g-gonna f-f-find you, p-pal," he told the boy. The nacreous, velvety lights in the sky seemed to brighten, tremble, waver.

"I love you," the boy told him, his breath warm on his neck. "I love you, Daddy."

"Was g-g-gonna f-f-*find* y-y-yuh-y-yuh—"

The boy's arms tightened around Charlie's neck. Charlie forced himself to smile, the flesh cracking and splitting and bleeding down his face and chin, and returned the boy's embrace with his one free arm. He squeezed the boy as tight as he could—

"…*find you*…"

—while the world around him went white, white.

BIOGRAPHIES

BRIAN KEENE is the best-selling author of many books, including *Ghost Walk*, *Dark Hollow*, *Dead Sea*, *Ghoul*, *Terminal*, *Kill Whitey*, and many more. The winner of several awards, his work has been praised in such diverse places as *The New York Times*, *The History Channel*, *CNN.com*, *Publisher's Weekly*, *Fangoria Magazine*, and *Rue Morgue Magazine*.

BRETT MCBEAN is the author of the novels *The Last Motel* and *The Mother*, the novelette *The Familiar Stranger* and the short story collection *Tales of Sin and Madness*. His stories have appeared in anthologies such as *Asylum Volume 3: The Quiet Ward*, *In Delirium II*, and in the upcoming *In Laymon's Terms*, and in magazines such as *Dark Discoveries* and *Post Mortem*. He lives in Melbourne, Australia with his wife and German Shepherd. Visit him on the web at: www.brettmcbean.com

NICK MAMATAS is the author of the novels *Under My Roof* and *Move Under Ground*, and the short story collection *You Might Sleep...*He lives near, but not in, Boston, and has lost several minor literary awards for his work. Visit him online at http://nihilistic-kid.livejournal.com/.

RONALD DAMIEN MALFI is an award-winning novelist and short fiction writer whose most notable works include *Via Dolorosa*, *The Nature of Monsters*, and the critically-acclaimed modern gothic novel, *The Fall of Never*. His most recent novel, *Passenger*, was published by Delirium Books earlier this year, and his forthcoming Medallion Press release, *Shamrock Alley*, has already been optioned for a major motion picture. He lives in Annapolis, Maryland and can be contacted at www.ronmalfi.com.

JOIN DELIRIUM'S HORROR BOOK CLUB

- Save 40% off all titles
- Shop online
- Major credit cards accepted
- Free book when you join

Discover the future of horror today
www.deliriumbooks.com/bookclub

Printed in the United States
134596LV00004B/4/P